MURDER
ON A
SUMMER
BREAK

Also by Kate Weston
Murder on a School Night

MURDER ON A SUMMER BREAK

KATE WESTON

HARPER

An Imprint of HarperCollinsPublishers

Library of Congress Control Number: 2023944475

ISBN 978-0-06-326032-0

Typography by Carla Weise

24 25 26 27 28 LBC 5 4 3 2 1

First Edition

For Nick Brookes

MURDER ON A SUMMER BREAK

CRIME SCENE CRIME SCENE CRIME SC CRIME SCENE CRIM

1

My pulse races at the sight of Annie's head poking out from behind a tree at the other end of Barbourough High Street. My best friend looks both ways from behind its trunk while I wipe away the beads of sweat forming on my forehead, the back of my neck prickling with heat and unease. The street is silent, lined with bunting that hangs perfectly still, without even the gentlest of breezes to rustle it. This is it. The calm before the storm, a sinister reminder of what's to come.

Finally, Annie steps out from behind the tree. My shoulders tense, jaw tightening as she strides toward me. I feel the air become closer, hotter. Soon this'll be over, we'll have done what we came here to do, but right now I'm sweating, my whole body fraught with nervous energy. I grip Herbie's leash tightly, holding him close to me, despite its leather slipping in my clammy palms. Annie and I lock eyes, and hope washes over me. For the first time I feel like we can do this. My fingers and toes tingle; I'm restless with anticipation. The ending is within our grasp, and my fight-or-flight instinct's telling me that we've won. Safety is coming.

"CUT CUT CUT!!!" Annie yells, waving her arms.

Taylor Swift's "Cruel Summer" cuts off, and I skid to a halt, immediately tripping over my own feet. In front of me, Annie goes to the phone she's set up on a tripod in the middle of the pavement. She struts with purpose in her cutoff denim shorts and pink T-shirt that reads *Mama's Nepo Baby*. Her pink plastic visor bobs on her head with authority.

"BACK UP! START AGAIN!" yells Annie, waving her arms—halting our reunion for what is now the tenth time, all for the sake of social media.

I throw my head back to the sky in exasperation. She may have been away for four weeks, but at ninety-five degrees, it's far too hot for this shit. Also *I* wasn't the one who left for an internship with the Ministry of Justice in London, so why am *I* being punished? She knows I'm shy. Appearing on a reel is my worst nightmare.

"Your eyes aren't glistening with emotion, and you're moving way too fast for this to pack the punch of a proper slow-motion, cinematic reunion," she shouts.

She spins on her heel and heads back behind the tree, ready for take eleven. Sure I missed her, but after this many tries at reuniting, any emotion that my eyes could have potentially *glistened* with has well and truly dried up. I am an emotional husk. The most she can hope for in this dry heat, at the end of a very long morning of interning at the glamorous *Barbourough News* office, is that a rogue bit of sweat might drip from my forehead in the vague direction of my eyes.

"Back up, Kerry! BACK UP!" she shouts from two meters away.

Annie refuses to come any closer to "preserve the

2

authenticity" of our first embrace for her ReelLife video. Heaven forbid we could just hug each other, without a video of it being available for strangers to watch and judge on the internet.

"This is the *last* time, Annie," I shout, realizing that a gaggle of old people have now gathered by the tripod, confused and unsure how to negotiate its presence.

Old Mr. Harris starts prodding at one of its plastic legs angrily with his walking stick as if it might move out of the way of its own accord.

"Go around!" Annie shouts to him. Her instructions are combined with a frantic gesture, but Mr. Harris just continues staring at her blankly, waggling his walking stick in the direction of the obstruction.

"GO AROUND!!!" she instructs again, even louder and with even more expressive arm movements.

Much to her continued frustration and my amusement though, Mr. Harris either can't hear her or is willfully ignoring her. To be fair, I think he's actually quite enjoying having something new to be annoyed at. I'm about to plead with Annie to abandon this whole thing altogether and just let us spend the rest of my lunch break at the pool catching up with our feet in the water like we'd planned, when she freezes, her lips stretching into a slow smile. I'm afraid she might have had an idea.

"What if we dance?!" she yells to me, deadly serious. "WE COULD WALTZ TO EACH OTHER!"

"You could bite me?" I reply.

Herbie, the little West Highland white terrier we share, confirms this sentiment by barking loudly. He can't figure out why Annie keeps teasing him by advancing toward him with a treat one minute and then backing away again the next. Really it's incredibly harsh for him—I'm surprised he hasn't called the RSPCA with his sad little paws already.

"*Why* are you suddenly so into ReelLife anyway?" I ask, slightly dreading the answer. "Is this a London thing?"

"Obvi, I want to be popular," Annie says. "Plus, how embarrassing would it be if we're the only people at the Festival of Fame without any followers?"

I look at the crowd that's amassed to watch us film this reunion, my face burning. "Yeah, really embarrassing," I mutter. "I mean I don't even have a profile . . ."

"Correction!" Annie says. "You *didn't*. Fear not, my friend! I have taken the liberty of creating one for you!"

Oh god. What's she done? I feel a bit sick and pull my phone out straightaway to take a look. Finding the profile, I can see that (A) she's used a photo with her in it as my profile pic where she looks great and I look bad, and (B) at least she's kept the bio short. But all it says is *the second half of the Tampon Two*. It could be worse I guess because (C) I only have three followers: Annie, Colin, and Audrey.

I should have known all this has to do with the Festival of Fame. The village has been covered in banners and posters for it all summer. Everywhere I look I'm reminded of the impending event where fans get to meet their favorite influencers.

I would be excited, because Winona Philips, feminist influencer and our hero, is hosting, so obviously Annie and I are going. And, of course, Annie's decided we're finally going to meet her. But it means camping for three days, with hundreds of other people, all of them making constant videos. And the possibility that I—very likely, knowing me—will do something absolutely mortifying in front of said hero. I'm terrified actually.

"Follow my lead and soon enough we'll have more followers than Les Populaires." Annie's eyes shine, and she stares dreamily into the distance, thinking of the most popular group in school. She spent six years trying to be part it, and last year she achieved her goal. Apparently she has a new one: becoming more popular than even Les Populaires. Which is a stretch, considering it took a murder investigation for her to get into the group in the first place. "Maybe even more than Winona Philips . . ."

"So you want to be an influencer now?" I ask, trying to keep the judgment out of my voice. "Was it not enough for you to get the glory from solving the menstrual murders?"

"It was a good starter. But yeah, I want to be an influencer. Just not a shallow one, like those 'Get ready with me' beauty blogger types." She turns her nose up at the thought as she speaks. "I want to be like Winona Philips. Smart! Political! Worshipped by all!" With each command, she slices her hand through the air, like she's already behind a podium commanding her devout followers or something. I didn't realize social media was so life-or-death.

"I've *been* places now, Kerry; I'VE BEEN TO LONDON! Seen things! I want more! I want . . . world domination!" Her eyes glisten, but as she says the words "world domination," a pigeon flies toward her head and she ducks out of the way, petrified. She'll not be deterred though. "Besides, we're the *Tampon Two*!"

I roll my eyes at the name *she* gave us after we solved the menstrual murders last year. It's a name that no one else has ever actually used, and yet she continues to try to make it happen.

"Anyway, ready for the next take?" Annie asks, seemingly recovered from her villainous monologue about taking over the world.

Reluctantly, I retake my starting mark as she aims the tiny remote at her phone from behind the tree with the precision of an assassin. "Cruel Summer" resumes, and Annie comes dancing out from behind the tree, shaking and shimmying in my direction. The crowd has now doubled in size, and their gaze moves over to me, waiting to see what I'll pull out of the dancing bag.

I silently plead for a sinkhole to open up in the hot pavement beneath my feet. There are so many people stuck watching our mortifying display who probably just wanted to get past. The air's beginning to feel thick with embarrassment (me), impatience (them), and sweat (all of us). I start my advance toward Annie knowing that the only way to get this over with is to power straight through it. Besides, it's been a whole month without mortification for me. (Well, apart from when my boss at *Barbourough News* made me walk the streets dressed as a giant newspaper to boost readership.) It's been good run, but I'd better get back to it. The only small mercy is that Scott went away on tour with his band this morning, so he won't be around to witness any of this.

Annie ramps it up, skipping enthusiastically and throwing in a couple of leaps like a ballerina racing to her long-lost forest nymph lover. I wish I could move with such ease and confidence—instead I'm just sort of bobbing a bit with every step, occasionally throwing a hand out to the side in a meek way when I feel jazzy. Spoiler: I'm not really a feeling-jazzy sort of person. I'm more of a feeling-tired-overwhelmed-and-shy person. And one of the things the last year of attention has taught me is that I'm actually okay with being all those things, thanks.

It feels like months have passed since I began bobbing awkwardly down this street, but finally Annie and I are close enough to each other that I can see an end in sight to this hell.

As our fingers touch, a tingle goes up my spine and my lungs open up, as if I can breathe more easily now that she's back.

"Good vulva to you, Kerry!" Annie beams, shouting Winona Philips's famous line.

"Good vulva, Annie," I whisper back.

We fling our arms around each other, and I inhale the scent of the same strawberry shampoo she's used her whole life. The rest of the world is a blur as we stand there in our embrace, just as the pigeon flies back toward us, seemingly intent on murder.

2

The air's thick with the feverish excitement of late summer as the two of us enter Rose Hill Farm, the farm where Heather—queen of Les Populaires—and her mum live. You might think after everything that happened last year she'd want to keep a low profile, hide from attention. But no, instead she's literally invited the whole world over. She says it's to try and get the farm known for something other than murder. Which means all summer I've been seeing videos and posts about people excited to spend their summer at the Murder Farm.

The tinny sound of a playlist containing all the current viral ReelLife songs plays across the acres of festival landscape stretching out in front of us—to be fair, it's completely unrecognizable from the last time we were up here, chasing the menstrual murderer. In place of barren fields and brambles are green lawns peppered with food stalls, fairground rides, flashing lights, stages, laughter, and music, all perfectly crafted to look like Instagram-ready sets.

As the two of us stride epically across the buzzing fields,

I feel intensely aware of all the people filming and earnestly talking into their phones. I'm nervous that any of them could capture me in the background at any time. I just want to find the campsite and put up the tent, then maybe hide in there. Just for a bit.

"Remind me again why we're here?" I ask.

"Apart from being in the same place as our hero and idol Winona Philips, you mean?!" Annie blinks at me and then returns to scrolling videos idly. "I need to learn my craft!"

She's gone all out, wearing a neon playsuit and neon face paint—as if she's seeking camouflage inside a rave—and a pair of wellies that seem to reach up so high they may as well be full-leg waders. It's definitely giving butcher rather than festival chic. To cap it all off she's got a camping backpack that's over half the size of her. I feel underprepared in my shorts and T-shirt with my small, modest backpack, and obviously the tent, which hopefully we're about to put up really soon.

"And anyway it'll be great for your career, too. You can write a piece about it for *Barb News*! You've been telling me all summer that they don't let you do anything apart from sharpen pencils and make tea. Now's your chance. You could review the most exciting event to happen in Barbourough since the menstrual murders!"

She walks on with confidence, further into the hordes of people.

"Annie! We've been through this—you can't go around calling the murders exciting." I sigh. "Besides, the review's not going to happen. I already pitched it to the editor, Ralph, and he turned me down."

"What? *How?*" Annie asks, spinning around to face me.

"Some of *the* most famous influencers are in our village. How is that not front-page news to him? I'd much rather read about that than Mr. Harris's massive turnip. This would never happen in London."

"He called it a *'new-fangled, trendy blight on our village that no one wants'*!" I say, looking around at all the people talking into their phones and making videos. He would hate this, but then, I think I do, too.

"So write it anyway?" Annie says. "You can publish it yourself. Maybe make it a blog?!"

Maybe that's not such a bad idea.

"I could write it while we're here and post it afterward. Like a real account of the UK's first massive influencer festival, from someone who was there. Maybe I could even delve into what the influencers are *really* like, behind the filters!" I feel the spark of excitement start to grow as I'm talking. What I don't say is that maybe I could interview an influencer or two . . . maybe even Winona Philips. I shake myself. I can't even dare imagine.

"Exactly! And I can share it with my followers!"

I don't want to point out to Annie that earlier this afternoon, when I was hard at work sharpening pencils and listening to updates from my desk mate, Carol, about the town BatCam (a camera filming the movements of the village bats—peak Barbourough excitement!), I looked at Annie's profile and she's only got two followers, Colin and Audrey. I'd follow her, but I don't want her thinking I intend to use my profile or tagging me in anything.

"Imagine if something really exciting happens, like another murder! You'll be the person writing about it from firsthand

10

experience! You'll get so many readers!"

"Annie, the only way a murder's going to happen here is if someone weaponizes a ring light," I say, gesturing to all the phone-gripped people around us.

"Excuse me! *VIPs coming through!!*" Annie shouts at the crowd of people.

Not a single one of them pays attention to her.

"Haha, VIPs. Yeah right," I mutter. "Can we please find somewhere to put up this tent soon?" I'm sick of hauling this massive thing around already.

"Oh, no, my friend! We won't be needing a tent! I wasn't joking. We're *obviously* going VIP," Annie announces.

"So we don't need this, then?" I nod to the fucking tent.

Annie's so blasé, but I'm actually not so sure the VIP thing is as certain as she thinks.

"Have you asked Heather or—" I'm cut off by Annie immediately.

"Don't need to! You don't think we're going to be camping with the common people when our friend's the person who actually put on this festival, do you? Besides, we *have* to be where Winona is!" Annie waves her hand, gesturing at the people around us. "Also, you're going out with Heather's brother. You're basically her sister-in-law!"

I'm still not sure any of this means we would automatically get a pass to the VIP section. Annie spins around to me, her eyes shining.

"Actually that's a good point," she continues. "Ask Scott to put in a good word for us—I mean, just in case Heather got distracted and forgot to save us a good yurt or something." She clutches my arm.

11

"Hmmm." I make a noncommittal noise as her fingers tighten on me.

"You'll never know if you don't try!" She's giving me puppy dog eyes, and I know that if I don't text him she'll never let it go, so I fire off an apologetic text to Scott purely for a bit of peace.

We walk further into the crowds, and I start to feel like I'm in some kind of montage video. Probably because everyone around us is recording "Come with me to the Festival of Fame" videos, phones raised, different voices talking earnestly or excitedly to screens. Thank god Annie's not got me doing one of those. It's definitely not part of her brand if she wants to be "less of a cheesy influencer." As we carry on walking, everything starts to feel more epic, like we're heading toward some kind of crescendo movie moment—it's as if I can hear the music building.

Actually, maybe I *can* hear it? Is that . . .

"Come with me to the FESTIVAL OF FAME!" Annie shouts.

Her nose is just inches from her phone, which has "Chariots of Fire" blasting out from it, far louder than her voice.

"WELCOME TO THE FAMOUS JUNGLE!" she shouts against the music, making Herbie's ears pin back and his head tilt in surprise.

This feels extra, even for her, and when I look at her screen she's got the "Iconic Flames" filter on so it looks like we're queens walking through a wall of fire. To be fair, with this many people around it does feel a little like that to me—just more scary and hot than "iconic."

"No, no, no," I say, shaking my head and taking the phone from her.

"Hey!" Annie sulks.

"I'm only doing what Colin and Audrey would do if they were here." I show her the WhatsApp messages Colin and Audrey sent to the Les Populaires group just minutes ago from their holiday in St. Barts as a reminder.

> **Colin:** Annie, don't do anything cringey at
> the festival while we're not there to rein
> you in.

> **Audrey:** No cheesy montage videos, babe,
> you are not diva enough to pull them off.

Annie rereads the messages and rolls her eyes before nodding her head in resignation.

"Fair point, well made," she says.

"Obviously *I* think everything you do is cool." I raise a hand to my chest to show sincerity.

"Natch," Annie says.

"But we know the rest of the world isn't as advanced as us," I proceed. "So maybe we should just keep a low profile while we're here?"

"Okay, fine," Annie agrees reluctantly.

If I'm going to be writing about the festival, I don't want to draw attention to myself. I want to be a casual and anonymous observer. I open the festival program on my phone and take a look at the events. I reckon I'll find out a lot from the "Creating Your Online Persona" event if I'm looking at what the influencers are really like compared to how they appear online. I decide to keep Annie well away from the "Dress Your Pet for Internet

Success" session for Herbie's sake, though. The first event, an "Influencers Under Twenty" panel, starts in a bit, and that's a good chance to quietly watch and get to know the influencers, or at least their public forms.

My research is hampered by Annie suddenly shoving her phone right in my face and whispering into it. "Come with me and my bestie to the Festival of Fame." She leans, wide-eyed, into the camera before realizing that I'm glaring at her. "What? I'm doing it quietly. Look! I've even taken the flame filter off."

"Annie . . . that's so not what I meant when I said keeping a low profile. I meant more, not posting it at all." I sigh.

"Okay . . . I'm going to need to explain to you sometime about how influencers work. Spoiler: they do kind of need attention," Annie says before suddenly stopping in the entrance to the main festival field and staring around her.

"What are we doing now?" I ask, watching her, nose in the air, sniffing her surroundings like a dog in the park.

"Just soaking in the atmosphere," Annie tells me. "Breeeeeeathing it all in . . . We're at our first festival, Kerry! This is huge!! MASSIVE!! You and me! US! AT! A! FESTIVAL!"

"Ten minutes from our houses." I mutter this bit of real talk because it would be cruel to be too forceful about it when she's this excited.

"We're finally part of the coolness," Annie says in a breathy whisper, looking around her, eyes shining.

"OUT OF THE WAY, TWATS!" someone yells at us, appearing from behind and giving Annie an almighty shove on the way past. The shove, plus the weight of her backpack, sends Annie flying to the floor. She scrabbles on the ground like an upturned beetle.

"Annie!" I shout, but as I reach down to grab her, I'm pushed forward by more impatient campers and knocked to the ground as well. I'm waiting for a break in the crowd so that I can get up and find my balance, but there are so many people, it feels like we're trapped down here forever. All I can see are hundreds of pairs of stomping legs, dangerously close to crushing us like insignificant bugs in the festival of life.

Then, somewhere from within the sea of fashionable wellies and platform Converse, a hand appears, reaching as if from heaven. Perfect fingers reach down and grasp me like it's almost holy, and as I ascend from the dusty ground, pulled by this sacred arm, I reach back and grab Annie's hand in my other. The two of us are yanked up from whence we were about to be squashed into nothing, saved from being influencer roadkill.

Out of the swamp of people, my eyes connect with his. My hero, my savior, my absolute fucking hottie.

"Scott!" I exclaim. "I thought you'd left already?"

We had our emotional goodbye hours ago. He's supposed to be on tour with the band for two weeks! What's he doing here now? Is he a sexy mirage? Am I *actually* influencer roadkill?

He smiles, the dent of his dimple appearing in his right cheek, and I feel my legs turn to jelly.

"Our drummer left his retainer behind; we had to turn back and get it. We were about to leave again when I got your text so I thought I'd just come and find you, seeing as you're here. Get one last kiss in . . ." His arms reach around me, pulling me into him tighter, further into safety and away from the hordes of wellie-wearing festivalgoers. I snuggle in, burying my head in his chest.

I give much less of a shit about the thousand people jostling past us now. Our lips lock, and I lace my fingers around his neck, running my hands through the back of his hair. As his hands settle on my butt, Annie starts coughing loudly next to us.

"Guys, come on!" she says as we pull away. "I thought we agreed, no tongues in front of me? I haven't even had a twosome yet; I'm definitely not ready for a threesome."

We lean back in for a kiss, ignoring Annie as she continues, "It's been nearly a year—aren't couples supposed to get bored of each other by now?"

"Nope," Scott and I say, pulling away at the same time and smiling at each other as he puts his hand in my back pocket, cupping my butt cheek.

I doubt I've got more than five minutes with him before he goes again. Annie's rules can wait.

"So, Scott!" Annie pops up next to his face just as our mouths are about to meet again. "What's it like being a big touring rock star?"

The two of us sigh and give up on trying to kiss. Annie's won, this time.

"Well, I've had a total of two days off, and now we have to race to Liverpool to be onstage there in about two hours," he says.

"Still, at least you had Kerry's place all to yourself while her parents are on that cruise, though." Annie does a gross little wink that makes me want to push her back onto the grass.

Actually Mum and Dad only left yesterday. Mum's been hired to work on a cruise for the over-fifties giving talks on how to keep things spicy in the bedroom after menopause, so she took Dad with her so he could have a holiday, too. Scott spent all day practicing and getting ready to go back on tour again, while I was at my internship. We saw each other briefly last night but were both exhausted, and all I could manage this morning was a wave goodbye on my way to work. This whole summer it's felt like just as we've managed to get any time alone we've been interrupted by something or other.

Annie takes another shove to the backpack and almost keels over again, proving that although she is small and mighty, a five-foot-one legend is really no match for a four-foot backpack. We grab her hands, and she straightens herself out.

"Oh my god, this festival is so fucking feral." She wipes sweat off her brow with a muddy hand. "I love it, you guys."

"How long till you have to go?" I ask Scott.

"Kind of now," Scott says sadly before leaning back in and kissing me again. "Jen's already texted saying that they're all waiting for me in the van."

"Oh," I say, trying my hardest to be cool at the mention of Jen's name.

Obviously I like Jen. She's one of the coolest people I've ever met in my life. When she joined the band a few months ago the number of gigs they got immediately went up because Jen knows people. Scott also thinks Jen's really cool. And that's fine, and normal. Understandable.

I'm so jealous of Jen, and I think it might make me the worst feminist in the world.

"I should go," he says, leaning down. I savor the kiss as his lips meet mine and his hand reaches up, cupping my face.

"Wait! What about the VIP area!" Annie shouts between our faces.

"Oh." Scott's voice is muffled by my lips before he pulls

away. "I can't get hold of Heather. She's in festival world. I guess just . . . good luck?"

"Urgh! What's the point of banging someone if they can't even get us backstage!" Annie mutters, stamping her feet.

Scott's quite used to her behavior now, so the two of us just ignore her, and he leans in to give me another kiss.

I feel a wrench as he pulls away.

"I should run!" He waves at Annie, and before my lips have time to catch up to what's going on, I'm watching his hot ass retreating into the sunset for the third time this summer.

"COME ON!" Annie says stridently, grabbing my hand and dragging me toward an area illuminated by the letters "VIP," formed from bright Hollywood-style bulbs, above a set of floral-decorated arches.

"Urgh," I groan. I'm getting flashbacks from all the parties we've been turned away from. There's no way we're getting into the VIP area.

As we approach the gates to the luxury glamp site, we see two huge security guys wearing bright pink Festival of Fame T-shirts stand with their arms crossed. I peer over their shoulders and spot some influencers I recognize just on the other side of them, already videoing content with each other. One of the security guards must notice me watching, though, as he adjusts his stance to block my view again. I've never felt so small in my life. I also can't help but think about how many people with hundreds of thousands of followers might capture this on video if we're rejected.

"Annie and Kerry, the Tampon Two!" Annie announces proudly to the security guards. "We're close, personal friends of Heather."

"Oh my god, don't say it like that." I screw my face up.

"You're not on the list," the security guard says.

"Try Les Populaires? That's our secret name for each other." Annie winks at the security guard, her confidence never seeming to wane despite the mortification starting to smoke away at my soul.

"Still no," the security guard says.

"Then I need to talk to Heather," Annie says. "She'll be *so* embarrassed when she hears about this oversight."

The security guards look at each other and then back at us, pity all over their faces as if we're delusional, which in Annie's case I cannot argue with. I notice with a gulp that some of the influencers are starting to look in our direction.

"Let's just go to the regular campsite and put up the tent," I plead.

"*No!* We should be in there! With the yurts and the influencers. *I'm* an influencer, you know! I *need* to meet Winona Philips, and for her to take me seriously. This is the *only* way to do it," Annie begs, turning back to the security guards. "You just need to ask Heather!"

I pray silently to myself that neither of the security men ask her how many followers she has.

"You can ask her yourself," the first security guard says, pointing behind us.

We spin around, coming face-to-face with two of three unpaid interns who Heather has "employed" to buzz around her all summer—helping her plan the festival and basically being her personal assistants. They stride toward us at the VIP entrance, accompanied by a swirl of bubbles.

While at the start of the summer the interns all seemed to

have their own identities, now they all look the same: like mini Heathers. They're even dressed the same, wearing black shorts, white tank tops with *Heather's Festival of Fame* emblazoned in pink across them, and pink sneakers. They have identical high ponytails, and each of them are talking at speed into black headsets and clutching clipboards as they march with purpose.

The interns part in the middle, and Heather appears, strutting through her entourage in a pair of gold sequin hot pants, a white T-shirt with *INFLUENCE ME* written across it also in gold sequins, and a gold headset and clipboard to mark her apart from her minions. The bubbles swirl around her in fits and starts as she walks, making her look like she's in some kind of super-perky music video. The reality, though, is that behind her, holding a massive pot of bubble mixture and huffing through three bubble sticks at a time, is another of the Mini-Heathers. She stumbles and coughs, spraying bubbleless liquid everywhere.

"For god's sake, Jessica, get it together," one of the other Mini-Heathers hisses in her ear. "If you can't hack it, there are others who can take your place."

"Sorry," whispers the Mini-Heather who I assume must be Jessica. "I just . . . keep . . . getting a bit dizzy . . ."

"Hi, Heather," Annie chirps, ignoring the entourage. "Thank god you're here; this man says we're not on the list to stay in the VIP glamp site, but obviously he must be wrong!" Annie tries to wave and get Heather's attention, but Heather doesn't look around and heads toward two influencers I recognize as Mystic Millie (has a follower count in the millions) and Dougie Trainor (ditto), as if she simply can't see anyone with less than 100,000 followers.

In some ways it's comforting being ignored by her; it almost feels like things are back to how they were before the murders.

"HEATHER!" Annie shouts, optimistically thinking Heather hasn't heard her.

Heather continues her determined stride over to the influencers.

"HEATHER! HEATHER!" Annie's waving her arms.

But Heather doesn't even look in her direction. A small twitch in her right eye is all the indication Annie needs, though, that she's heard her. Unfortunately the influencers *have* heard us and, unlike Heather, are looking right at us.

"HEATHER STEVENS, DON'T YOU DARE IGNORE ME AFTER EVERYTHING I'VE DONE FOR YOU. I EVEN GOOGLED WHETHER HAVING SEX UNDERWATER MEANT THAT YOU'D GET STUCK TOGETHER LIKE SEAHORSES WHEN YOU DIDN'T WANT YOUR MUM TO FIND IT ON YOUR SEARCH HISTORY!"

There's a collective gasp from the Mini-Heathers as Heather spins around, lowering her sunglasses pointedly. She glances in our direction before shuffling quickly toward us, with Jessica and her bubbles in pursuit.

"Christ sake, Annie, you said you'd never tell," Heather hisses, the bubbles still popping around her angry face.

"And *you* said you'd never ignore me in public again," Annie says, hands on her hips in confrontation.

"I literally do not remember saying that," Heather whispers.

"Well, I do!" Annie announces loudly to everyone around.

Heather looks around her, smiling through gritted teeth at Mystic Millie and Dougie, who have now stopped filming, and are watching with amused interest.

"What do you want?" she asks out of the corner of her stretched mouth.

"Let me stay in the VIP glamp site." Annie narrows her eyes, and Heather copies her. The two of them stand for a moment, as if about to duel.

Annie goes to open her mouth again, and Heather's eyes widen as she steps toward her. "Urgh, look, fine—yurt number ten has become unexpectedly free at the last minute," Heather says with a sigh.

I can feel excitement radiating off Annie, but I can't help wondering what exactly happened that made yurt number ten suddenly free?

"Is there a reason why—?" I start to ask nervously, but I'm cut off by Heather snapping over me.

"But, oh my god, just don't, like, do anything embarrassing, capisce?"

"Capisce," Annie says, beaming at her.

"They're in," Heather says to the security guards.

Annie flashes them a grin, but I can't help feeling incredibly sheepish as we pass.

"I'm sorry," I mutter, my head down. I'm not entirely sure what I'm apologizing for, I just feel for some reason like it's appropriate.

3

"We're going to be staying in the same place as Winona Philips!" Annie squeals, skipping ahead of me as we pass under a tunnel made of flower arches that links the VIP area with the rest of the camp. "I wonder if her yurt'll be near ours! I can see it now: us having important feminist discussions around the campfire with her."

I side-eye her as I continue lugging the cumbersome tent that Annie clearly had no intention of ever using. But she doesn't notice because she's too busy daydreaming out loud.

"She can be my mentor, and when I get into university she'll come and do talks and we'll be old friends. She'll call me to join her onstage in front of all my peers; they'll worship me by association . . ." Annie's eyes are sparkling as she spirals dangerously into a fantasy world.

I feel a wave of anxious nausea hit me, and I think I might be sick.

"Here's a thought!" Annie snaps out of her daydream. "Now we're here among the influencers, you can interview them!" She stops and spins around to me, clutching my arm. "YOU

COULD INTERVIEW WINONA PHILIPS!"

I smile and nod, trying not to let on that I'm way ahead of her and that, in fact, since this thought first occurred to me ten minutes ago, I have created an imaginary scene in my head with Winona and me. We're sitting on a sofa, me interviewing her with confidence and poise, asking intelligent and insightful questions, and her complimenting me on their intelligence and insightfulness.

"Oh my god, look at it!" Annie exclaims as we pop out of the tunnel and into the lush, green VIP area.

It's so much quieter, much less chaotic, and even more beautiful than the main festival ground. A circle of large pink yurts, probably each the size of a small house, are gathered around a central firepit. Logs to sit on circle the pit while long strings of bulb-style fairy lights hang around the camp. And I can't help but notice that as soon as we got in here away from all the crowds, I felt much more chill about everything.

"Oh, and there's yet *another* reason to thank me for getting us in here!" Annie beams with pride. "We get access to the VIP spa block rather than those gross porta potties like everyone else!"

I smile as she stares back down at her phone, once again immersed in scrolling ReelLife while I'm left to do the practical stuff, like looking around for our yurt. I clutch Herbie to me, trying to see if there's some kind of map.

"HEY, GUYS!" A bubbly female voice comes from the yurt next to us as its flaps are thrown open and an influencer who even I recognize immediately emerges, talking into her screen.

Annie's so caught up in her ReelLife feed and thoughts of Winona and world domination that she's not even seen her.

"Honestly, Winona's definitely going to connect with me far more than all these other vapid influencers," Annie's saying as she scrolls through the Festival of Fame hashtag. "I mean look at *this* one! She's just obsessed with mascara and shopping!"

I look down at her screen and realize she's talking about the very same influencer I can see just a few feet away from us now.

"Welcome to the Festival of Fame! I'm so excited to be here!" the stunningly beautiful influencer says into her phone. She has perfectly beach-waved auburn hair decorated by a crown of daisies.

Both she and Annie are walking backward, so locked into their phone screens they're not looking around them, and now they're getting perilously close to one another.

"Annie . . ." I warn, hoping I can get her to at least not crash into the person she's hate-watching. "*Annie.*"

"God, she's so shallow!" Annie laughs. She twists her voice to mimic the influencer: "Hey, GUYS, I'm *so* excited that I'm going to get *loads* of money from this post about a glorified cotton bud. So basic."

"Annie!" I warn, but it's too late, she goes crashing into the auburn influencer, sending both their phones flying into the air.

The two of them tumble to the ground, their phones landing beside them seconds later. Annie looks furious, while the influencer still looks perfect, her skin glowing, cute freckles glinting in the sunlight. But that would make sense considering how many free beauty products she receives on the regular, because she's Celeste—just the one name, like Madonna, or Kylie—the biggest beauty and wellness influencer in the UK right now. But Annie clearly hasn't figured that out yet since becoming an influencer five minutes ago.

Annie looks up, scowling, ready to have a go, but then she looks from Celeste to the ground, where her phone is still playing one of Celeste's videos, and then back to Celeste again, realizing that *this* is the very person she was just mocking. Her mouth hangs open as she slowly reaches out a hand to grab her phone.

"Oh crap, sorry!" Celeste's the first one to speak while Annie's jaw simply hangs open.

"Mmmmph," seems to be the only sound Annie's able to make as the two of them scramble up.

"I should have been looking where I was going," Celeste continues.

She stands, brushing dirt from her neon cycling shorts and T-shirt—with the slogan *Bitches Get Riches*—her business that supports young women in business born off the back of her makeup brand Bitches Get Contours. There's a pair of oversize daisy-shaped sunglasses dominating her face, to match her flower crown.

"Mmmmmurgh," Annie mumbles again, staring at the darkened screen of her phone like a cat that's been caught in the litter tray. She pushes her hair behind her ears awkwardly and then, clearly changing her mind, pulls it back out again. Her lips purse into an awkward pout. I've never seen her so flustered.

Ahead of us, Heather and the Mini-Heathers have seen what's going on and diverted from their glory lap around the glamp site to make a swift beeline for Celeste, clearly convinced she needs rescuing.

"Are you okay?" Celeste asks Annie kindly.

"Yes, thank you, you?" Annie says so politely and disjointed that she doesn't sound like Annie at all.

Heather's face looks thunderous as she and the Mini-Heathers approach. I notice that each of the Mini-Heathers have numbers on the backs of their shirts. They're no longer individuals with their own names and identities; they're simply one, two, and Jessica at the back is number three. Like a dystopian women's football team. They all trot behind Heather obediently, poor Jessica literally drowning in the sea of her own hard-blown bubbles.

"I'm Celeste." Celeste beams.

Annie's cheeks flush even darker red.

I'm guessing Celeste didn't hear Annie's little impression, at least I really hope she didn't.

"Annie." She eventually puts her hand out and does an awkward little shake.

They continue shaking hands, looking like they're not sure who started it or why they're still doing it.

"Kerry," I say, opting for an equally awkward wave and immediately wishing I hadn't.

"Celeste! Are you all right?" Heather squawks before narrowing her eyes in Annie's direction. "What was she doing to you?"

But Celeste doesn't appear to notice Heather and her entourage because she's already resumed filming again. She's leaning into the camera, talking about some kind of bubble tea, which I know is her favorite cold beverage. I also know that she doesn't actually like hot beverages at all. I stop myself. Why and *how* do I know so much about this person? I thought I didn't know much about influencers at all. Is it kind of creepy to have this level of knowledge about a person I've only just vaguely met?

"I'm so excited to meet some of the fans over the next few days and talk all things beauty with you guys! And I *cannot wait* to share some exciting Bitches Get Contours exclusives with you all . . . PEACE, BITCHES! Love ya!" She does a peace sign to the camera and blows a kiss before she stops filming.

I can practically feel the eye roll that Annie does at the word "bitches" from next to me. I hope Celeste doesn't see.

"I'm Heather! CEO of the festival," Heather launches in again as soon as Celeste's finished filming.

"CEO?" Annie and I mouth to each other.

"It's *so* lovely to meet you," Heather gushes.

"Oh, great, yeah I noticed my yurt doesn't actually have the silk pillowcases I requested. The ones in there are linen. It's really bad for my skin not to have the silk ones," Celeste says while tapping away at her phone.

Heather stares at her briefly in horror before shouting into her headset. "SOMEONE SORT OUT THE PILLOWCASES IN YURT NUMBER FOUR. THEY SHOULD BE SILK, NOT COTTON. NEEDS TO BE FIXED, NOW!"

Next to her, Mini-Heather One mutters into her headset. "On it, Heather, rectifying now. So sorry."

"I'm *so* sorry about that," Heather says. "I hope everything else is to your liking."

"Sure, gotta go post this," Celeste says, before turning back around. "And, hey, great job getting Winona to host! She's an absolute babe!"

"Oh, thanks so much! Yes you were the real coup obvious—" Heather cuts off when she realizes that Celeste's already left.

She shoots Annie and me one final angry look before turning on her heel and scuttling off, shouting into her headset.

"God, diva much?" Annie mutters in Celeste's direction. But I can tell that Celeste's mention of Winona threw her a bit. After all, she wouldn't have expected someone so "vapid" to even know who she was, right?

I finally spot yurt number ten ahead of us and I'm relieved to have a reason to get away from everything out here.

"Maybe we should dump our stuff in there before you make any more content?" I suggest, pointing to the backpack that's preventing her from moving her arms freely.

"Good plan," Annie says as the two of us walk into the yurt.

The two of us stand between the entrance flaps observing the luxurious space, complete with beds and a sofa and tiny fairy lights.

"Which bed do you want?" I ask Annie, but she's staring at something on her phone still.

"We'll take the one farthest away from the door, then, Herbie," I say to him, plonking my bags on the bed. "What do you reckon, boy?"

"Cool!" Annie eventually says, coming over and dumping her bag.

I collapse onto my bed at the same time, knowing that I need to get up and start exploring the festival. I'm here on business, I need to get businessing and journalisting! I am a professional woman! But my god these beds are comfy.

"Hey, guys!" I hear what sounds like Annie's voice from my bed, but it's so perky that I find myself jumping up and staring at her like she's a stranger. Next to me Herbie cocks his head as if wondering whether to do his intruder bark.

There's something kind of sinister about the way Annie appears to have had a complete personality transplant whenever she records something for ReelLife, and I can't help but wonder if Herbie thinks so, too. He makes a small growling noise, and I worry he might be trying to tell me something. They say dogs can sense danger, don't they? Or is it ghosts they can sense? Either way, he's definitely feeling uneasy about something here.

"Come with me to take a look around the VIP section of the Festival of Fame!" Annie's saying into her screen before she spins the phone around to try to capture the inside of the yurt, and I race to cover my face with the bedsheets.

Somehow Annie's got me back out of the yurt and making "content" with her, so in the name of influencing we're currently walking around the VIP section while she films our every move and I try to hide.

"Just out with my bestie, Kerry—we've got some iced teas, and we're ready to explore the Festival of Fame!" Annie says again. She tries to capture me in the shot, but I duck out of the way just in time to preserve whatever's left of my dignity today.

"Just out with my bestieeeeee," a guy's voice behind us mimics Annie to an immediate chorus of male laugher around him.

We turn, and the moment I see who's behind the voice I know this whole festival is going to be one of the worst mistakes of my life. It's Timmy Eaton—the most popular and dickish of all the influencers attending this weekend. And he's laughing at us with his group of look-alike friends, known as the Tim-sciples. The world's most toxic entourage. Even without them, he's a man constructed purely of fake tan and ego, who describes himself as a "prankfluencer." And as if all that wasn't bad enough, his most viral video, which everyone in the entire country has seen, involved him "finding" tampons that he'd soaked in red paint on girls' seats after they stood up at his high school. Disturbingly, he was recently voted as the world's sexiest influencer. Even more disturbingly, I can kind of see why but only if we're purely going by looks. Definitely *not* personality. Either way, I hate that I know that his favorite food is pasta, because he "loves to carb load, man."

"Here with my bestieeeesss," he repeats jarringly, the Tim-sciples laughing even harder, as if it was somehow funnier the second time even though the first wasn't funny at all.

The smug ass laughs along, radiating arrogance in a baseball cap. He's holding out his phone in front of him and flexing his muscles as he films. He must be on a livestream. My stomach bottoms out. He does more than five livestreams a day, at least one of them is some kind of live workout. After every workout, he eats a protein bar from a company that sponsors him. I can't believe I know all this about someone's daily routine when I don't even like them. ReelLife is a curse.

Annie gapes at him, and I have to admit I'm doing the same.

"What's your mouth open for, love? You'll have to open much wider than that if you're wanting to give me a blow job!" he shouts.

The pack of identically dressed men behind him whoop and cheer, slapping him on the back in congratulations for his awful attempt at humor. They're like his personal laugh track.

Annie slams her mouth shut like a bear trap and glares. I

will her to ignore him and not give him the reaction that he so clearly wants. Now would be a good time for that psychic link straight into my brain I've always been scared Annie has to kick in.

Ignore him, I think. Walk away. Right now.

"Excuse me?!" Annie shouts at him.

Dammit.

"We weren't talking to you, so maybe keep your grubby comments to yourself. Shoo, little boy." She puts her hands on her hips and glares at him.

"Shoo, little boy!" Timmy repeats in a high-pitched voice, and the crowd of Timmy look-alikes break into loud, patronizing male-pack-like laughter, like directionless sheep. "All right there, grandma? Shoo, SHOO! NAUGHTY LITTLE BOY!"

His minions fall about laughing again.

"Could we not just leave and go explore the rest of the festival? Winona's got to be here somewhere. There's no reason to stay talking to him," I whisper to Annie, trying not to make any eye contact with Timmy or any of his band of douchebags.

"I'm not stopping filming for that misogynist piece of shit," Annie retorts, making brief, defiant eye contact with him.

"Don't worry, I'm not going to stop filming for you, either, sweetheart," Timmy says, gesturing to his phone camera that's angled directly at Annie and me.

"You don't have our consent to film us. STOP," Annie says, her face going red.

He smirks and brushes his hair back like a guy who thinks he's god's gift to humankind and swaggers toward us, getting closer and closer to her with the phone.

"You could always leave, unless that is, you don't want to

because you're enjoying what you see." He winks and runs his hands over his defined chest and abs. It's the grossest act I've seen since two slugs mated in front of me in a biology class. "A lot of girls do find me irresistible. She's not normally my type, but I love a fiery temper."

"GROSS! Just STOP FILMING ME!!!" Annie suddenly shouts, as if all the possible options for comebacks exploded in her head. "STOP FILMING ME NOW! I DO NOT CONSENT TO BEING IN YOUR REELLIFE!"

Behind Timmy, the Tim-sciples burst into laughter, delighted with the way that she's caved in and lost it like they wanted.

"Calm down, sweetheart! Someone on her period or what?" he says to the camera. Then he puts on a David Attenborough voice, speaking into his phone. "The village local in its natural habitat, in heat, stalking her male."

"Annie." I try to hide behind her while I talk because I'm simply not as brave as she is. "Let's just go, at least then he can't film us anymore."

"Yeah, Annie, let's go!" The nameless copycats behind Timmy start imitating my voice, and I can feel the redness threatening to engulf my entire face.

"Yeah, Annie, time to change your tampon, babe," Timmy says. It's this final blow that seems to spur Annie into action. Not her most rational of actions, though.

"DICK!" Annie suddenly whips around to face the dickhead, her eyes flaming hotter than the sun. "For your information I *AM* MENSTRUATING and in this ten-*thousand*-degree heat. Which by the way should actually be ILLEGAL. There's no way *you'd* be able to hack it. SO WHY DON'T YOU AND YOUR GANG OF MERRY DICKHEADS JUST BACK! OFF!"

There's a brief moment of silence as Timmy's mouth turns up at the corners, the self-satisfied grin of victory spreading like a fungus.

"Bro, she is MENTAL," one of the Tim-sciples shouts to him.

"Right? They're all crazy when they're on their period, though, bro. It's, like, science or something. It's Timmy versus the Mental Menstruator, guys." Timmy laughs, his head thrown back, his mouth open like a gaping maw as he howls with laugher at our expense. "Go cool off a bit, Annie babe, I've clearly made you too hot."

Without a second thought Annie spins around, iced tea in hand, and dunks the entire thing—ice cubes, straw, and all—over Timmy's head. The gathered crowd along with his Tim-sciples watch open-mouthed as brown liquid drips over his perfectly sculpted arms and gold iPhone, even catching some of his bro-tourage behind him.

"You're the one who needs to cool off," she snaps.

As the liquid runs down his now transparent T-shirt, I cringe, expecting anger. Instead, a smile starts to form back on his face. Dimples accentuating each of his cheeks, he hands the phone off to his bro, stepping up next to Annie—into frame, I realize as my stomach lurches—and reaches for the bottom corners of his shirt before slowly peeling it off himself and over his head, exposing a perfectly formed six-pack. I could count them. I start to but then realize what's happening and try my absolute damnedest not to look, even though the whole thing feels like it's moving in slow motion.

"If you wanted to get my clothes off, babe, all you had to do was ask." He smiles, licking his teeth with the tip of his tongue.

"ARGH!" Annie stamps her foot and grabs my hand, storming off back across the VIP glamp site away from the most infuriating dickhead either of us have ever met.

I'm absolutely not going to turn around and look back at his perfectly formed six-pack, not even for one last glan— Oh, whoops.

4

The two of us storm away from Timmy so fast that I get a stitch. I have to stop and bend over, clutching my side. While Herbie watches me with concern for my welfare, Annie seems more concerned with a giant poster containing Timmy's face. For a moment I think she's about to start kicking and punching it, but instead she takes out a black Sharpie.

"Now what are you doing?" I pant, looking over my shoulder to check that none of the Tim-sciples have followed us.

"Just a little bit of fan art. Won't be long," Annie says, scribbling away.

"Well, I'd say this is going swimmingly!" I pant, grabbing Herbie and clutching him to my chest like a comfort blanket. "We've not only pissed off the most popular influencer here, we've also borderline assaulted him with iced tea. Oh, and now we're being stared at by strangers."

"No one's staring . . ." Annie says, trailing off when she spins around and realizes that there are actually quite a few people around the VIP area looking at us. Their glares burn through me, and I wonder if I might be about to find out how spontaneous combustion happens.

Behind Annie I can see what she's been busy scribbling on the wall as well, and it definitely isn't about to help our cause any. On the poster of Timmy Eaton, she's drawn a very detailed giant phallus protruding out of his forehead in thick black Sharpie. She's also written the word "D I C K H E A D," in perfectly spaced caps next to his name.

"Wow," I say. "Hang it in the Louvre."

"Show me the lie." Annie gestures to the picture with her added improvements.

"Now that you've made that important political signage, maybe we should head back to the yurt for a bit?" I ask. "It's half an hour till the first event, and I'd rather we didn't piss off any more influencers before then."

"I mean, once Winona gets here I'm pretty sure she's going to applaud me for throwing that iced tea, you know, but until then, let's make new friends," Annie says, looking around her with intent.

"Yes, interacting with others has gone well for us so far," I mutter. "Let's definitely do more of that."

"It's networking, babe! We have to get connections so I can get followers and you can get scoops! Look! That lady over there." Annie points to a woman who's hanging sage sticks and crystals on the outside of her yurt. "She was here earlier when we came in. Who is she again?"

"Mystic Millie," I say. Why, when Annie's the one who wants to be an influencer, am I the one that seems to know all this?

The blond woman stands, surveying the crystals in the doorway to her yurt. She's wearing a large tie-dye kaftan, round purple-lensed glasses, a matching tie-dye scarf tied around her hair, and huge crystals hanging from her earlobes, hands, and neck. Mystic Millie gives daily horoscopes and predictions to subscribers as well as offering things like classes in crystal healing, her own range of crystals, and even séances. She also paired with Winona Philips on her vaginal-steamer product line.

Mystic Millie pulls out her phone and holds it up to film, posing in front of her new crystal arrangement.

"SPIRITS! Welcome to behind the scenes at the Festival of Fame! I'm giving you the inside scoop on the vibes, the auras, and who's touching whose chakras!"

She gives the screen a coy smile, and before I know what's happening, Annie's headed in her direction, barreling toward influencer number two for the day.

"Now I've got some predictions for the festival ahead!" Mystic Millie's still talking into her phone, blissfully unaware of Annie's proximity. "I can see what's coming in the near future, and you're all going to love it!"

"Hey!" Annie says, popping up around her phone screen and making Mystic Millie jump so she drops her phone.

"Oh Christ, I nearly pissed myself!" Mystic Millie says, clutching her chest and going to pick up her phone.

"Oops! Sorry!" Annie says with a cheeky grin. "Sorry! I'm Annie, this is my friend Kerry, we're the Tampon Two! You're Mystic Millie aren't you? I just love your horoscopes and content!"

I try to maneuver my face into something approaching neutral, knowing that Annie has never seen any of Mystic Millie's content.

"Oh, right," Mystic Millie says, brushing off her phone and stopping the recording. She looks angry, not exactly like she's enjoying this conversation.

"I loved your post this morning, with tips about what to do when Mercury's in the microwave and you're having a bad hair day," I butt in. Seriously, how do I remember all this stuff?

"Oh, thank you! That's so kind—not even I can foresee every bad hair day!" Millie says. With that, she raises her phone again.

"Oh my god! You're the ones who chucked iced tea on Timmy!" Another figure I recognize from earlier appears from the inside of Mystic Millie's tent, entirely shirtless. Up close he's so tall that I'm nose to abs with him. I raise my head slowly, swallowing excess saliva as I scan the shaggy, sandy hair, chiseled cheekbones, and shining brown eyes of Dougie Trainor, reality TV and influencer heartthrob. And he's talking to us. My mouth hangs open, breathing hot air somewhere around his navel.

An influencer since birth, Dougie Trainor is Timmy's best friend and cohost on their podcast—the imaginatively titled *SausageFest*. As the name promises, it's a podcast where they have never, to my knowledge, had a female guest on. He seems far nicer than Timmy, though—not that that's hard. For instance, on this year's season of *Romantic Rambles*, a show where the contestants go for half-naked walks in the wilds of Wales in the middle of winter, with the aim of finding love wearing only their underwear—honestly not sure if I've ever seen him fully clothed—he was nicknamed the Adorable Adonis, because he kept tearing pieces off his already tiny boxer briefs to add to his female contestants' outfits. He didn't find love, but he did win the lust of a nation. It's wild to me that he's best friends with such an enormous dickhead.

"Erm, yes. That would be us," Annie says, trying to maintain a professional and cool exterior.

I realize he's smiling at me, flashing his white teeth, and I'm still staring, mouth open like I'm at the dentist. Annie elbows me.

"I'm Kerry," I say, but it comes out like a puff of air with *erry* on the end. I find myself twirling a strand of hair around my finger and tilting my head slightly.

Oh my god, what am I doing? I don't know. It's like hormones are transforming me into a hair twirler. My brain goes into overdrive.

Am I flirting?

Is flirting cheating?

Am I cheating on Scott?

I'm just touching my hair.

Stop touching your hair, Kerry.

Why am I still twirling it?

"You guys have blown *up* on ReelLife!" Dougie's enthusiasm rings alarm bells even through the haze of lust, and I look down at my phone to see several messages in the Les Populaires WhatsApp, indicating that we could be in quite a lot of trouble.

Les Populaires

Colin: Oh Christ. You're VIRAL.

Audrey: I cannot believe you did that to
TIMMY EATON. He's like SO FAMOUS.

Heather: I am going to KILL you.

"I'm viral!" Annie breathes into her phone.

"Nice to have achieved your goal. At least you can die happy now, because Heather is going to murder you," I mutter, as she seems to have willfully glossed over Heather's message.

I look over Annie's shoulder at the ReelLife video on her screen, depicting the moment she was so overcome with rage that she showered him in her cold beverage. Timmy must have saved the live as evidence. It's only been five minutes and it already has thousands of likes and comments from people outraged at Annie's "attack" on Timmy. Yet not one of them seems outraged by his blatant harassment of us I notice.

"Look at my follower numbers!" Annie says. "How did they find me?"

I flick to Timmy's video again and notice a comment from none other than Colin, always one to fan the flames of a drama. On closer inspection I see that he's responded to people asking who Annie is and tagged her profile.

"I've got over a thousand followers!" she gasps quietly, trying not to flag to Mystic Millie and Dougie that this is more than she's ever had before.

"Yeah they're not exactly 'fans' of yours, though, are they?" I point out the comments saying that they will "unleash a million iced teas" on Annie as payback in Timmy's honor.

"Oh man," Dougie says, looking up from his phone to Annie. "Oh, you're in trouble."

"What?" Annie asks, edging closer to a man so incredibly hot that he has been voted as such multiple times at multiple award shows, without so much of a hint as a weakness at the knees.

"He's declaring war," Dougie says, turning his screen to us.

On the screen Timmy's surrounded by his Tim-sciples in pretty much the same space that we left him in. As they stand jeering excitedly behind him his voice is drowned out, but the captions on the screen spell it all out in great detail.

"Some of you may have seen my earlier incident with some kind of 'feminist activist' called @AnnieTamponTwo." He does bunny quotes with his fingers while talking to the screen, flexing his muscles for good measure. "She seems to think what she did was really big and clever, and I've heard someone else saw her defacing a poster of me by drawing a dick on my face as well. Pretty childish. Well, guess what, babe, I'm a rubber and you're lube, whatever you say just makes me slicker. So @AnnieTamponTwo, it's time to put your pranks where your mouth is! I gave you the first for free, but now it's on. I declare prank war. Best prank in the next twenty-four hours wins. Good luck to you, @AnnieTamponTwo, you'll need it."

"Oh, it's on," Annie says, glaring at the screen so intensely I physically gulp back nervous spit. "It's really on."

Behind her I can see Mystic Millie lighting a small stick of sage and wafting the smoke in our general direction, and as I watch the comments from Timmy's fans growing on Annie's profile, I can't help thinking we're going to need all the sage smudging we can get.

Timmysbabe4eva: I've got two large iced teas with your name on if I see you around this festival.

TammyLovesTimmy: You're going to need more than a tampon to soak up all the iced tea we've got for you babes.

TimmyEatonsMineBackOff: I'd literally eat my lunch off Timmy Eaton's dirty underwear, let me know if anyone's selling any. $$$$$

Next to me I can feel Annie's confidence waning. She gulps, trying to keep up with all the new comments as they appear every few seconds. Each of them details how they intend on avenging her attack on Timmy Eaton. While I probably wouldn't mind a cold drink to cool me down, I think a thousand iced teas is way too much.

Annie and I poke our heads out of the yurt, clutching the flaps tightly around our faces in case we need to disappear back inside urgently. We look left and then right, both of us wearing bright yellow raincoats that Annie just happened to have in her massive camping rucksack, with the hoods pulled up and tied tightly around our faces, and big black bug-like sunglasses over our eyes.

"We can't go back out there without full protection," Annie had told me, and I believe her. Even if the protection is a little more high-vis yellow than I'd hoped.

So now here we are, cautiously poking our heads out into the festival from the safety of our yurt, trying to work out if we can make it to the VIP backstage area without getting pranked, soaked, or otherwise humiliated again before the "Influencers Under Twenty" panel event. Herbie joins us in sticking his little head out of the flaps and sniffing the air.

"This isn't just a prank war," Annie says, peering over her lenses dramatically. "It's, like, he's put a virtual hit out on me. All five million of his fans are going to be buying iced tea as we speak."

"There's only a thousand people at this festival," I point out to her. Despite my nerves, I am still trying to find some kind of perspective in all this.

"I COULD STILL DROWN IN A THOUSAND PEOPLE'S ICED TEA, KERRY!" Annie panics. "There are Timmy fans EVERYWHERE. It could come at me anywhere, anytime."

Her terrified face is squished by the tightness of her hood as she continues peering over her sunglasses at me. And her eyes flit from left to right as if expecting the iced tea blow to land right this minute.

"I think we should go," I say. "I'm worried we're going to miss Winona. If we have to be here in peril, I want to at least get something out of it."

"Oh god, look, I know you're right; we just need to watch each other's backs, right?" she asks me.

"Right," I agree.

"Right, Herbie?" Annie asks.

"Right," I say, using a fake Herbie voice.

"Then onward we go, for feminism, friendship, my world domination, and your blog," Annie says, putting her hand down between the two of us.

I lean down and add my hand over the top of hers, then add Herbie's little paw over the top of us all.

"For feminism and friendship," I confirm, not adding the rest because it seems less catchy.

Herbie barks, because he's nothing if not a feminist dog, and the three of us proceed, waterproofed and ready for whatever liquids come our way.

"Wait." Annie holds up a hand dramatically at the yurt opening. She looks left to right three more times and then flings the yurt flaps open wider. "Coast's clear, proceed."

I follow her out. Ahead, she's skipping and muttering to herself excitedly, despite the possible peril. "I can't believe we're going to meet Winona Philips!"

We walk through the VIP campsite with little drama. Having Annie and Herbie beside me makes my confidence grow with every step. We're halfway through the flower arch when someone approaches us with a cup in their hand. I feel my shoulders tense but realize pretty quickly that they're not even looking at us. Despite this, Annie throws herself on the ground in front of me.

"Nooooooooo!" she screams, skidding across the grass while

the guy walks past, bemused, holding what I can now see is a completely empty cup.

"I saved you," Annie says, beaming up at me and Herbie— who stares at her with puzzled eyebrows.

"Yep, from the invisible danger. Your love really knows no bounds." I pick her up from the ground and help her dust herself off. "I missed you, dude."

5

"I'm here, and I'm not afraid of you, Timmy Eaton." Annie speaks into her phone screen with the seriousness of someone about to enter the Hunger Games of prank wars.

I don't think she even realizes how ridiculous it is that she's addressing a public video to someone who's just a few feet away from her. He can surely hear her from where he is—but he's not even looking in her direction, he's far too busy flirting with a female fan.

The inflatable sofa we're sitting on in the green room (a small pink mobile behind the stage area) squeaks and farts under Annie as she moves around animatedly, and I hope to God that no one thinks those noises are coming from me. I take the hood of my raincoat down because it's actually impeding my view, and I'm trying hard to observe the influencers preparing for the "Influencers Under Twenty" panel and mentally take notes for what I'm sure will be a prize-winning exposé, although it's becoming increasingly difficult not to be distracted by Annie's dramas.

"Whatever you try, I'll always be ten steps ahead," says

Annie, phone pressed to her face, presumably speaking to Timmy and his flock of rabid fans. "And speaking of steps, maybe it's time you watch yours." She stops filming and turns to me, still encased in her raincoat and bug glasses like an angry glowworm. "You gotta give your public what they want."

"Oh no, whyyyy?" I groan with my head in my hands as she hits Post. "Surely Winona Philips will be here any second now. And what would she think of all this? Her first impression of you is going to be that you're pranking with a fool."

"Surely when she sees that I've taken Timmy Eaton down a peg or two, she's going to think that I'm an absolute queen and rather than me trying to make friends with *her*, *she's* going to be trying to make friends with *me*."

I have a really, really bad feeling about this.

"Have you even got anything planned?" I ask, because I'm pretty sure she doesn't.

We both hate pranks, and we've never been any good at them.

"Of course I do." Annie bristles in a way that lets me know she's got absolutely nothing.

"Hey, guys!" Celeste marks her entrance with her trademark greeting as she films her way into the backstage area. "Welcome to the green room at the Festival of Fame, where we're all getting ready for our first panel. If you're here and you're ready for fun, COME JOIN US! WHOOP WHOOP!!"

Next to her Dougie waves into the camera.

"Did you know that the two of them have been best friends since birth?" I whisper to Annie. "They were the highest-earning baby influencers way back at, like, the start of the internet." Immediately I wince. I've unwittingly become some

48

kind of encyclopedia for influencer knowledge and I'm scaring myself.

Mini-Heather One cuts short Celeste's video-making by running in and attempting to herd all the influencers like sheep. "Everyone get ready for curtain up! All the influencers to the stage! Does anyone know where Mystic Millie is?"

"Sorry! Someone wanted to talk to me!" Mystic Millie says, rushing in and nodding up to the sky mournfully. "Someone with an important message, from the beyond."

"Right, yeah," Annie mutters. "Wait, where's Winona? They can't go on without her."

"Maybe she's already onstage?" I suggest.

"Maybe she's got a really cool way she's going to appear onstage? Like what if she's flying in on something?!"

I find it unlikely, but I want to hope, as Annie and I follow the influencers out of the green room and through to the side of the stage. We wait in the wings. I look out at the crowd from the sidelines and see hundreds of excited people out there. I definitely wouldn't cope among all those people. It makes me even more relieved to be a VIP now.

Music suddenly blares out of huge speakers, silencing everyone. The buzz of anticipation from the crowd is infectious, everyone waiting for the first sighting of Winona Philips and the other influencers. But when the lights go out, it's Heather who walks onstage, and the crowd's faces change from anticipation to confusion in an instant.

"GOOD EVENING, BARBOUROUGH!!!" Heather shouts. I can tell she's waiting for a cheer, but what she's greeted with is silence. The light from the audience's iPhones goes out when they realize that she's not an influencer or a celebrity, and they stop filming, saving their battery for something more exciting. It's weird not to see people treat Heather as if she's the main event. And you can tell it's jarring for her—she's been Barbourough's main event her whole life.

"I'm Heather Stevens! The She-EO of Festival of Fame!"

I cringe so hard I want to turn myself inside out.

"Oh my god," Annie breathes, wincing as Heather continues to force perkiness despite the crowd's disappointment.

"This weekend's all about getting to know your favorite influencers, finding out what makes them tick, and, crucially—how you can go viral! We're so proud to be hosting this event here at Rose Hill Farm, the original home of V-Lyte period products." She turns to a cameraman who's filming everything just below the stage for one of the livestreams and throws up a peace sign while staring earnestly into the camera's lens. "FESTIVAL OF FAME SPONSORED BY V-LYTE PERIOD PRODUCTS!"

She pauses, I'm not sure if she's expecting a laugh or a cheer or something, but there's just discomfort and restlessness. They just want her to hurry up and get off so they can see Winona.

"God, it's so awkward," Annie whispers. She starts winding her finger around and mouthing "Wrap it up, babe."

But Heather can't see.

"It's like watching a car crash in real time." I put my hood back up to obscure my view.

"So, without further ado . . ." Heather begins, and we both finally exhale.

"Thank the baby Beyoncé," Annie whispers.

"Here to host the first event, our 'Influencers Under Twenty' panel, it's . . . Winona Philips!" Heather gestures behind her as the crowd waits for Winona to walk onstage.

I'm standing on tiptoes, straining to see where she might be coming from because she's certainly not backstage with everyone else. Annie bobs into my peripheral vision like a meerkat, head turning so fast I'm surprised she's not dizzy. And it's not just her; everyone's becoming more frantic, because Winona's nowhere to be seen.

"Where is she? What if something's happened to her?" Annie whispers, chewing on her thumb, her eyes wide.

As the moments pass, and the stage remains empty, I'm starting to think Annie could be right. Around us the Mini-Heathers are tapping away furiously at their phones. A concerned murmur travels the length of the green room. Onstage Heather's smile hasn't budged—if something *is* up, she's not going to let it show. I see Celeste and Dougie whisper to each other, brows furrowed with concern. What has happened to Winona Philips?

There's a loud buzz from the wall behind Heather, making an already tense crowd jump. The screen lights up, enveloping the stage in a blue illumination before pixilating dramatically. A mixture of relief and disappointment settles over the audience as Winona's face appears twenty times larger than life, but not really here.

Far from the danger we had started to imagine her in, Winona's safely holed up in her house, hosting from the pink armchair that her fans have seen her in so many times before. She looks cool, calm, and, as ever, extremely stylish. Once the initial confusion peters out, the crowd goes flat. I'm feeling pretty disappointed myself. Sure I was nervous about meeting her, but maybe I was also excited, too. And that won't happen now that she's not in Barbourough. Even backstage you can hear the mutters from people who feel like they've been lied to. Finally she speaks with a slight delay, her lips not matching the words projecting across the festival site.

"Good evening, Barbourough! Winona Philips here, ready to host your gala event—the 'Influencers Under Twenty' panel! Obviously we need to address some elephants on this stage. No, I'm not under twenty—but it's rude of you to even mention it! Haha! And secondly, I'm so sorry that I couldn't be there with you all today. I've had some last-minute things come up, so I'm having to attend the festival remotely."

"Fuck's sake," Annie mutters next to me. She kicks at the dusty ground petulantly with the tip of her butcher-grade wellington boot.

"I think that went well?" Heather says brightly, appearing next to us in the wings just as Annie's anger about Winona's no-show reaches its peak. "The atmosphere out there is just ELECTRIC you know. You've not lived until you've been on a stage in front of hundreds of people, all idolizing you."

"You didn't think to mention to me that Winona wasn't going to make it?" Annie bites out.

"I only found out today! She's hurt her foot or something," Heather says. "It was *such* a pain in the ass that no, Annie, you weren't the first person I thought of getting in touch with."

"Wait, was yurt ten—our yurt—supposed to be where Winona was staying?" I ask, but it's as if neither of them hear me.

Annie and Heather are locked in eye contact in a way that I've only seen before when they've argued about whether Jacob Elordi is hotter than Timothée Chalamet.

"OMG, that was so good, Heather." Mini-Heather One comes over with her clipboard, interrupting their stare-down to lie

52

about Heather's performance, and thus crawl further up her ass.

"SO GOOD!" Mini-Heather Two pats powder onto Heather's face while Mini-Heather Three fluffs her hair.

I see Annie snapping a pic for Colin and Audrey so that they can see the way they've been replaced by much more subservient underlings in their absence.

"Did you get it on ReelLife?" Heather asks.

"Of course," Mini-Heather One replies.

"STATS?" Heather presses.

"No likes yet," Mini-Heather One replies.

She glances at me nervously, like I can save her. I shrug back to indicate that I cannot.

"But," she continues, her voice trembling, "I'm sure it's just buffering."

"Who's ready to meet our inspiring influencers under twenty?!!" Winona shouts from the stage, and the crowd roars.

"First up, we have DOUGIE TRAINOR!!!" Winona Philips announces to whoops and whistles.

Dougie walks across the stage, arms out to embrace the wall of sound.

"Dougie is the *star* of the last season of *Romantic Rambles*, where we all hailed him as the Adorable Adonis!" Winona crows. I note that Winona looks like she's reading off a script and probably didn't write this.

As Dougie reaches his seat, a bra comes hurtling out of the crowd and catches on his nose. He waves a thanks to the bra launcher, smoothly detangling himself, as if this is an everyday occurrence for him. Winona ignores the underwear and moves on, but you can see it makes her a little disappointed in humankind.

"Next we have Dougie's lifelong best friend, another influencer since birth, it's CELESTE!!!!" Winona shouts over the crowd that doesn't feel ready to move on from their Adonis.

Unfazed, Celeste strides across the stage, her legs perfectly long and sculpted in a way I didn't realize real humans could be. She reaches Dougie and gives him a hug as the crowd cheers the two of them on.

"What's their deal?" Annie asks.

"I know that the internet's been dying for the two of them to get together, but they never have. As far as we know anyway . . . although there was that weekend when they had a gifted spa trip together and it did actually look pretty romantic to me. . . ."

Annie gives me a look, and I instantly wipe the smug smirk from my face. God, what's wrong with me?

"A good journalist immerses themselves in their subject, and I am a good journalist," I say weakly.

"Okay, babe, maybe you should start writing," Annie says pointedly. I stare down at the empty Notes app page on my phone, because despite immersing myself in all of this, I've so far observed absolutely nothing I feel I can write about.

"And our spiritual guide for tonight is MYSTIC MILLIE!!!" Winona calls, saving me from being roasted further.

A puff of smoke covers the backstage area, spilling out onto the stage, as Mystic Millie in her purple kaftan sweeps out from behind the curtain. The smoke obscures her feet and adds to the illusion that she's not walking so much as she is gliding, a higher being, too spiritual for feet. But backstage we know it's just an illusion. Beside us a smoke machine splutters, filling the area with an overzealous amount of smoke that makes everyone waiting in the wings and Mystic Millie herself cough.

"Are you *trying* to be incompetent, Jessica?" I hear Mini-Heather One scolding Mini-Heather Three, who's seemingly been forced to ditch her bubble wand and haul a smoke machine around behind Mystic Millie for the vibes.

Somehow, the crowd seems to know to make a spooky "OooOOOOOOOoooooooohhhh" sound as Mystic Millie swooshes to her seat.

"And fourth up we have feminist influencer, female ally, all-around good egg, and Mystic Millie's OTHER HALF!!!! ETHAN WOODS!!!" Winona Philips announces, giving him a far nicer introduction than all the others.

"She seems to like him," Annie remarks wryly.

I shrug. "It's nice to have another feminist at the festival, right?" I don't know much about him, but with Winona's stamp of approval, my interest is certainly piqued.

Ethan Woods walks across the stage in a black turtleneck with a sign across the front that reads "Hands Off Our Bodies." There's a pair of round glasses perched on his upward-pointing nose and a copy of *The Feminine Mystique* poking out of the back pocket. He's got a thoughtful expression on his face, as if he's solving the issue of world peace as he goes to sit next to Mystic Millie, taking the book out of his pocket and placing it on his lap in a way that feels a bit performative if I'm being honest.

"What do we think of him?" Annie asks me, her tone scrutinizing.

"From one feminist to another, thank you," Ethan says to Winona. "I'm so happy to be here representing women, using my louder, stronger male voice to fight for equality for you."

"No." The noise punches out of me immediately, instinctively. I don't need to expand on that with Annie.

"Agreed," Annie sighs.

Winona glances down at her script, her eyes crinkling. "And last we have TIMMY EATON."

I snort. Last and clearly least, in Winona's eyes.

"I wish she was here so we could find out what she really thinks of him," Annie says, basically reading my mind. "And Ethan the 'male feminist' come to think of it." We share a look, and I nod, trying not to let on how suddenly I'm reminded of the prank war. "Where is Timmy anyway?"

The crowd's cheering becomes more insistent, but I notice that while Timmy was here about ten minutes ago, now he's completely disappeared. I sweep the backstage; I can't see him anywhere and neither can the frantic Mini-Heathers. I wonder where he's gone, and my gaze immediately turns to Annie.

"What?" Annie asks. "You're giving me your suspicious eye."

"Did you do something?" I narrow my eyes.

"What do you think, I like tied him up and locked him in a box or something all while still standing here next to you, just so he couldn't make his appearance, as a prank?"

"Did you?" I ask, but Annie simply smiles at me. I groan. "You can do incredible things when you put your mind to it."

The audience starts chanting his name. They've been burned by Winona already, and they'll definitely lose their patience if Timmy's now gone AWOL. If he doesn't show up soon, it'll turn nasty out there.

"Annie," I murmur, something like fear prickling at me.

The screen onstage flickers, and a furrow the size of a

capybara appears in Winona's gigantic brow. She opens her mouth to speak, but everything freezes. Someone screams, and I jump, then realize it's coming through the speakers. As the screen flickers again the image splits in half. Winona stays on the lefthand side, while a new video appears on the right. A girl turns around to the screen, one of Timmy's fans. Tears roll down her cheeks as she faces the camera. She raises a shaking hand and points down to something beneath her on the floor, something that looks worryingly like Timmy Eaton.

"She's killed him!" she wails, staring straight into the camera, her expression haunted. "She pranked him with a trip wire and . . . @AnnieTamponTwo's KILLED TIMMY EATON!"

6

Annie swallows and clutches my hand. The crowd has gone silent, and backstage every single eye is on us. It feels like the walls are closing in. My chest tightens as the image of the two of us in prison-issue jumpsuits flits into my head. After all, wherever Annie goes, I go too. I clasp her hand tightly in mine, our fingers shaking against each other.

"What's going on?" Winona asks from the screen, clearly as confused as the rest of us. "Sorry? Can someone help sort this out? Whatever it is?"

The crowd turns. A wave of angry whispers, and chatter, sets over the festival ground, and I hear Annie's name over and over again. Her face is green, and her bottom lip starts to tremble. I actually think she might cry, and Annie's not a crier. She saves tears for things that really hurt, like when she rode into a holly bush on her bike at age six.

Dougie stands up on the stage and shouts at the screen. "SOMEONE DO SOMETHING!"

This is it; we're going to be burned at the stake. Heather's approaching us at speed. I look around for an escape, but we're

58

completely hemmed in by the intimidating sea of cross faces. She's less than a meter away now, the Mini-Heathers flanking her, and I can tell she wants blood. They all want blood. Annie and I gulp in synchronization, while Herbie stands tall at my feet, barking at the tension. I look from Annie to the raging faces, willing this to be a bad dream that we'll wake up from soon. I close my eyes, screwing them up tight, but I can still feel the glares and accusing looks. I open them again just as there's a loud bang, a puff of smoke and a spark of fireworks onstage, and as if by twatty magic, Timmy Eaton reappears.

"HE HATH RISEN!!!!" he shouts into the crowd. "PRANKED YA @ANNIETAMPONTWO!! TIMMY EATON HAS WON THE PRANK WAR!!!!!"

I think I might pass out. Around us people gasp, and shocked laughter fills the festival as Timmy parades across the stage to cheering and whoops. I feel Annie's sweaty hand clamped in my own, and a rush of blood and adrenaline hits me all at once. The faces of people around me blur and swim in my vision, twisting with relief and laughter. The noise around us starts to sound far away, almost underwater. Then I feel my shoulders sinking from around my ears and eventually things start to refocus, the adrenaline settling.

Did that really just happen? I look at Annie, her eyes fixed firmly on the stage. She looks unsure if she wants to scream or cry.

The second half of the screen disappears, and Winona's face goes back to taking up the entire space, making her eye roll even bigger than it would be normally as Timmy laps up the cheers and praise from the crowd.

"For fuck's . . ." I see the words cross Winona's lips before she catches herself. "What a relief."

"YES, MAN! HE LIVES!!!" Dougie shouts from the stage, relieved and slapping Timmy on the back.

Timmy's victory strut goes on forever, with the crowd cheering along. Around us in the backstage area there's a mixed reaction from people who think he's gone too far this time, to people who think that this is the funniest thing they've ever seen. In the middle of it all I see Heather, her smile fixed but showing no real emotion. I wonder if she's thinking she'd like to kill Timmy Eaton herself now. This festival was supposed to distract people from murder, not the other way around.

"Timmy Eaton, sponsored by BigBoy condoms guys!" Timmy announces to the crowd with his arms spread out. "And don't you forget it. Once a BigBoy . . . always a BigBoy!" He winks to no one in particular.

As the crowd simmers down and Winona Philips starts the panel session, Annie gradually releases my hand from her grasp. But I see her fingers still shaking, even as she forms them into balled-up little fists. The prank war's either over, or it's only just getting started. I fear it's the latter.

The whole crowd silently weeps, their iPhones raised in an emotional illumination of the moment, as Celeste talks about the heartbreak of a lawsuit that she was recently embroiled in when she had to sue a nail salon for ruining her nail beds. Next to her, Dougie has his arm around her shoulders while she delicately sniffs, dainty tears dropping from each eye. Her voice is earnest as she discusses the trauma that she went through and the fight that she's had to gain compensation for, ads that she could have done involving her hands, had her nails not been recovering from the terrible ordeal.

"God, Dougie's so sensitive," I hear Mini-Heather Two sighing before Mini-Heather One lightly slaps her on the arm.

"Number two! No. Heather's into him," Mini-Heather One says. "Girl code."

"I'd have bad nail beds just for him to comfort me," Mini-Heather Three adds to the conversation, this time prompting a savage glance from actual Heather.

"Nice one, Jessica," Mini-Heather One hisses.

I actually don't see why everyone's falling over themselves about Dougie. Sure, he's conventionally hot in that muscled, perfectly sculpted physical specimen kind of way. And *sure*, he has perfect hair that I want to run my fingers through, but I *definitely* don't think he's hot. My phone vibrates aggressively in my hand, and I realize that I'm biting my lip while staring at him, again.

Les Populaires

Colin: OH MY GOD TIMMY'S DEAD!!!

Audrey: OH MY GOD!! I CAN'T BELIEVE IT!! ANNIE? WHAT DID YOU DO?

Colin: ANNIE OH MY GOD ARE YOU ARRESTED???

Colin: Oh right it was a prank. Drama over.

Colin: Fuck me that was a great prank though.

Audrey: So good! Like I actually almost peed myself.

                     Me: Guys it was terrifying.

Annie: I don't want to talk about it. He's dead to me.

Colin: I mean maybe be careful about writing stuff like that after what just happened.

Heather: Guys did you see how great I was onstage? Like I OWNED it!

Colin: What you gonna do as payback Annie? What prank?

Audrey: I mean I don't think anyone can better what he did? Pretending you actually killed him? Does it get better than that??

Colin: I'm so gutted we're missing this. Don't get me wrong, St. Barts is great, but we're missing literally the most exciting

thing to happen in the village since the
murders!

Heather: Guys???

I look up from the phone to Celeste still gravely discussing her nail beds.

"It's so completely awful," Ethan pipes up from the other end of the row, also wiping away a tear. "My heart really goes out to you and to *all* the women who are held to unrealistic nail standards on the internet. No one should ever feel that they aren't enough, and I know that in this online world so many women do. I fight for women to have the right to be ugly."

"God what a prick," Annie mutters, lifting the words right out of my brain.

At the other end of the row, Timmy Eaton looks confused. He's cleaned himself up after his prank and doesn't seem to know what to do when all the attention isn't focused on him. So he pulls his own finger and farts. He laughs to himself, and about half the crowd laugh too.

"Another prick," I say with a sigh. I'm really unsure how I'm going to write this blog. What's my angle supposed to be? Two of them are pricks, but the rest of the influencers seem . . . fine?

"I think we're coming to the end of our time now," Winona says, cutting off Timmy's fart laugh. "I'd just like to thank you all for coming. Thank you to Celeste about reminding us of the perils of the fake beauty industry. I know everyone is so excited to meet you all out there over the next couple of days and have the discussions that really count." This feels very pointed after Timmy's finger fart. "The influencers will be popping in and out of the signing tent, and they'll be up here and in the photo sets over the weekend. So say hi whenever you see them. We'd love to help you make content that counts!" Winona finishes.

"Let's make content that counts!" the influencers all shout from the stage as the crowd joins in.

It feels like some kind of content cult. Celeste blows kisses toward people as the other influencers wave, and the crowd whips up into another ear-shattering round of applause.

"That was so emotional," Mini-Heather One says to Mini-Heather Two before I hear Heather's voice screeching out of their headsets.

"What are you guys doing?! GET MOVING!! THE INFLUENCERS NEED WATER AND SNACKS!!!"

But as they file off the stage, it's clear that Timmy is interested in something else entirely.

"Ready to concede yet?" He swaggers over to Annie wearing the smuggest smile I've ever seen in my entire life.

"Never." Annie shakes her head firmly, maintaining eye contact. "I said it's on, and it's on."

The two of them are locked in a staring contest so fierce that she doesn't even notice Heather and the Mini-Heathers appearing next to her.

"Ahem." Mini-Heather One stands with her clipboard poised and Heather behind her. "Heather wants you to know that while she doesn't condone what's going on, she does see that it has improved traction and tags of #TheFestivalofFame online. So, she is happy for you to continue, but legally she does not take responsibility for any harm to your person, persons, or belongings. She just asks that you carry on with your obligations to the festival. We have you down to hang in the sets for the next few hours to mix with the public for photo and video opportunities."

"Right," Celeste says. "Come on, then, guys! Let's go!"

"Let's go," Annie whispers to me, a spark back in her eye. Which, to be honest, is never a good sign for me.

7

I'm smacked unawares in the face by a rogue inflatable sheep that nearly knocks me straight off my hay bale.

"Sorry!" The inflatable sheep's flinger gives me a casual wave, and I feel my cheeks start to burn.

How I ended up on these Instagram sets is beyond me, but now I'm taking farm animals to the face. Honestly, Nellie Bly would have never. I regain my balance just in time for Timmy Eaton to start circling on a small child's plastic pedal tractor. Next to me a fiberglass chicken clucks from a speaker nestled in its beak, while two poor people (I'm not ruling out Jessica being one of them) walk around in a cow costume. I'm calling it: the farm set definitely feels like the most surreal of all the Instagram sets so far.

Obviously Annie really wanted to ride the tractor, but Timmy beat her to it. He's supposed to be taking selfies with fans like the other influencers are, but he threw a diva tantrum and declared himself exhausted. So instead he's riding around by himself, hunched over the tiny pedals, knees up to his chest, asserting his "masculinity" by winking at all the female fans he passes.

"COW-TIPPING TIME!" Timmy shouts, pedaling with intent toward the two unlucky people in the cow costume. Even without seeing their faces I can sense the alarm as the two of them attempt to coordinate enough to race away.

It does seem to me from watching all the others, though, that influencing is actually quite a tiring job. Great observations here, Kerry. I can add that to my blog post along with—some of the influencers are dicks, and some aren't. I'm starting to wonder if I'm really up to the blog after all. What if I'm all ideas with no substance? I'm not even sure if I have any ideas now.

"HAHA! BURGER TIME!" Timmy shouts as the cow falls over, and I briefly wonder about attempting to save it from the pedals of Timmy's slaughter tractor. But to be honest, I've had enough run-ins with him today.

"What do you think?" Annie asks.

She's posing with a straw hat perched on top of her head, despite still wearing the sunglasses and raincoat with hood pulled up. The inflatable sheep under her arm, wader wellies, and small bit of hay poking out of her mouth really complete the ensemble.

"Cute!" Celeste says on her way past us.

"Oh . . ." Annie blinks, fiddling with the brim of the hat awkwardly as her cheeks grow red.

Celeste bustles off, clucking chicken under her arm, ready to take more selfies with her fans.

"God, she's so shallow." Annie whips the hat off and throws it onto a hay bale and makes disgusted faces at Timmy posing on the tractor, at the feet of the tipped cow, like a twatty hunter with its prize. None of the other influencers seem to bat an eyelid at his behavior, but I notice they're not exactly going over to hang out with him either.

Over in the magic forest set opposite, Mystic Millie's got a queue; she's been offering festivalgoers palm and tarot readings and pictures of her holding crystals to people's heads. Despite not believing she's actually in possession of any "special powers," I'm still tempted to join the line. Maybe she can give me some insight into how I'll get over this writer's block.

"I've got to go and sort some things for . . . something," Annie says, looking around her shiftily.

"Gosh, I wonder what that could be. You're so stealth," I say sarcastically.

She won't tell me anything about the prank that she's got planned, but she's never been the queen of subtlety. I actually don't want to know anyway. The less I know the easier it'll be for me to plead plausible deniability.

"I know!" she says, before stalking off away from everyone to a more secluded area of the farm, glancing over her shoulder as she goes like some kind of secret pranking agent.

I think it might be time to take my own selfie for Scott. I click a picture of myself holding one of the inflatable cows and send it to him. Just as I raise my phone, Dougie peels away from Celeste and the fans and sticks his head in the picture as well, and the photo captures me in a state of shock rather than a smile for my boyfriend.

"You're welcome," he says with a grin, as if he's doing me a favor rather than photobombing.

"Er, thanks," I say.

"It's Kerry, isn't it?" he asks.

"Yeah, that's right," I say.

I'm surprised he knows my name. Maybe he really is a nice man who cares about everyone. That's not going to help the article, either. It would make it way more interesting if he was a secret monster.

From behind one of the hay bales I see Annie's head popping up, her phone conversation clearly finished. She walks back over to me with a dangerously smug look on her face, and I feel a churning in my stomach.

"Annie's friend, right? So, what's with the tampon thing?" Dougie asks me.

At least, I *think* he's talking to me, but I'm not totally sure because he's completely focused on his own bicep as he flexes it, much to the joy of the girls giggling around him.

"It's kind of a weird handle."

Annie arrives next to me and opens her mouth to reply, but she's cut off before she can even get a word out.

"They promote tampons," Ethan shouts over from where he's hanging around next to Mystic Millie, lapping up her fans' attention. He joins Dougie and Celeste with the air of someone about to teach a lesson. "They want more positivity for periods, and so they use things like period products in their names. And I think it is a *travesty* in this day and age that women have to *beg* for tampons. LIKE LITERALLY JUST GIVE THEM TAMPONS."

Annie and I look at each other.

"Eerrrr *no*, that's not what it is," Annie says. "Kerry and I solved the menstrual murders last year. *We're* the Tampon Two . . . The Tampon Two are a crime-fighting duo."

I wouldn't have exactly put it like that because it makes us sound like we don capes made out of splatted tampons or period pads or something in our spare time, but at least it's more accurate than Ethan's first guess.

"Oh my god, that was you guys?!" Celeste gasps.

Annie and I are both somewhat taken aback by Celeste's extreme reaction, but Annie still beams with pride.

"Cool, dude," Dougie says, brushing his hair off his face and taking a selfie with another couple of fans, lunging over a bale of hay in the manliest display yet.

The way his eyes sparkle when he smiles for all the pictures is quite endearing actually. I bite my lip watching his strong hands gripping a fan's phone, helping her get the best angle.

"We know them! We were there, too," the two girls who he's selfie-ing with pipe up.

I recognize them from the year below us, but we've never spoken to them, and they've certainly never paid us much attention before.

"I actually had a relationship with one of the guys who was murdered," one of them says solemnly, clutching her chest. It takes me a while, but I recognize her as Felicity, the old volleyball team captain.

"You and everyone else, Felicity," Annie mutters, rolling her eyes.

I could have sworn that I just heard Celeste let out a small snort next to Annie as she sets up her phone to record a Reel-Life.

"I can't believe you're the Tampon Two and I get to meet you! This is *so* exciting!" Celeste squeals. I feel like she might find everything exciting, though. She's like a permanently

triggered puppy. "I *have* to get you guys in my stories immediately!"

Annie looks shocked that someone she's previously called
vapid is so interested. Celeste grabs a ring light from behind the
hay bales and moves it around to the front of us, clearly finding
the light in here unsatisfactory for our faces.

"I need to be in the picture, too," Ethan shouts over us. "I
am the feminist here!"

He pushes his way into the frame, despite not knowing who
we were until about ten seconds ago. But just as the flash goes
off, Timmy rides his tractor into him, knocking him out of the
shot.

"Prick," Ethan mutters from the floor.

All the other influencers barely seem to notice anything's
happened.

By the time I've stopped seeing stars in my eyes from the
glare of the ring light, Celeste's phone is rammed in my face and
I'm watching a very well-lit version of my own startled expression reacting to itself in real time. I actually might throw up.
The spotlight is truly not for me.

"Oh my god, guys! I said this Festival of Fame was classy,
and *now look* who I've bumped into! It's Annie and Karla, THE
TAMPON TWO!" Celeste shouts into the screen.

I'm sorry, Annie and *WHO*? I give Annie a side-eye.

I literally introduced myself to this woman today; how can
she still have no idea who I am?

"Kerry," I mutter. I'd intended it to be loud and confident,
but instead it comes out like an apologetic squeak.

"The *actual* girls who solved the *actual* menstrual murders!"
Celeste enthuses.

Suddenly she pauses the recording.

"Hang on, let's just break there for a sec. Karina, do you mind not doing that with your face? You're just looking a bit . . . yeah . . . um . . . weird. You know?"

It takes me a moment to realize that Celeste's actually talking to me. She stares at me expectantly, seemingly baffled by my inability to be on camera. I'm baffled because as far as I can see, this is just my face.

"'Course," I say, taking a massive gulp of air and not even bothering to try correcting her again.

Why isn't Annie trying, though? I look over at her, and she's just so focused on her own face in the video. Who's vapid now, Annie? She probably didn't even hear a word of what Celeste said. I try to arrange my face into a smile, but the effect is that I look scared.

"Gosh you look like you're about to get eaten by a giant shark! Bless you, hon!" Celeste does a small cheerful giggle.

"Oh, yeah, sorry, right," I say, putting all my effort into having no expression.

"Annie, you're doing such a great job!" Celeste says, and Annie beams at her, the smug grin of someone who isn't wasting everyone's time with their uncontrollable facial features. "Let's just go again."

Celeste starts filming again, and I hope she doesn't expect me to talk as well as look "normal" because it feels like I have the most saliva in my mouth right now that anyone has ever had. What if I choke on all this excess saliva and then I die, live on ReelLife? The last thing I will have done is an interview with someone who didn't even know my name. What a legacy.

"Say 'Bitches Get Riches,' guys!" Celeste practically shrieks into the camera, placing an arm around Annie's shoulders.

Annie says the phrase along with her, but I simply find myself performing a series of large swallows, trying to clear my windpipe of saliva so that I may breathe and hopefully survive this ordeal.

Celeste turns off the camera and posts the video in one fluid movement. I'm in awe, because whenever I post anything on social media, I sit for half an hour first thinking about how long it's going to be there for (basically forever), whether it's something that could get me canceled and ruin my university applications, whether I've said anything that could be misunderstood or taken out of context or that might not age well, and whether it's going to get me the kind of attention I don't want—which is any attention at all, by the way. Maybe it's no wonder I can't even start a blog.

"Oh, here you are!" Heather arrives on the set with the Mini-Heathers around her. "I've been searching for you everywhere."

For a minute I think she's talking about me and Annie, but I come to my senses and realize it's the influencers she means. Mostly Dougie. Unfortunately for her, though, Annie and I are the only people who notice her presence. Mystic Millie doesn't even look up from the tarot reading she's giving to one of her fans.

Then I hear the chirp of several phones going off at the same time, and all the influencers immediately stop what they're doing to look at their screens. Suddenly they're all standing up from where they are and moving en masse, without even saying a word to each other. Mystic Millie swiftly wraps up a tarot reading, derailing her promise of a long and healthy life filled with love by whipping out the death card and saying, "The end!" The poor girl looks rather shocked.

Without even so much as a glance to one another, they all move to the disco set, while fans, Mini-Heathers, and Heather follow.

"The talent is heading through to the disco. I repeat, talent to the disco," Mini-Heather One shouts into her headset next to Heather, waving her arms in a kind of herding motion as if she has any kind of control over the situation.

The disco set is exactly what it says on the tin. There's a DJ playing music, huge glittery balls spinning around, and colorful lights. Somehow, Annie and I have gotten swept up with the crowd. As we enter, I look to my left, expecting to see Annie watching the scene with the same disinterest I feel curling my own lip, but she's already in the thick of it, on the dance floor, pretending to surf underwater with Celeste and Dougie, laughing and joking her way through "7 Rings" by Ariana Grande. A queue starts building for Timmy, who's perched on the edge of the disco. It seems weird that he doesn't go and dance with the others, especially when they're all having such a good time.

I settle myself down at the side on yet another inflatable sofa—I can't shake the worry that poor Jessica was probably forced to blow all these up—and take out my phone to message Scott. He'll be so excited when I tell him about the blog.

Me: So me and Annie had an idea!

Me: I'm going to start a blog!

Me: I thought the first post
could be about the festival!
We're VIP so I can write about
being behind the scenes with
the influencers.

Me: What they're REALLY like!

Scott: OMG I LOVE THIS IDEA! You'd be
so good at this! Share it with me!!!

Me: I'll send you the link
so you can see it while I'm
writing that way you can see
all the ridiculous stuff we get
up to while we're here.

I normally hate showing people stuff before I've finished, but Scott's always so supportive, and actually it helps to have someone to bounce things off that I can trust.

Scott: I'm so proud of you <3 you're like
Gloria Steinem.

Scott: I can't wait to read it <3 I can be
your cheerleader while you write it.

I feel a warm glow and then remember that so far I've got nothing for this blog. No real angle about what the influencers are really like, apart from that they're entirely controlled by their phones. But that doesn't feel like the most groundbreaking news. The feeling of failure that I know so well begins to creep over me, and I try my best to brush it away. Instead, I turn my attention to my subjects. I look up just in time to see Heather dancing with purpose over to Dougie, who simply grabs Mystic Millie's bejeweled hand and twirls her off and away.

Annie comes over and tries to woo me onto the dance floor with the rest of the influencers as they start a famous Reel-Life dance, but I shake my head. I tell myself it's because I'm observing from the outside, but deep down I know it's because I don't think I'd fit in to that dance. Even though I've seen it thousands of times, I wouldn't even know what to do. I feel like the only person here that's not dancing and having a good time as I stare at my empty Notes app. What if the real reason I'm stuck on the outside is because if I exclude myself, then others don't get the chance to exclude me?

I shake off the thought and use my ReelLife profile to watch all of Winona Philips's latest videos, reminiscing about what could have been. I could have been talking to her right now—although I'd probably be too shy to. She's so classy. Every single video is perfectly poised, the background often shot in the same bit of her house, where she does her feminist musings. Always the same thick-framed stylish glasses, gold earrings, and matching gold necklace. Although, it looks like she's got a new one lately because I notice a change from a green emerald to a light white stone. Obviously she probably has multiple necklaces. Her style is simple and elegant, like her. I find myself lost, addicted to scrolling on and watching more and more of her videos. When I grow up, I want *to be* her. God, bit creepy actually, Kerry. Maybe it's a good thing she's not here after all.

Everyone's having so much fun that they don't spot the first sausage. It's not until the third one comes flying past my cheek that I really stop and take notice. And then it happens—a group of people invade the disco set, sausages in hand, flinging them at Timmy. In an unfortunate misfire, one hits me on the head, which knocks me a step back, but for the most part, these three sausage-wielding heroes know what they're doing, and Timmy's getting absolutely pummeled with them. As he falls to the floor, Annie beams with pride, shimmying across the dance floor like a victorious gladiator, until she reaches where I'm lurking.

"WELL, YOU DO LOVE A SAUSAGEFEST!" she shouts at him. Then she leans over to me to whisper, "I promised them pictures with Dougie if they threw the sausages. We can handle that, right?"

Why do I get the impression that what she means is she wants *me* to handle that?

Behind the Filters Blog—Notes App

Some honest thoughts about the other influencers that we're hanging out with (Maybe I can use this to help write an actual post. There has to be something here . . . anything??)

Dougie Trainor: Does seem as adorable as he is on TV—personality wise—but I still don't fancy him. Obviously.

Celeste: Absolutely obsessed with her brand. Lost count of the times she said "bitches" tonight. I feel bad saying it, but I think Annie's right: she seems kind of shallow. But also nice enough.

Mystic Millie: Seems okay ("nice" and "okay," find better adjectives, Kerry) but definitely doesn't have any of the "special powers" she claims. Although people do seem to swear by her predictions, and everyone on her page only talks about how accurate she is. Maybe I'm missing something?

Ethan Woods: A complete fake. Honestly clocked it as soon as we met him. He doesn't know a thing about feminism, and I'm not sure how he's managed it this long. Have noticed however after some secret research that most of his fanbase is male and that he has considerably less followers than the other influencers.

Timmy: Where to even begin . . .

8

"Kerry . . ." Annie whispers, and I try hard to pretend I'm asleep. "Kerry . . . KERRY."

"What?" I whisper back, slightly pissed off and stirring from the beginnings of a nice dream about Scott.

"Are you awake?" Annie whispers.

I feel my teeth grit in frustration as I turn over to face her. Next to me Herbie sighs and puts his paws over his face. This whole sleeping-in-a-yurt-under-the-stars thing really isn't ideal for an anxious person. For starters, there's no lock on this yurt, so anyone could walk in at any time, and that includes wild animals. Just because no one's ever seen a big cat in Barbourough village doesn't mean that it couldn't happen. I lay here for ages imagining a lion smashing through the tent and ripping us from our beds. Finally getting to sleep was nothing short of a miracle. A miracle that Annie's destroyed.

"I guess I am now." I sigh, still clinging hopefully to the luxurious cotton sheet draped over me. "What's up?"

"I need a wee," Annie whispers, sitting up in her bed.

"So go for one," I whisper back, determined that I won't be

leaving the soft nest I've created for me and Herbie, no matter what Annie thinks.

"But then I'd have to go outside . . . In the dark . . . Plllleeeaseee? There's safety in numbers? Don't forget what happened here before . . ." Annie gulps, and I can see even through the dark that her eyes are actually wide with fear. To be fair, Heather's deranged father was chasing us around these very grounds with a gun not too long ago.

"Fine," I whisper in harassed tones, throwing the covers off. My movement prompts Herbie to stand up, and he looks appalled. For a second, I think he's going to bark, so I put a finger to my lips, and he understands. He sits at attention, licking his lips, ready for adventure.

"We need to be quick. I've really been holding it," Annie whispers, leaping out of bed.

"At least the ground is wipe-clean tarp," I say, pointing to the floor.

"Ha. Ha." Annie laughs sarcastically.

I shuffle my shorts on, lace up my Converse, and join Annie at the entrance to the yurt. She races out into the camp in her poo-emoji pajama shorts and top and her massive rainboots, and we walk through the quiet camp toward the spa block where the VIP toilets are located. Despite the fairy lights illuminating our path, it still feels eerie out here, and I find myself quickening my pace as we walk, the hairs on the back of my neck pricking up. I have an urge to look over my shoulder with every step we take. In fact I'm looking behind me when the fairy lights all turn off.

We're plunged into total darkness.

"Great, this isn't horror movie–like at all," I say sarcastically, scooping Herbie off the ground and clutching him to myself, more for his comfort than mine. I feel him nuzzling into my shoulder with a whimper—although he likes to consider himself a fierce guard dog, we both know he's not.

"Wonder what happened to the lights," Annie whispers.

"Maybe they were programmed to go off when everyone's asleep?" I suggest reasonably, because I really want to convince myself this is all normal.

Behind us I swear I can hear something rustling, and I'm trying to tell myself it's just my brain being overactive, but the sound intensifies and is joined by an animalistic kind of keening noise. I spin around with my phone flashlight on, ready to defend myself from some kind of flying attack squirrel horror, when I see the source of the noise: Dougie's yurt. For a disturbing second, I see the silhouettes against the canvas of two figures doing whatever the hell it is that they're doing in there, before I spin around, facing my phone the other way.

"Gross," Annie whispers into the night.

A second later though, a twig snaps behind us, followed by more rustling, and we spin around again. I could swear there's something or someone moving in the trees . . . Are they trying to use Dougie's carnal noises to cover their tracks? But when I shine my flashlight back over there, there's nothing to be seen.

"I think I peed a little bit already," Annie whimpers. She clutches my arm tightly.

"Let's just get this over with and back to the yurt," I breathe.

We walk faster, and it sounds like the rustling moves faster, too. I can't tell what's the noise of my own feet and what's coming from behind the bushes. I feel like I'm one rustle away from running in the opposite direction screaming, though.

"Hello," a robotic voice booms out at us.

"What was that?" I ask, prickles dancing down the back of my neck as I wheel around, searching for the source of the noise.

And then I realize—it's Timmy. It has to be. And I'm ready to defend myself from whatever prank he's about to pull. He probably turned the lights off, too. I peer into the bushes, trying to work out where he might be hiding.

"It's my phone," Annie says, waving her phone screen at me.

"Really?" I lean over to watch the livestream from Timmy's ReelLife account.

Timmy's not on-screen but at least I know that was where the voice came from and I can stop craning my neck searching for danger like a panicked meerkat.

"I can't believe you're watching ReelLife videos right now."

"It's a good thing I am," Annie says. "Look! Timmy Eaton's live in the spa block now, creeping on Celeste! He's hiding in one of the changing rooms or something?"

Captions fill the screen, and the robotic voice speaks again.

"I think I've probably pranked poor Annie Tampon Two enough for one day . . . so I'm here ready to prank Celeste. She just came in to film her 'Get un-ready with me' video. But little does she know she's being watched . . . Who knows what'll happen next, guys, maybe she'll take her clothes off hahaha! Or maybe I'll scare the shit out of her and pretend to be the ghost of one of the menstrual murder victims! Stay tuned!"

Annie looks full of rage, which I hadn't thought possible when she's so clearly full of pee.

"Why the voice?" I ask.

"He's probably just typing rather than talking, so Celeste doesn't hear him when he's in there," Annie says. "The voice will just be reading out what he types."

Celeste begins removing her makeup in the mirrors in front of Timmy, completely unaware of his presence as he carries on typing onto the screen.

"And here we see the influencer in the wild using her Bitches Get Contours magic cleansing cloth, supposed to remove all traces of makeup, but lo! What is this? She's stopped filming!"

The video zooms in further, and Celeste takes out a disposable makeup wipe from another brand.

"Hang on, guys, why isn't she filming this bit of the cleansing routine? And why isn't she using her own products?"

"Oh my god, this feels so unfair and creepy!" Annie says. "I'm going to DM her on ReelLife now. She followed me earlier! Put the video on your phone so we can still watch while I message her!"

I find Timmy's stream on my phone while Annie messages Celeste. His commentary seems to have stopped, which is making it feel even creepier. Even worse than him videoing a woman without her consent, though, is the amount of people who are watching him do it. The figure in the corner of the screen tells me that there are approximately half a million people tuned in to this live. I feel dirty to be adding to that number. I can't believe that even at this time of night, and when he's being an obnoxious letch, he gets an audience. I hope she sees the message soon so it gets shut down.

"Come on—we need to help her!" Annie says.

The two of us start running for the spa block, Annie typing as we go, past the creaking and snapping of branches in the woods surrounding the camp. Annie's moving at twice the speed that she was before, clearly feeling purposeful in her rescue of Celeste from Timmy Eaton or her need for a wee. Watching her gait, I think it may be more led by the latter actually.

"Where is he even filming from?" I ask, squinting at the screen. "How's he doing it without her seeing?"

"I don't know!" Annie huffs back at me breathlessly. "This is hands down the creepiest thing he's ever done, and he's a pretty creepy dude already."

"TIMMMY! WHERE ARE YOOOUU?" Celeste's voice booms out of Annie's phone as she opens another livestream but from Celeste's account this time. I don't hear it on Timmy's stream, so I guess he must have muted his microphone.

We pause outside the spa block holding the two phones next to each other. It's dark like the rest of the campsite, and I'm wondering how it's possible that the lights can be off for this long without all the Mini-Heathers and OG Heather causing a stir.

"Come out come out wherever you are, Timmy."

Celeste's face is visible in the mirror as she holds her phone up in front of her.

"Hey, guys, for those of you who have just joined us, Timmy Eaton's currently creeping on me in the changing rooms like a jerk. Big thanks and shout-outs to everyone who messaged me to let me know, especially @AnnieTamponTwo, total queen. But don't you worry, I WILL find him. OUT YOU COME, TIMMY! THE GAME'S UP!"

84

Annie and I look at each other in trepidation and then race in through the spa doors, our footsteps echoing down its dark bergamot-scented corridors. On both feeds I can see that Celeste's still trying to find Timmy to no avail, and on my screen there's still no movement from Timmy whatsoever—definitely committed to the prank, which makes my blood boil. I imagine he's silently giggling to himself, the dick. Annie flies through the door into the changing room, Herbie trotting with purpose behind her, eager for his big detective moment.

"We've come to help!" Annie announces to Celeste as Herbie runs around the room sniffing all the corners and barking.

"If we look at the angle that he's filming from we can work out where he is," I say, standing in the center of the room, turning around to check the view from every which way until I get it. "It's looking this way so it has to be . . ." I look behind me and point to a large full-length mirror. "There!"

But I can see Herbie's already ahead of me, sniffing at the mirror with abandon, a properly clever boy who found it all first before any of the rest of us. Annie rushes over to the mirror and knocks on it like she's a building surveyor testing the construction.

"It's just propped up; it's not actually screwed into the wall. There's a hollow space behind it!" Annie says. She thrusts her finger against the glass. I watch it blot out a spot in the livestream, her fingernail eclipsing the room. "And it's a two-way mirror."

"Come out, Timmy!" Celeste says as we all crowd around.

"You're surrounded!" Annie says.

I stand behind the two of them hoping that I'm not in shot on any of the livestreams.

"If you don't come out, we're coming in!" Celeste says.

We all stand for what feels like minutes staring at each other in the darkness.

"FINE!" Celeste says.

She and Annie grab either side of the mirror, pulling it away from the space to reveal a tiled shower cubicle. I blink against the darkness; as my eyes adjust, a figure resolves out of the shadow. It's only when the main lights to the block click on a few seconds later that the whole thing is revealed. At first I only see his phone, recording on the tripod, but as I look beyond that, I freeze. Because there in the shower cubicle, perched on a small pink chair, slumps Timmy Eaton, dead, one of his very own sponsored BigBoy condoms stretched over his face, proving that it really does fit all sizes. #Ad.

9

Annie and I have two very different reactions to the situation. I freeze, contemplating running in the other direction, while Annie does what she always does: she heads straight toward the danger. After a moment of dithering, I head into the shower cubicle after her, like I always do.

"It'll just be another of his stupid pranks," Annie says, still trying to catch her breath. "As #SponCon goes, I hope this gets you canceled, Timmy."

She walks over to where Timmy's slumped.

"I mean at least it's an original prank; I'll give him that," Celeste says, phone still in her hand filming. "Or it would be if he hadn't faked his death like two hours ago already." Celeste furrows her brow and then she seems to rally. "Timmy, this isn't funny! You need to stop pulling stuff like this because one day you'll be in real trouble and people won't come to help you!"

She's talking right into his face, but there's no reaction. He doesn't even twitch. So she grabs him.

"SAY SOMETHING!!!"

The three of us stand over him, and even Annie's starting to look concerned. Considering everything that's happened in the past twelve hours, I never thought that today would end with us actually willing Timmy to speak.

"Is he . . . dead?" I ask, my voice shaky as I step back.

"He can't be," Celeste says, paling.

"You've had your fun, Timmy! Time to get up!" Annie bends closer to him.

But he doesn't move and he hasn't this whole time. A sinking feeling settles over us and Herbie rushes to hide behind me, whining. Celeste turns off her livestream recording.

With caution, like she expects him to suddenly jump and scare her, Annie picks up Timmy's wrist. She moves her fingers around looking increasingly troubled. Then she reaches around his neck, just below the condom.

In a haze of swishing kaftan and clacking earrings, Mystic Millie appears rushing through the door to the spa.

"What's happened?" she demands. "What happened to Timmy?"

"He's . . . he's dead," Annie says, staring straight ahead at Timmy's body. "Phone the police."

"Annie," I whisper, "his phone."

But it's too late. Timmy's livestream is still running, and Annie has just announced Timmy's death to the world.

"I sensed something was wrong!" Mystic Millie howls, crouched over his body with a chunk of clear stone in her hand. She presses it into his hand and starts wailing, "TIMMY!! CLEAR QUARTZ FOR HEALING! LET IT HEAL YOU, TIMMY!!!"

"He's dead," Annie snaps. "No amount of crystal healing's going to bring him back to life. We need to make sure that we're not tampering with the body."

Around us the whisper from social media quickly turns into a real-life torrent of alarm faster than anyone can control, and the room fills up with people—other VIPs, fans, everyone else who saw the video. We stand awkwardly around the body, unsure what to do, as Annie tries to prevent people from getting too close. Two security guards race through, but the crowd's already far too big. There's nothing they can do to stop the flow of people into the VIP area and through to the spa. They're overwhelmed and outnumbered.

Journalism mode kicks in quickly. I didn't know what I was going to write about before, but now I know: I have to write about this. I open the Notes app on my phone to quickly jot down what I know and what I can see at the scene.

Timmy Eaton: Murder Scene
Body behind a mirror in a small shower cubicle. Not much room in there.

Auto text captions appeared on his phone, but at some point this stopped—rewatch to ascertain when this happened.

There was a livestream going the whole time: phone on a tripod but he never appeared on the screen. He was behind the camera the whole time.

The stream started when I heard him say hello after Annie clicked on it, and he was already in the shower then.

"What's going on?" Dougie pushes his way through the crowd, shirtless (apparently never missing a second to show off his Adorable Adonis physique, no matter how inappropriate the circumstance). I briefly wonder what happened to his yurt friend, if they've already been forgotten.

Around him phones are raised capturing the moment. It seems even death is content these days. A look of shock seizes Dougie's face and he leaps toward Timmy's lifeless body.

"TIMMY! TIMMMAAAYYYY!!! MATE! MAAAYYYTE!" He falls over, grabbing Timmy and pulling him to the floor before Annie can stop him. Celeste watches from Annie's shoulder, whimpering, her hands shaking with shock.

"Maybe he's not gone. Maybe we can save him!!" Dougie grabs Timmy's shoulders and shakes them before leaping on his chest.

He begins attempting some kind of CPR, but clearly without any skill or training because even I know he's pushing on Timmy's diaphragm rather than his chest. Then he blows on Timmy's mouth with the condom still on his head, which is the final evidence that I need that he doesn't know what he's doing. But everyone else stares, gripped by Dougie's attempts at "lifesaving."

"Wait? Timmy? TIMMY??!" Dougie stops pumping and looks down at Timmy, realization dawning. Maybe he thought this was another prank. "HE'S DEAD! HE'S ACTUALLY DEAD! WHAT THE HELL, MAN?! TIMMY!!!"

Mystic Millie appears next to us; she places an arm around Celeste's shoulders and begins rubbing the clear quartz across Celeste's face. Despite it all, I almost laugh at Millie's determination to heal someone with that crystal today.

"To cleanse you of your trauma, my sweet," she says sagely. "I always told him that he would come to a sticky end if he continued behaving in the way he was. Now look. Always listen to Millie."

At the front of the crowd, someone thrusts their phone forward, trying to get a closer shot of Timmy's body, but Annie puts a hand over their camera to stop them.

"Please don't take pictures or post anything," she says sternly. "Things that you post might have an effect on the case."

No one listens to her, though, and I realize hundreds of phones are currently capturing me standing here with my mouth open as Annie tries to take control of a crime scene in wellies and poo pajamas. Around us stewards wearing Festival of Fame T-shirts have appeared, but both they and the security team still seem to be wildly out of their depth. Where's Heather? Surely she should be here by now.

"Excuse me . . . excuuuuseee meeeee. I need to get to my girlfriend! She's in there!!! EXCUSE ME!!!" I can hear Ethan Woods's voice from down the corridor. "MILLIE, MY LOVE?!" he asks, finally pushing through the crowd and into the marble changing room. I can see people parting to let him through, but it still takes him much longer than the other influencers. "Sorry, ma'am, I absolutely did not mean to touch your breast. So sorry, I am a male feminist, and that's also my girlfriend over there, I did *not* mean to touch your ass at all. But as a male feminist, may I say what a firm butt that is. Well done you!"

"Timmy's DEAD!" Celeste wails at him as soon as he reaches them, before flinging herself into Dougie's arms next to her.

Dougie clutches Celeste tight to his chest, with his chin

neatly rested on her head. He strokes her hair soothingly. There's something about the protective way he holds her as Ethan approaches that makes me wonder if he's keeping her out of Ethan's way. Ethan tries to get Millie's attention, but she's too busy rubbing crystals against people and wafting things in the air above Timmy's condom-clad corpse to notice.

There's a loud male gasp that makes us all stop and turn as the Tim-sciples appear at the front of the crowd. Annie holds out a hand to stop them from tampering with Timmy's body, but without their leader they look lost. They stand speechless, the once intimidating pack now just scared little boys. I can't help but feel sorry for them.

Finally Heather arrives beside us, flanked by the Mini-Heathers talking frantically into their headsets, although I don't know to whom. Everyone's here, and I can't help but notice that Heather's got a fresh face of "natural"-looking makeup on and her hair is in the most perfectly put-together messy bun I've ever seen. She looks very glam for a murder scene in her cashmere yoga pants and T-shirt. No wonder they took so long to arrive.

"Oh my god, Dougie! Are you okay?" Heather races to him to offer a hug but he simply continues holding Celeste and staring at Timmy, his expression blank as if he hasn't even heard her. I watch as this irritates her maybe even more than someone dying at her festival has.

"I think Dougie's fine. It's really Timmy that we should be worried about right now," Annie whispers to her loudly and points to the dead body.

The faint sound of sirens flows into the spa from outside, followed by the shadow of blue flashing lights on the white walls. There's a rush of activity behind us as police officers and paramedics weave their way through.

"STEP AWAY FROM THE BODY!" a man's voice booms into the shower room. "EVERYONE PUT YOUR PHONES DOWN AND STOP FILMING! WHAT YOU'RE DOING IS ILLEGAL!"

When they reach us, I'm comforted by the familiar sight of graying hair and the raincoat that I've seen many times before.

"DI Wallace!" Annie exclaims, reaching out a hand for him to shake like they're old colleagues.

He rebuffs her outstretched hand, instead turning to the short woman next to him who seems inappropriately smiley considering the context. "Let's get everyone clear of the scene ASAP please, Detective Constable Short."

Annie stands open-mouthed as DI Wallace continues to ignore her, instead talking to the paramedics attending to Timmy's body.

"Okay, everyone!" DC Short shouts into the corridor, a sea of poised smartphones videoing her. "We need you all to go back to your tents and stay there until we've spoken to you. NO ONE leaves the festival ground, and no one comes into the festival ground until we've spoken to all of you. HAVE I MADE MYSELF CLEAR?"

A ripple of nods travels around the crowd like a small domino wave of resignation as people begin to disperse. I can hear people recording the moment for ReelLife, talking animatedly about being "held captive by the police."

I watch DI Wallace talking sternly to Heather as everyone files out of the spa. I'm in conflict with myself, itching to run away but wanting to stay as long as possible to find out more for the blog. It's clear to me that it's no longer just a peek behind the filters, but an investigation into Timmy's death. If

I was Annie right now, I'd be imagining myself collecting a Pulitzer Prize.

"Let's get all security manning the gates, I repeat all security manning the gates." Heather strides away from DI Wallace shouting into her headset.

"ON IT!" the Mini-Heathers reply into their headsets and dash away into the crowd.

"The body was found . . ." Annie starts explaining to DI Wallace despite him not asking her any questions.

He walks away from her and she follows him.

"DI WALLACE!" she shouts. "DI—"

"Annie." DI Wallace cuts her off abruptly, and she looks like she's just taken a brutal slap to the face. "Go back to your tent. Let the professionals do the investigating this time, that way maybe we won't all end up nearly getting killed."

DI Wallace walks away without so much as looking back at Annie. He's sort of right—last time, our investigation did end with the three of us stumbling into a secret drug ring and facing the kingpin with only a Dictaphone to defend us.

"Wha—?" Annie's too shocked to form sentences; she's just blinking furiously.

"Come on," I say, putting an arm around her shoulders to guide her. "Let's just do what he says, hey? Better not to make him angry so early in the investigation . . . there's plenty of time for that, I'm sure." I'm surprised to find myself a little disappointed, too, though.

With the crowd cleared from the spa block, Annie and I are left standing outside with the influencers in the blue-tinged night, the cool air settling over our shock. Ethan goes to put his hand around Mystic Millie's shoulder, but with an almost imperceptible shrug, she brushes him off and he's left looking wounded. I note it for later. It seems odd she doesn't want him to touch her. I mean, I wouldn't want him to touch me, either, but they are allegedly a couple.

I decide it's time I found out more about their relationship, so I go onto their profiles to try to establish a timeline. It's incredible what you can piece together about people's romantic lives from even the tiniest of clues.

"What do we do now?" Dougie asks.

"Go back to our tents like they said," Celeste says.

"Contact the spirits and ask them to help guide Timmy into the light," Mystic Millie answers at the same time.

"I'm going to do a nature wee," Annie whispers to me before shuffling off with urgency into the woods.

My phone vibrates with a message from Annie the moment she's out of sight, and I already know what it's going to say.

> **Annie:** Just to check we're on the same page. You think this was murder too right?

> **Me:** Definitely.

> **Annie:** Classic locked room mystery.

> **Me:** There's no way he'd get a condom on his head but not off, surely?

> **Me:** Also it's a weird way to want to scare someone . . . pretending to be some kind of condom ghost . . . but that's just my opinion, not fact or evidence.

Although I'm not normally one to always jump to the most dramatic conclusion—that's Annie's department—it does strike me as the most likely explanation.

> **Me:** And the influencers are our suspects.

> **Annie:** I've taught you well . . .

> **Me:** I mean it could be anyone, anywhere really.

> **Me:** Oh my god, Annie, be careful in the bushes! Keep your wits about you!

Annie comes racing out of the bushes at high speed, grabbing my hand and dragging me swiftly in the direction of the camp to be with the influencers. There's safety in numbers, I guess.

10

"Why do bad things always happen to good guys? It's just so sad," Dougie whispers, his eyes red-rimmed with tears. Something about him crying and vulnerable like this makes him more attractive to me. It also makes me wonder if I need to worry about myself. Am I a terrible person? Do I find sadness sexy? Do I like sadbois? Is Scott a SADBOI?!

In lieu of being able to take part in the actual police investigation, Annie and I are observing the suspects around the firepit in the VIP glamp site. We've opted to sit opposite each other, slotting in between the influencers in the hope of connecting with them easier. But perched next to Celeste and Ethan, I feel like I shouldn't be here.

"Such a tragic accident," Dougie mutters.

Annie's name appears on my phone the second the words are out of his mouth. I try to shield my screen so that the others don't see it, but I'm not sure why I bothered; they're far too absorbed in their own phones to notice mine.

Annie: Oh god, they can't actually think
this was an accident.

Annie: Is this really happening again?

Me: I'm getting déjà vu.

I hear the buzz of several phones vibrating all at once and
see the influencers' brows furrow at their screens.

Annie: Are they all getting messages at
the same time?

Me: Yep. This happened earlier
too when they were in the sets.
They all got a message at the
same time and suddenly just
upped and moved to another set.

Annie: That was why we moved? I thought
it was weird.

There's another collective buzz—and a wolf whistle from
Ethan's phone—as another message arrives. As subtly as I can,
I sneak a glance at Celeste's phone next to me and the word
"MOTHER" pops out at the top of what looks like a WhatsApp
chat.

Me: MOTHER? That's who's
messaging them.

I see Annie straining unsubtly to look at Dougie's phone on the other side of her. Then she nods.

Annie: Is MOTHER telling them what to do?

Me: I think so.

Annie: They all have the same mum? Is that possible?

Me: I doubt that. They're all aged 18-20. How could she have so many kids of the same age?

Annie: What other explanation is there?

I catch Annie's eye across the fire, and she shrugs at me.

Celeste's the first to speak. "That's that, then."

"Ethan, she told you to stop doing that," Dougie says, looking over at where Ethan's tapping away at his phone.

"Just replying to a comment," Ethan says.

"She told you not to reply anymore," Celeste says. "She can see what you're doing. She can see what all of us are doing."

Annie: They're like puppets on a string . . . but the string's just snapped.

I try to ignore the dramatic face she's pulling across the fire. Timmy's not a string; he was still a person, even if he was a dick of a person. She's worryingly savage sometimes.

"I can't believe my best friend's gone," Ethan suddenly wails.

"He hated you," Mystic Millie snaps.

> **Annie:** Lover's tiff or no love lost between Millie and Ethan?

> **Me:** It's gotta be a fake relationship.

> **Annie:** Show your work?

> **Me:** I was suspicious after I saw her brush him off back there so I took a closer look at their profiles while you were having your nature wee. Likes on their posts went up by around 50% when they announced they'd started dating.

> **Annie:** Interesting . . .

> **Annie:** Oh god, incoming.

I look up to see DC Short approaching the campfire.

"Dougie, we're ready to interview you now," she says, her face illuminated by the campfire. She seems almost excited.

"I sensed you were coming for him," Mystic Millie declares, her arms raised as the two of them walk away.

"Sure." Dougie stands up and heads toward the detective.

If I'm not mistaken, DC Short's staring at him with a thirst I've not seen since Annie discovered Reneé Rapp for the first time. The two of them walk away, Dougie towering over the small detective, as the influencers around the campfire fall silent, waiting for the police to be less present.

"I'm a huge fan," DC Short whispers to Dougie, clearly assuming she's out of earshot.

I see Annie roll her eyes at the detective's lack of professionalism. I'm willing to bet she's also fuming she wasn't the first one to be interviewed, but she'd never say that out loud.

I'm about to text Annie again when Celeste leans in toward me.

"Annie? Kathy?"

Oh for god's sake.

"What should we do? You guys solved the menstrual murders. You have to help us."

Annie swallows her surprise and is about to speak when Ethan butts in. "You think it was *murder*?"

"You think he suffocated *himself* with a condom?" Mystic Millie snaps.

"You tell me. You're the one who's supposed to be allseeing," Ethan retorts sarcastically.

Celeste rolls her eyes at them. "Instead of arguing, we should be looking for clues. Surely we'd be the first suspects. They'll be thinking it was one of us, right, guys?" She looks to us for confirmation.

"Actually, I'm pretty sure I'd be the first person they

suspect," Annie says, looking inappropriately proud. "I mean we *were* in a prank war—people thought I'd killed him before. I'm one hundred percent suspect numero uno."

The influencers all start tapping away at their phones and I join them, feeling like I should be doing whatever they're doing, I guess. They all have such purpose with their phones all the time. Not one of them is sitting playing Tetris or staring at a lack of messages forlornly. Except I don't have anyone to text—with my parents away on a cruise and my boyfriend probably fast asleep—so I go into ReelLife to search for anything that's been posted about Timmy Eaton.

"The internet says it was you," Ethan says, looking up at Annie before my search has even loaded.

He's not wrong—hundreds of videos start loading on my screen, reposts of either Celeste's or Timmy's livestreams with people presenting over-the-top, frame-by-frame analysis. And all of them mention Annie and the sausage attack. They think it was another of her pranks, but this time Timmy's death was real. It's wild; this morning I was sharpening pencils, barely trusted to make a cup of tea, and now we're at the center of the biggest drama ReelLife has ever seen. And we're sitting around a campfire with some of the most famous people on the internet. But I've still only got three followers and haven't written a single word or posted a single photo.

"Did you do it? Did you kill my friend?" Ethan suddenly stands and squares up to Annie.

"Errr, obviously not," Annie says coolly. "I solve murders, I don't commit them."

"Prove it," Ethan spits, crossing his arms and stamping like an overgrown toddler.

"I was the one who discovered the body and I was with Kerry the whole time," Annie retorts petulantly.

"Obviously it wasn't her," Celeste adds calmly.

"I don't see murder in her past," Mystic Millie concurs.

"This is sick." Celeste winces at her screen, scrolling.

As she speaks a new video pops up on my feed showing a close-up of her face with the caption "Bitches get murderous?" I guess it's not just Annie who's a suspect, although I'll admit most of these videos are about her. Weird that anyone would think it's Celeste when she has the strongest alibi. She was literally being watched live at the time he died.

"The way people have analyzed this footage! Everyone so excited and jumping on Timmy's death for followers and likes! It's disgusting!" Celeste cries.

"Disgusting," Annie echoes with a nod. But I can see a glint of something I fear may be excitement in her eye. Hopefully it's just a reflection from the fire.

I also know that when we're alone later Annie and I are going to be joining these "sick," "disgusting," individuals by watching and rewatching this footage, examining and analyzing it ourselves. Just far more privately, obviously.

"What can we do to find out who really did it?" Celeste asks, looking up at Annie.

"They haven't taped his yurt off yet," Annie says, looking a little offended by everyone else's dismissal of her as the killer. "We could just go in there and take a look."

Before Annie even finishes speaking, Celeste has sprung up from her seat and is striding across the glamp site. I go to trade a nervous look with Annie, but Annie has that same gleam in her eye and is making her short legs work hard, so

I do my best to follow.

"You're tampering with evidence!" Ethan shouts, but everyone ignores him, which seems like the best way to deal with him generally to be honest.

"Wait." Celeste stops just as we reach the yurt. "Maybe only one of us should go and the other two keep watch from the fire? We don't want to look sus . . . And I don't think I should go in there, either—I'm too recognizable. Someone might see me."

"I can't go in there," Annie says. "Everyone thinks I did it, and I've got way too many followers now." She turns to me. "It needs to be someone no one's ever heard of."

I can feel Celeste staring at me while I lock eyes with Annie. I'm trying to communicate to her psychically that she's being an asshole. I don't actually mind going into the yurt—after all, the more firsthand evidence I can collect for my blog the better. What I *do* mind is that Annie's just going to send me in there on my own. Sure I'm a *nobody*, but I thought at least we were always nobodies together. I guess I was wrong.

"I've got gloves." Annie pulls a pair of disposable gloves out of her poo-emoji pajama pocket.

I can't believe it. And she doesn't even seem bothered that while I'm in there, she'll be out here, possibly sitting around a campfire with a murderer.

"Fine," I say, plucking the gloves from her grasp and giving her side-eye. "Let me know when someone's coming."

"Will do," Annie says, already walking away.

"Urgh." I brace myself.

"Good luck, Kerry!" Celeste calls after me. I almost don't notice that she's finally got my name right.

Timmy's yurt looms in front of me, but I know the longer I

take to get the job done the more likely I'll be caught. So, with one last hopeful look from Herbie, I disappear through the yurt flaps.

For a moment, I just stand in the center of the yurt and glance around. Where am I supposed to start? It's almost empty. I'm not sure what I can really get from this. And surely the biggest clues to be found would be on the actual live footage that we have from when he was murdered. Is it weird that it's so empty and clean, though? Timmy was such a messy and gross guy that I sort of expected his yurt to reflect that, too. But instead there's just one suitcase propped up neatly in the corner and a glass of water by the bed next to a huge box of BigBoy condoms. I guess he can't have spent too much time in here before . . . well . . . before he got condom-ed.

I open his suitcase as carefully as I can, so as not to disturb anything. On top of the neatly folded clothes is a bag of toiletries that I open first, poking through with one gloved finger, relieved to have the gloves protecting me in case I find anything gross in there. But nothing seems to be out of the ordinary. I put the bag to one side and see two books lying on top of his clothes. One is a manual for picking up women called *Get Lucky and Never Get Dumped Again*. The other is a red hardcover A5 notebook with an elastic band across the front. I slip my hand under the elastic band and flip the notebook open to a page marked by a fabric ribbon. On it is a detailed breakdown of the prank that he played on Annie, including sketches and timings. I wouldn't have thought of Timmy as someone who would plan so meticulously. I just assumed it was all more spontaneous. But then I also wouldn't have expected his yurt to be this clean.

I turn back to the previous page, and there's a list of the all the influencers who are just outside this yurt right now, under the title "The Great Dirt Dish."

Celeste—Friday, August 26, 11:30 p.m.
Mirror

Millie—Saturday, August 27, 10:00 p.m.
App
Crystal
Speakers

Ethan—Sunday, August 28, 7:00 p.m.
Webcam
Log-in details
Chipolata

Dougie—Sunday, August 28, 10:00 p.m.
Pants

Winona—Monday, August 29, 10:00 a.m.
Vagina steamer

The date and time next to Celeste's name is exactly the time he was pranking her in the spa block. And the mirror was what he used. These must be pranks that he was planning on doing to the other influencers.

I flip through the rest of the notebook and it's full of prank plans, all with detailed notes and diagrams, like the one on Annie. But the influencer list doesn't have any other information—it's more like a summary page. Then I take a closer look and realize that something's been ripped out. There's a stump for around ten or so pages that are missing. Maybe he tore the pages out so he could have them in his pocket when he was doing the pranks? Remind himself of his plans?

Or what if someone else *has* been in here before me? Someone who wanted to hide them . . . We didn't see anyone coming out of here. What if they were already in here when we got back to camp, what if they're still . . . I look around me for places someone might hide. Cautiously my eyes fix on the bed, or more specifically, under the bed.

"KERRY!" Annie starts hissing from the other side of the tent flaps. "KERRY! SOMEONE'S COMING! QUICK!"

I hastily take pictures of the prank pages, put the notebook back in the case, and zip it up, standing it back exactly where I found it.

"Kerry! Hurry!" Annie whispers from outside the tent, and I panic, jumping through the yurt flaps.

Outside I immediately collide with Annie and Herbie. Annie strains her neck to peer past me into the yurt, clearly regretting her decision not to go in with me. That's the price of fame I guess, Annie.

"What did you find?" she whispers as I take off my gloves and the two of us head back to the campfire.

"I'll send you pictures. Make sure no one sees," I whisper, sending the pictures to her as we walk.

I can see DI Wallace and DC Short in the distance coming back with Dougie just as we reach the fire, and I breathe a sigh of relief. Mystic Millie appears to be hanging some kind of long thin crystals from the strings of fairy lights around camp.

"What are those?" Annie asks.

"Crystals for protection," Mystic Millie responds. "They will guard you from any dangerous energies."

Mystic Millie finishes hanging the crystals and then stands and stares at the top of Celeste's head in a really sinister way. Celeste and everyone else look at the area above her head questioningly.

"When I've finished, I'll cleanse your auras. Celeste first, yours is murky." Millie starts waving her hands around Celeste's face with concern.

"I'm okay, thanks, Millie," Celeste says with a confidence I'm not sure I would have if my aura was being called murky. Millie is oblivious and produces another stick of sage as if from thin air, lights it, and starts wafting it around her.

Dougie and DC Short arrive back at the campfire, while DI Wallace walks past with some uniformed officers and directs them into Timmy's yurt. I got out just in time! Then he joins DC Short at the campfire, ready to call their next witness. I can feel Annie getting agitated. She clearly thinks she's next. Especially now that the internet's declared her the chief suspect.

"Ethan Woods, we'd like to speak with you next, please," DI Wallace announces.

Ethan stands up, pushing his glasses up his nose with an air of great importance, as Annie slumps back down around the firepit, her eyebrows knitted together in fury.

Once Ethan and the detectives have left, Celeste leans over to me.

"Well?" she whispers. "Did you find anything?"

I shake my head. "Nothing. Apart from that it was a lot tidier in there than I thought it would be."

I hang back from sharing what I've found with her because something doesn't feel quite right here. Obviously Celeste has the strongest alibi, but something feels a bit off about how eager she is for us to investigate. Besides, how do we know we can trust any of these people? They're all strangers. In the back of my mind, "Bitches get murderous" continues to circle, even though it's built on nothing but a catchy headline.

"What are you talking about?" Dougie asks, sitting back down next to me at the fire. He's so tall he casts a shadow over me as I sit there. The Adorable Adonis, sharing my log. Get a grip, Kerry.

"Kerry had a look in Timmy's yurt, to see if there were any clues." Celeste fills him in.

Dougie stares at us blankly. "Clues for what?"

"For what happened to Timmy, duh!" Celeste says.

"Oh, right, yeah man . . ." Dougie looks confused as he puts a protective arm around Celeste.

"I didn't find anything," I lie again. That's the second time in as many minutes. I'm getting good at this.

"What did the police ask you?" Mystic Millie asks Dougie.

"Just what I was doing before he was found, how I found out he was there," Dougie says. I almost scoff aloud. It's clear DC Short just wanted to get him alone and stare at him shirt-less. He wasn't even there when we found the body.

Millie turns her attention to Annie and me. She waggles one of her evil-warding crystals over our heads, wafting her hands with a serious concentration. Then she circles us, squinting at the top of my head with a puzzled expression, moving her face closer to mine and then further away.

"Your aura is very thin," she says. She looks like a doctor who's just given me bad news. "I am sorry."

As she shuffles off away from me with a solemn look on her face, I feel panic rise. What does a "thin" aura mean? Is my aura thin because I'm in danger? Am I going to die? Why can't I just have a murky one like Celeste? I type "thin aura" into Google, and there's no such thing. My pulse slows back down and I chastise myself for getting so worked up. I don't even believe in all that stuff, and even if I did, I wouldn't believe it from Millie.

Dougie's phone vibrates, and all the other phones around the campfire, and I see the name MOTHER appear again just before he shields the screen.

"Shit," Dougie says. "Who's taken that?"

"Someone's watching us." Celeste looks spooked.

Dougie wraps his arm around Celeste's shoulder, pulling her into him protectively and resting his chin on top of her head. It's easy to see why people want them to be together, I guess. It is quite adorable the way he looks after her.

"That's so creepy?" says Mystic Millie.

I have never wanted to know what's in a text message more in my entire life. Who *is* MOTHER?

"What's up?" Annie asks, but everyone ignores her.

Dougie's so focused on comforting Celeste that he's being slack about protecting his phone, though, and I can slyly get a look at the message. It's a picture of us all taken from afar, sitting around this fire chatting. The text with it says, "STOP TALKING TO STRANGERS." It can have only been taken minutes ago because Ethan's not in it and I'm back from my yurt investigation.

I guess that's why they're not talking to us.

"There's spies everywhere," Dougie says. "We're always being watched."

"Who's watching us?" Annie asks again, but no one says a word, it's like they've shut down, closed ranks. We're no longer in their circle.

I add "Who is MOTHER?" to the notes I've already started on my phone and shudder. Peering around us into the darkness beyond the fairy lights and phone screens, I wonder who's watching . . . and even more worryingly, did they see me going into Timmy's yurt?

"God, get your fingers out of my aura, Millie," Celeste says, swatting away Mystic Millie as she persists in cleansing her darkness without consent.

We've been sitting around the campfire in awkward silence for what feels like hours—since the influencers received that last message from MOTHER. In reality, it's probably only been ten really uncomfortable minutes. But I feel a glow of warmth and relief when I see Scott's name *finally* appearing at the top of my screen, giving me something to do.

> **Scott:** Are you OK? Jen just showed me these ReelLife videos about the festival and some dude Timmy being dead?!

> **Scott:** I went to find my phone because I didn't know where it was and then I saw

you'd been trying to call me. I'm so sorry!
It's been wild, there was this MASSIVE
crowd tonight.

Scott: But that's not important right
now! What's going on? Jen says there
are videos saying that you've all been
imprisoned on the farm as suspects.

Scott: Some other dude on ReelLife's
saying that Annie killed a guy.

Scott: With a condom? I didn't know she
had it in her.

I thought hearing from Scott would make me feel better, but something rankles me. Rationally I know that Scott doesn't have any social media profiles, so of course he's having to rely on Jen for all the details. But why didn't he call me when I texted him about it?

My phone vibrates again right away with a response to my messages, though, and my worries immediately slip away.

Scott: Should I come home?

I so badly want to say yes, but I know I don't *need* Scott to come home. And would that be selfish of me? After all, he's off living his dream. How many people actually get to do that? I can't stand in his way.

Me: No, I'm totally fine. I promise. 🖤

Annie nudges me, and I see DC Short heading back over to us with Ethan in tow. He's been with them far longer than Dougie was.

"You know, DC Short"—Ethan projects his voice because whatever he has to say is clearly very important—"it's absolutely wonderful to see a woman out there serving on the force, solving crimes and doing it for sisters everywhere. What an asset to feminism and the female species you are."

I notice DC Short isn't as starstruck by Ethan as she was by Dougie. If anything I'd say her body language is giving off pure hate, and I can relate.

"Celeste, we'll take you for your statement now," DC Short says, trying to ignore Ethan. Her eyes light up again in Celeste's presence. "I absolutely love your work, by the way."

"Oh, thank you," Celeste coos. "Would you like an autograph? I've got some Bitches Get Riches T-shirts in my yurt. I can just get one for you?"

"OH MY GOD I WOULD LOVE THAT!!!" DC Short practically screams in her face.

"Fab, one sec." Celeste gets up and heads to her yurt, reemerging seconds later with a T-shirt while Annie looks on, slack-jawed.

DC Short immediately puts the T-shirt on and turns back to us, a ball of excitement. It's then that DI Wallace appears behind her with Heather hot on his heels. I can't imagine he'll be too impressed to learn that DC Short's fawning over the suspects.

"DI Wallace? Heather has some questions!" Mini-Heather One arrives across the camp, shouting at him. Heather follows close behind, letting her interns talk for her. "We need to know what's going to happen with the events tomorrow. Obviously, as I'm sure you can appreciate, there's a lot at stake here."

"As much as a person losing their life?" DI Wallace snaps over Mini-Heather One's head.

"Depends whether that life was worth the hundreds of thousands it cost to put this on," Heather mutters under her breath but it's loud enough that everyone hears it and stares at her. "What? I missed out on this season's Dior bikini for this thing, and the Versace sunglasses. We've all made sacrifices."

She shoots Annie and me a look to show she's deadly serious, but I never would have doubted it anyway.

DI Wallace coughs to regain everyone's attention and starts speaking again. "In my professional opinion it's tricky because when you look at the footage, the time between when Timmy last speaks—or captions, or whatever you folk call it—and when Celeste started looking around the spa block for him is only a few minutes. How could someone have gotten in the room, behind that mirror, and then out again in that time without Celeste noticing them or it showing up on the video?"

"So it's an accident and we can carry on?" Heather pushes.

"Yes," DI Wallace confirms, already turning away from Annie.

"WHAT?!" Annie shouts. "Why would it be an accident?"

"How could it not be an accident?" DI Wallace spins on his heel and stares Annie directly in the eye.

"Why would he put the condom on his head in the first place?" Annie asks.

"Because he was playing a prank on his friend and he wanted to scare her." DI Wallace crosses his arms like he thinks he's won, but Annie won't be convinced.

"You've been wrong before," Annie points out.

"Shut up, Annie," Heather mutters.

"Shut up, Annie," Mini-Heather One repeats.

"Annie, unless you have any evidence to back up a different theory, I think you'll have to conclude the same thing that I have," DI Wallace says with superiority. "Do you have any evidence?"

"Well for one thing, the whole internet thinks I did it, and I'm chief murder suspect," Annie says, stamping her foot for emphasis. I resist the urge to grab her by the scruff of her neck like she's a little kitten, rescuing her from nosing into something that's bad for her. Seriously, what is she doing?

"We don't think you did it, Annie," DI Wallace says so calmly it's almost an insult.

"We'll discuss that in my interview," Annie says through gritted teeth. DI Wallace just stares at her. Neither of them are backing down.

A loud bang erupts in the sky, and I almost leap out of my skin. DI Wallace swears, and everyone else jumps. Herbie scoots into my arms, shaking while the sky lights up around us. Everyone stares upward as DI Wallace loosens his tie and tries to look like he hasn't just absolutely crapped himself.

"I KNEW THIS DAY WOULD COME!" Mystic Millie shouts as more bangs pop off and more lights fill the sky. "I'VE ALWAYS SAID THE FUTURE WAS HAZY AND THIS IS WHY! BECAUSE WE'RE ALL GOING TO DIE! RIGHT NOW!!!! IT STARTS WITH TIMMY, BUT IT ENDS WITH US!"

"I'm too handsome to die!" Ethan frantically shields his face with his hands and then goes to seek shelter in Mystic Millie's arms, but she wiggles away, instead concentrating on rubbing crystals on her temples and swirling the burning sage around her head, creating a frantic tornado of the strong-smelling smoke.

"Whoa," Dougie says, staring at the sky, his eyes glittering like a beautiful emoji.

"It's fireworks," Celeste says to Mystic Millie.

As if on cue, more fireworks illuminate the sky, their sound drowning out whatever DI Wallace is attempting to shout to Heather and the Mini-Heathers. All around us the fireworks are coming thick and fast, zooming into the center of the festival ground. We're entirely surrounded.

"THIS WASN'T PLANNED!" Heather manages to reply to DI Wallace and DC Short in between the bangs. "I DON'T KNOW WHAT'S HAPPENING!!"

The fireworks continue, a circle of noise surrounding the festival, colors forming perfectly in the center, making different patterns. At first it's hard to see what those patterns might be, but then one thing becomes clearer: The word "Timmy," glowing in the sky.

I look over to the Tim-sciples, standing topless and aimless without their leader. Each of them wears a black armband on their right arm as a sign of mourning. They stare at Timmy's name in the sky, raising their left hands in peace signs, their right hands clasped in a fist, punching their chests emotionally over their hearts. Small sparks of light slice through the black sky and explode. The colors and sounds intensify in every direction, and I feel that there's no escape. As the light of Timmy's name fades away to dust, yet more bangs continue around it. The festival ground comes to a standstill, held captive while a picture emerges above us all. It's that of a perfectly drawn cock and balls, made entirely from the light of the fireworks. A sobering reminder of everything that Timmy Eaton stood for. Even in death, he's a massive dick.

11

"EVERYONE GET THE FUCK UP!" A woman's voice echoes around the camp making Annie, Herbie, and me sit up in our beds immediately.

I'd been lying in bed, regrettably scrolling ReelLife, unable to tear my eyes away from video after video about Timmy. I probably should have been doing other things. But instead I just kept scrolling. Even when it moved on from Timmy to videos of people just filming their typical day-in-the-life stuff and watching everyone being so busy on there made me feel kind of lethargic, I still couldn't stop.

I must not have slept for longer than an hour last night. It was about 6:00 a.m. when the police finally finished our interview because DI Wallace insisted on talking to us last; Annie called it a power play, but I wonder if it was because he knew that the two of them would be locked in combat over his insistence that Timmy's death was an accident for over an hour.

After that, we stayed up for a while watching and rewatching the livestreams, searching for clues. But there was nothing aside from what we saw already. Timmy was filming Celeste from behind the two-way mirror in the shower cubicle and then the captions stopped just a few minutes before Celeste started looking for him. As for Celeste's livestream, we were there for most of it, so I was hoping there might have been something I missed while we were searching for Timmy's location, but there didn't seem to be anything. Even Annie's fresh determination to prove DI Wallace wrong couldn't help us. How is it possible that someone can die with millions of people watching and there's not even a hint as to how it happened?

"GET THE FUCK UP!" yells the voice again.

After so little sleep it feels more than a bit rude that a stranger's now shouting at the top of their lungs outside our tent. Still, Annie and I get out of our beds, rubbing our eyes as we traipse across the yurt, followed by Herbie, who's reluctantly stirred from his curled-up croissant position. The three of us peer our heads through the yurt flaps to look into the camp, where there is a woman who, despite the heat, is wearing a black pantsuit complete with blazer and shoulder pads. She's marching around shouting and shaking yurt covers, trying to rouse all the inhabitants. Although so far, she only appears to have succeeded in waking Annie and me.

"Who's that?" Annie and I whisper to each other while Herbie rushes back into the tent, seeking solace from the shouty person.

She doesn't seem to notice us, and continues on her rounds until she reaches the other side of the firepit, where she briefly hesitates at Timmy's yurt for a second. It's been taped off so that no one can enter, but there's no actual barrier or police guard stopping anyone getting in or out, which seems sloppy if you ask me. But then we also watched them take everything out of there piece by piece (eventually) last night.

"Wakey, wakey, rise and shine, someone needs to explain to me what the fuck happened here last night!"

"Morning, Joanna," Ethan says, crawling out of his yurt first and stretching. His dark curly hair's popping out at wild angles.

"Joanna?" Annie mouths up at me from our little yurt flap bubble and immediately starts googling a combination of the influencers' names and "Joanna."

Ethan's already wearing another terrible black turtleneck T-shirt with a paper sign he's made pinned to it. Today's reads, *No Uterus, No Opinion*, and it makes me wonder. I wouldn't be surprised if on the back it had: **Except for my opinion*.

"*Is it* a good morning, Ethan? When one of your colleagues has stupidly asphyxiated himself with a condom? *IS IT?*" Joanna shouts right in his face, so close that he blinks at her breath on his eyeballs.

"Probably not, no, Joanna," Ethan says, looking at the ground like a small child who's just been told off.

It actually brings me a lot of joy to see him taken down a peg or two, and although I don't know who this woman is, I do wonder if I might like her.

The woman we know to be Joanna doesn't stop there. "And who were you talking to last night? After I told you specifically not to talk to anyone? There were two thirsty-looking teenage girls in those pictures with you!"

"How *dare* she," Annie whispers, still tapping away at her phone. "I was well hydrated yesterday actually."

"MOTHER?" I whisper back, though, tent flaps clutched tightly around our faces. "I think that's MOTHER."

Annie suddenly thrusts her phone at me, displaying a picture of Joanna. It's a more poised version of her, but unmistakably still her. The Google search says she's the manager of Dougie, Celeste, Ethan, Millie, and Timmy. We make a small *ahhh* noise and then retreat our faces slightly back inside in case the terrifying yet quite impressive Joanna sees us. I feel like she's not our biggest fan.

Celeste comes out of her yurt in a big black hoodie and black cycling shorts, yawning. Her long ginger hair waves over her shoulders perfectly as if she really did just wake up like that. From the yurt next to her Mystic Millie emerges, too, wearing a black tie-dye kaftan with black crystals and rocks dripping from her earlobes, fingers, and neck.

"They already had outfits for mourning prepped and ready to go," Annie whispers.

"I was just trying to contact Timmy in the spirit world," Millie announces like it explains her lateness. She sounds like someone trying to pretend to their mum that they've been doing their homework all evening when actually they've been watching reality TV and eating snacks.

"Right, right," Joanna says as Celeste stifles a snort of laughter.

"Come on, sleeping beauty, time to get up!" Joanna stands outside Dougie's yurt. "It's like trying to herd fucking cats," she mutters to herself. "Dougie, if you don't get up, I'm going to presume you're dead, too, and come in there myself!"

Dougie eventually emerges from his yurt looking tired and bemused in just a pair of boxers. As a girl traipses out behind him, he leans down and gives her one last kiss before she heads back to the main camp.

"Bye," he says, eyes sparkling.

"Yep, off you go, love. Sorry, influencers only. I thought I'd made myself clear about mixing with the riffraff last night," Joanna says harshly. A cloud of vape that she's sucking on aggressively floats around her face as she talks. "Consoling you, was she?"

Dougie doesn't answer her. He stands with his abs out, all shirtless and just kind of . . . I need to stop staring at him. He seems smaller in Joanna's shadow, vulnerable, yet still muscly . . . oh god, I need to be stopped. What is *wrong* with me? Have I no self-control? Or is this just human? Just a human feeling when faced with a man with abs like . . . STOP IT, KERRY.

"Right," Joanna says, more vape smoke swirling around her angry face. "Someone needs to explain to me how Timmy ended up apparently suffocating *himself* with a condom? Seriously? Was no one watching him? Can I not leave the country for one VERY IMPORTANT meeting and let you guys get on with it for a SECOND?!"

Annie and I stay completely still, yurt flaps wrapped around our faces. I'm amazed and relieved that we still haven't been spotted.

"COME ON! SPEAK!" Joanna shouts, making Herbie bark. Annie and I freeze; I fight the instinct to shrivel up on myself. The game's up. We've been rumbled. It's too late to disappear back in the yurt because she's locked eyes with us now. "AND FOR GODSAKE SOMEONE EXPLAIN TO ME WHO THESE TWO WITH THEIR HEADS POKING OUT OF THEIR FUCK-ING YURT ARE!" She waves aggressively at us.

This is worse than being told off by a teacher, and I have that urge to laugh that always happens at the most serious and inappropriate of times. Except I don't know what we're being reprimanded for aside from merely existing?

"Annie and Kerry," Annie says, swooping out of the yurt flaps in her pajamas like she's doing a big reveal.

I find myself following her, reluctantly, just like always. "We're the Tampon Two. I'm an influencer, and Kerry's a blogger slash journalist."

"Never heard of you," Joanna says brutally, and I feel Annie ball up her fists. "Who manages you? How many followers do you have?"

"Ermm . . ." Annie checks her phone. "Fifty thousand."

"Three—" I stop talking and turn to stare at Annie. "Wait HOW MANY?"

"I KNOW RIGHT?!" Annie jumps below me shoving her phone in my face, my eyes nearly popping out of my head at the number on her profile. It's true. She's got fifty *thousand* followers.

"She was having a prank war with Timmy. Everyone on the internet thinks she killed him," Ethan says snidely.

"Oh, you're the iced tea girl," Joanna says. "God, anyway—fine, whatever. You'll be forgotten by lunchtime." She doesn't even look at me, but it's clear she doesn't think we're worth bothering with. And she definitely doesn't seem to think Annie's a cold-blooded killer, much to Annie's disappointment.

"They actually helped last night, massively," Celeste says, defending us. "They're pretty cool, and they're friends of

Heather, who planned the festival."

"Fine. Where is Heather anyway?" Joanna looks around her, absolutely furious. "You'd think that what with one of my influencers accidentally dying at her festival, she'd be rolling out the red carpet for me, but she doesn't seem to be anywhere."

I look at Joanna's stern face, her mouth a grim line of disapproval. Maybe she'd be a little less angry if she weren't wearing a full black suit on a boiling hot day, but who knows? She takes a deep inhale of her vape and continues talking in a more professional tone.

"The important thing is that we need to be posting content about Timmy—be respectful and sad et cetera, but make sure we're calling it an accident. Try to stamp out the silly rumors. And we can't neglect our normal duties." Joanna says this as if Timmy's death is just a minor inconvenience to their regular posting schedules. "Dougie! Where was your morning workout routine this morning? PUSH-UPS! NOW!"

Dougie immediately drops to the ground and starts doing push-ups.

"So, we're not going home?" Mystic Millie asks.

"No, why would we?" Joanna looks perplexed as to why her clients wouldn't want to stay at the scene of a murder. "Ethan, put an arm around Millie to comfort her for fuck's sake. Someone could be watching. You two need to amp up the love, be supporting each other through your grief and so on. Do I have to literally spoon-feed content ideas to you?"

Ethan looks delighted as he heads over to Mystic Millie and puts an arm around her shoulders. Millie on the other hand looks like his arm is made from some kind of ripe smelling cheese.

"A tragedy brings in the likes and the morbid interest," Joanna continues. "We need to give the public what they want: a united front and a small drip feed of exclusive information. Everyone at the festival will feel part of something, those at home will feel jealous. Spectacular!"

I doubt Timmy sees it as "spectacular," though. Next to me Annie's phone lights up with a ReelLife DM from Celeste.

> **Celeste:** It's not an accident. You have to investigate. Please. We need to find out what happened to Timmy.

The two of us read it and try to remain neutral, so as not to draw attention to anything in front of Joanna, but Celeste's staring at us, so Annie does a small nod of recognition. Joanna doesn't notice—thankfully she's far too busy explaining to everyone that the morning's events are canceled and instead they're all taking part in a panel event to honor Timmy.

Next to me Annie's gesturing at her screen while scrolling through theories about how Timmy was an AI robot that malfunctioned. These actually seem to be eclipsing the ones about her being a murderer, but I don't want to point out that she's already becoming old news just when she's "enjoying" her moment in the spotlight.

"Celeste!" Joanna commands. "You need to fix the damage done last night. Post a video explaining that you were doing a compare and contrast to show how effective Bitches Get

Contours products really are when pitted against rival brands. And double down on the use of Bitches Get Contours in all your videos."

"But"—Celeste walks closer to Joanna and whispers—"but they're not great, though, are they? Bitches Get Contours products just aren't all that? Can't I just let it die?"

"You do that," Joanna whispers, getting intimidatingly close to Celeste's face, "and I'll have to reconsider your contract. I'm not about to waste my time with someone who's not making me money."

I fight the urge to let out a low whistle. After a tense moment where I'm not sure anyone breathes, Joanna straightens up and Celeste blinks, looking slightly rattled.

"Right, everyone get away from me," says Joanna, heading toward an empty yurt. "Go and create respectful grief content. Ethan, for the love of God send me anything before you post it. A baby has more self-awareness than you. And *no one* talks to the press." She turns back to Annie and me and shoots two fingers in our direction that I can practically feel jabbing my collarbone. "That includes you two."

The influencers disperse, leaving Annie and me standing in the camp. I can hear my own breath as overwhelm sets in. It's not just Joanna's comments; it's knowing that we're investigating again. Knowing that I've finally got an angle for the blog now, but that angle puts me and Annie back in danger for the second time in less than a year . . .

Be brave, Kerry! I am a serious journalist, with a serious topic to write about and a serious job to do. But I'm also in the middle of a field, camping with a possible murderer and a load of strangers. Annie suddenly grabs my hand in hers, clasping my sweaty fingers tightly in her own clammy paw.

"Are you ready to investigate a crime, Velma?" Annie whispers.

"Ready, Daphne," I reply to my bold friend, just like her Scooby-Doo counterpart.

The two of us look down at Herbie, who mostly looks ready for breakfast.

12

We turn to walk back inside our yurt, ready to solve the mystery of the condom killer, when something falls from above my head. Its smooth hard surface brushes my arm on the way down before stabbing into the ground, just millimeters from my left foot. Annie shrieks in surprise as we stare down at it, poking out of the grass like a dagger.

Herbie comes over to investigate, his little nose twitching as he sniffs around the perilous object, and as I go to pull him away, I recognize it. It's one of the protective crystals that Mystic Millie hung around the camp last night.

"OMG you could have *died*," Annie gasps as I pull it out of the ground. "That could have *killed you*!"

"Errrr, okay, yeah thanks," I say, turning the crystal over in my hand, comparing it to the other ones still hanging up. The end has broken off somehow, which is why it's so sharp and stabby.

Annie joins me in staring at the offending crystal, while Herbie sniffs at its perilous four-inch-long shaft.

"Imagine that," Annie says. "Nearly maimed by one of

Mystic Millie's protective crystals."

I shudder, because actually there are a few things that have started to trouble me about Mystic Millie. Not just that she's a spiritual fraud and her relationship with Ethan's fake. For one, she was first on the scene after Timmy's death and all dressed up. She immediately tried to tamper with the body (admittedly she wasn't the only one to do this . . .). And she was next on that list of pranks that I found in Timmy's yurt yesterday. Her aura's growing more murky by the hour.

"Maybe it thought you were the danger, and it was trying to take you out?" Annie says, taking the crystal from me. She weighs it in her hand, considering its bulk.

"Oh yeah . . . very comforting, thanks, Annie," I say.

"Is she selling these or something? Is that why she's got them everywhere?" Annie asks.

"Not sure," I say, but Annie's already googling "Mystic Millie crystals" anyway.

Her website comes up advertising crystals, tarot cards, crystal balls, scarves, kaftans, mood rings to really "get in touch with yourself," and aura-cleansing water. You can buy the entire Mystic Millie starter kit to become exactly like her for the sum of just one thousand pounds, including three tarot-reading workshops that might be with her but also might be with someone who she has apparently specially trained to channel her vibe. I've never heard of such a con in my entire life.

"Oooh! Can I get a mood ring?" Annie asks, jabbing her finger onto the screen. "I've always wanted one of those!"

"ANNIE!" I chastise with a loud whisper. "We're not shopping; we're investigating!"

"Sorry," Annie mumbles. She lowers her head sadly but still

swiftly clicks Add to Basket, thinking that I won't notice.

"It's weird, but I can't see any similar crystals on the shop at all. Everything on here's more like a chunk of rock, whereas these ones"—I point to the crystals hanging around us—"they're more kind of a long, thin . . ." I take the crystal from Annie, studying it.

"Maybe she's only just got them in and they're new? And now she's using Timmy's death as, like, the soft launch?" Annie suggests. "After someone's died is a time when people feel vulnerable, I guess."

"Inappropriate, but it does seem like the sort of thing Joanna would suggest." I snap a photo for a reverse Google image search. "Wait? If she had these ready, though, does that mean she knew they'd be needed?"

Annie and I lock eyes while the search loads.

"Don't you think it's kind of ironic that Timmy was also killed by something used for protection," Annie says thoughtfully. "I mean it was *sexual* protection, but protection nonetheless."

I fake a gag. "Please never say *sexual protection* around me again. It just feels kind of . . . icky."

"Sexual protection," Annie says, blinking at me. "*Sexual protection. Sexual protection Seeeeeexxxxuuuuualllllll. Protection.*"

I shake my head and look down at my phone, but what's loaded there makes me squeak with a mixture of surprise and embarrassment. When I turn the phone to show Annie, she immediately throws the crystal on the floor.

MYSTIC MILLIE'S CRYSTAL DILDOS DISCONTINUED AS INFLUENCER APOLOGIZES FOR THRUSH.

Annie slaps her hand over her mouth before laughing so hard she falls to the ground next to the offending article. "Oh my god, imagine if you'd been killed by a crystal dildo? That would be how they'd have to tell your mum you died. I'd definitely make sure it was on your gravestone!"

"Thanks," I say, narrowing my eyes at her. "I feel better knowing that if I had died, you would have found great amusement in it."

I click into the article. I guess it's my duty to read more about the crystal that launched literally a thousand yeast infections (actual stats from the article). It could be evidence.

"'Discontinued in 2020 after it was discovered that they were incredibly bad for vaginal health,'" I read from the page.

"It's like being in a cage of dildo," Annie says, looking up at all the crystals hung around us in a circle. I would pay money for her to stop saying the word "dildo."

"Can we go inside?" I flap a hand toward our yurt. "They're starting to make me feel a bit claustrophobic actually."

Annie smirks, and the two of us head back inside, where the temperature's really ramped up since we've been outside. The bright sun's turned it into a massive fabric oven. The two of us sag into a pair of white beanbags, and Annie's phone vibrates in her hand.

"Oh," she whispers, crestfallen.

"What's up?" I ask. "I mean apart from the obvious."

"I'm no longer a suspect in Timmy's death because apparently a woman could never have the strength to pull a condom over a man's head like that." Annie shakes her head angrily. "Fucking patriarchy."

"Fucking patriarchy," I agree. "What do we do now?"

"I need to put a condom on your head."

"I think we should interview— Wait, what?" I suddenly register what she's said.

"To see if you can get it off again." Annie pulls a BigBoy condom out of her pocket. "If you can't, then it could have been an accident; if you can, then it was murder, simple. An exercise in scientific proof."

"We already know it was murder," I say. "Even if it was a prank, if he got the condom on, he must have been able to get it off himself. The only reason he wouldn't have been able to is if someone or something was stopping him."

"Yes, but we need to prove it," Annie says, avoiding eye contact with me.

I glare at her. "Are you just trying to get video evidence that you could have done it for ReelLife by showing yourself stretching it over my head?"

"NO." Annie tsks at me in an overly theatrical way.

There's a moment of silence while Annie stares at her follower count starting to decrease and turns to me.

"Ok, FINE. I'm a brave girl." Annie gulps nervously. "Condom me."

She sets her phone to record and stands with her eyes shut, but as I approach her head with the condom, I just can't do it. Last time I saw one over someone's head they were dead. I don't want to do that to my best friend. Not to mention the fact that I reckon the whole thing would feel and smell terrible.

"I can't do it," I say, lowering the condom.

"Urgh, fine," Annie says, and looks around the yurt. "What's like a head?" She settles on a small kettle in the kitchen area.

Flexing, she stretches the condom on and off with no trouble.

"Happy now?" I ask.

"Yes," she says. "Let's start the murder board."

"Dude, we cannot start a murder board in a yurt," I say.

"Why not?" Annie asks.

"Floppy walls? Also there's no security, so anyone could come in at any point and find it. Let's just use my laptop. We can do a virtual murder board on PowerPoint."

I pull out my laptop, smiling at the colorful, cartoonish picture that Scott drew of me and him and stuck to the lid before he went away.

"Ew, vom!" Annie says, spotting it.

"I love it, shut up," I say, not missing a beat.

"This feels less fun to me," Annie sulks. But her sulk soon turns to a cheerful smile as I start copying and pasting pictures of suspects from the internet onto the murder slides. "Actually I guess this is easier because if anyone else dies, you can just delete them."

"Wow, brutal," I say, but she has a point. Even though I'm very much hoping no one else dies. Obviously.

"Do you think we should put Heather on there again? Maybe the Mini-Heathers?"

"I doubt it's Heather after last time, but we'll add her for good measure. The Mini-Heathers are definitely going on there, though. They're all kinds of sinister."

"Do they remind you a bit of the twins in *The Shining*?" Annie asks.

I shudder. "Brrrrr, yeah, actually—definitely One and Two anyway."

I put all three Mini-Heathers down on the board but without knowing all their names I can only put them in as numbers one, two, and Poor Jessica. So now I feel like *I'm* part of the problem. I also feel bad about putting Jessica on there at all—she's been through enough already.

"The main focus is on the influencers, though, so we need to start putting in where they were during the murder," I say, and start to type. "I still maintain that there was definitely someone rustling around in the bushes when we were on our way to the spa block as well. So we need to think about who that could have been."

"Let's start with Celeste," Annie says. "Least likely to have done it because she was in the spa and we have her on film the whole time."

"Do you think she's actually a bit smarter than she appears online, though?" I ask. I've certainly been surprised by her since the murder.

Annie doesn't hesitate. "No."

"Even though she wants us to investigate?" I ask.

"Still no. I stand by my original point. She's literally always filming herself putting on makeup and shouting 'Hey, guys!' at her phone."

Celeste

Makeup influencer with small businesses Bitches Get Riches and Bitches Get Contours.

Best friend of Dougie, who in turn is best friends with Timmy.

Timmy told the world that she doesn't actually use her own beauty products.

Location at time of death: Being pranked by the deceased and filmed the entire time.

Dougie
Timmy's best friend.

The Adorable Adonis. Also not smart.

Location at time of death: With a girl in his yurt, "entertaining."

Ethan
NOT a feminist. No way.

Definitely not in a relationship with Mystic Millie but pretending to be.

A total creep.

Location at time of death: Not sure but at a guess, alone in his yurt?

Mystic Millie
Not an actual mystic. It seems very obvious that she doesn't have any special "gift," and they all know it.

In a fake relationship with Ethan.

Using Timmy's death as a chance to relaunch a failed "product" as protective crystals.

Location at time of death: Possibly nearby? Was the first at the scene of Timmy's death suspiciously quickly and fully dressed and made up. Was she going somewhere? OR coming back?

Joanna/MOTHER

Their manager, in charge of all of them.

Wants everyone to think that this was an accident when it clearly is NOT.

Location at time of death: Not at the festival site. Celeste says that Joanna was in the US at the time, at a meeting. But yet still sent creepy pictures to everyone of someone keeping an eye on them for her?

"Okay," I say, clicking and adding in the images from Timmy's notebook that I took last night. "And these are the pranks and the order that they were due to be done over the weekend. It looks as though he had something planned for all of them."

Even though I imagine everything he said about Celeste's fake makeup products has been completely forgotten in the drama of his condom death.

"Does that mean he had dirt on everyone?" Annie asks. "He was trying to ruin careers?"

"Maybe."

"I don't know if I really get the whole Celeste thing. Timmy just doesn't strike me as the kind of guy who would be bothered about someone faking their beauty routine. He was hardly a beacon of morality," Annie says.

"Good point, but he also didn't seem the type to plan out his pranks in technical detail. Maybe there's more to him and we need to find it?" I suggest. "We can start by working out what the notes under people's names mean."

"Because the type of prank links to what he was going to expose?" Annie asks.

"Exactly," I confirm, editing the picture and breaking it up so that each prank that Timmy had listed goes next to the respective suspect. "And then we can see who had the most to lose. Millie was next on the list. And she was first on the scene. So we should look at hers first."

> Millie: Saturday, August 27, 10:00 p.m.
> App
> Crystal
> Speakers

Annie and I stare at the list, trying to work out what the words might mean.

"Well, the crystal could be the 'protective' ones?" Annie suggests.

"Yeah, but then what about the speakers and app?" I ask.

"Maybe he was going to announce it was actually a dildo over some speakers?" Even Annie sounds unconvinced by this.

"And the app?" I purse my lips and wrinkle my forehead.

Annie purses her lips and wrinkles her forehead back at me, and for a short while we stay like that, staring at each other, until she cracks first.

"Yeah, no, I don't know." She sighs.

"Whatever he was planning was listed in much more detail on the pages that were ripped out," I say. "And we'd know what the secrets he was trying to expose were if we saw those."

"Maybe that's why someone took them?" Annie asks.

"Someone knew about the pranks and went to great lengths to protect their secrets?" I follow on.

"So we find the missing pages, and we find the murderer?"

"Maybe?" Could it all be that easy? "But how do we figure out who has them?"

The two of us sit in pensive silence with Herbie at our feet, his little chin resting on his paws. After a few minutes where neither of us comes up with anything new, he sighs.

"The Timmy panel Joanna's got them all doing starts in ten minutes. We should head there now," I say, feeling slightly defeated. I'm sure there's an answer staring us right in the face.

"Yeah, let's see what it is that Joanna's been training everyone to say all morning." Annie peps up at the idea.

My phone beeps for the ten millionth time today with messages from Les Populaires, and I realize with a jolt that there's been nothing from Scott. He hasn't replied since I messaged him around 6:00 a.m. to tell him Annie had waged war on DI Wallace.

The two of us are about to leave the yurt when Annie stops suddenly.

"Oh, wait." Annie picks up her phone and starts recording, speaking solemnly into the screen. "Hey, guys. Just wanted to touch base after the sad events of last night. We're on our way to 'Timmy's Memorial Panel' at the Festival of Fame now so, come with us to mourn."

I wait for her to stop recording to flick her on the arm. "Annie!"

"What?" Annie asks innocently, rubbing the spot I just flicked.

"Come with us to mourn?! It just feels a bit crass."

"Everyone else is doing it." Annie fiddles on her phone before playing one of Celeste's videos.

"Hey, guys," Celeste says, sitting at one of the backstage mirrors, all in black. "Obviously things are super sad at the Festival of Fame today. Everyone's really struggling to get to grips with what's happened. So, get ready with me to mourn my dead friend. RIP, Timmy. I'm going to be serving grief with my Bitches Get Contours waterproof mascara!"

She does a peace sign to the camera as she reaches for her Bitches Get Contours blush stick, and my mouth hangs open as I watch the viewer count tick up and up. It looks like everyone is benefitting from Timmy's death.

13

"Do you think we can go over there?" Annie gestures over to where Joanna's giving Dougie, Celeste, Mystic Millie, and Ethan a very stern-looking backstage pep talk.

"I'm still scared of her." I gulp, looking in Joanna's direction. She's currently pacing around shouting things at the influencers between puffs of her vape. I personally wouldn't want to get in the middle of that.

All the influencers stare at the floor sulkily, with the exception of Celeste, who's filming herself putting on more Bitches Get Contours products. I watch as she pulls out an aerosol can and sprays a tiny amount before wrinkling her nose.

"Nah, I won't let her scare me off," Annie says, taking a deep inhale and shoving her shoulders back. She advances toward them before choking on the cloyingly sweet smell of Joanna's smoke cloud. She flails a bit, managing to nearly scratch off my face. "Get behind me, I'll protect you," she hacks.

I slink behind Annie like the wuss that I am as we approach. The shouts and smells get more intense the closer we get, and I have to choose between covering my nose or my ears. Another smell's started to overpower the vape, though; I look over and see Celeste spraying more of the aerosol before coughing and putting the lid firmly back on it. Whatever's in that can smells gross.

"Celeste, whatever that is smells vile!" Joanna huffs hypocritically considering she's the source of the literal cloud of smell. "So, remember what I said, look sad, shed a tear if you can without looking constipated—Ethan—and please, please don't try to make any jokes, it's not appropriate. Ethan, again!" Joanna finishes her lecture before realizing that we're right behind her. She whirls around so sharply I swear we're buffeted with air from her shoulder pads. "How did you two get in here?"

"We still have backstage passes, and I'm still an influencer." Annie flashes her gold wristband. I attempt to do the same while chewing my fingernails to the cuticle. I feel hot and shaky under Joanna's scathing gaze. I need to get everything I can for this story.

I try to focus on the influencers rather than Joanna; after all, they're the story. They're all still wearing black—Dougie's in a deep V-neck black T-shirt, so low and tight that if he were a woman, the tabloids would say he was "flaunting his chest" and that it was inappropriate given the somberness of the event. Celeste's in a black T-shirt and shorts with black sunglasses on and black nail polish (when did she have time to change her nail polish to mourning colors, because it was luminous green yesterday? What about her nail beds?), and Mystic Millie is wearing a dark-colored dress with some kind of pattern on. I squint at it, trying to work out what it is, and when I finally do I have to push down an inappropriate titter. It's the death tarot card, all over her dress. And in her ears are small death-card earrings, paired with an even smaller matching death-card pendant on a chain around her neck.

"Time to go!" Mini-Heather One shouts. The influencers trail from the green room to the stage, and we follow in hot pursuit.

Annie and I watch from the wings as the influencers shuffle out in front of a huge crowd—maybe even bigger than yesterday. Winona Philips's somber face appears on the big screen as the influencers take their seats.

"Welcome, everyone, to a very special panel this morning honoring our dear departed friend Timmy Eaton, may he rest in peace. Please note that anyone who was hoping to come to the 'Feminist Fiesta,' we do hope to reschedule it to another time."

I search her face for a hint of irritation, and there is the tiniest of twitches at the corner of her mouth as she speaks. But mostly she is doing an excellent job of looking sad, when everyone knows that she was no fan of Timmy's work.

"We wanted this to be a chance for us all to talk about Timmy, how much we loved and cared about him." Like yesterday, Winona's eyes are flitting from side to side as if she's reading from a script. "But before we start, let's take a few minutes to have a look back at Timmy's best bits."

The way she says it feels more like we're welcoming someone home from the celeb jungle, where they have been forced to eat bull ass for the sake of a reality TV show. Winona disappears entirely, replaced by a blank screen that flutters into a black-and-white video of Timmy.

It starts off with him as a child, a picture that he posted

recently for National Goldfish Day of him and his old pet goldfish, Titan, who apparently met a watery grave shortly after the picture was taken. It moves swiftly on to him growing up and more recent events—Timmy in an office with the CEO from BigBoy condoms, posing with a giant penis sculpture; watching bottles of his new fake tan coming along the conveyer belt. Emotional music ramps up, and the video moves quicker through outtakes of him laughing at people and dangling tampons in their faces. There's a more recent clip of him receiving a Best-Looking Influencer award before pictures flood the screen of him at that same ceremony photographed with Winona, Celeste, Dougie, Millie, and Ethan. A clip pops up from yesterday, and I pray we're reaching the end; it feels like it's been going on forever. We watch Dougie and Timmy doing a dance in the VIP glamp site. I'm about to switch off entirely when something in the background of their dance catches my eye. I nudge Annie.

"Oh, yeah, it's us," she whispers, pointing to where our hooded heads are poking out of our yurt.

"No, it's Millie!" I whisper, squinting at the scene behind Timmy. "And she's coming out of Timmy's yurt in the background."

Her small figure is quite far away, but it's still possible to see that it's Mystic Millie because of the kaftan and huge crystal earrings and rings. She looks around outside Timmy's yurt and then hurries out of shot.

"What would she have been doing in there?" Annie whispers, and narrows her eyes.

"I'm telling you," I say, making a note to add this to the board. "She's one shifty psychic."

Up on the screen an image of Timmy with his bum out posing in front of the Angel of the North statue fades out and the screen starts to fuzz at the edges, a blackness shifting at the sides into the shape of a heart. It closes in around Timmy's face, a tampon dangling from his mouth, the string between his teeth, and then freezes as the music finishes and his name, date of birth, and date of death appear at the bottom. The festival ground is subdued, and the only sounds are sniffs and sobs as people stand in the bright sunlight waving their phones in the air, flashlights illuminated, making no impact against the actual sun.

The silence and the image stay for far longer than even the other influencers find comfortable. I look over at Joanna, busily typing away on her phone as if it's just another crisis to manage.

Finally Winona reappears on the screen, her foot propped in front of the camera as she picks at the varnish on her toenail, before quickly dropping her leg and staring woefully at the screen.

"Very moving," she says after a long pause. I stifle a snort at the appalling awkwardness.

Joanna looks up and types frantically some more. I'm assuming Winona's getting a lecture. Unfazed, though, Winona continues to address the influencers on the stage.

"If you can bring yourselves to, please share with us what Timmy meant to each of you and share your best memories of him. I'm sure everyone in the audience will have their own favorite memories too. Celeste, let's start with you."

On the screen above them all, hashtags start rolling along the bottom: #RIPTimmy #RIPthePranking.

"Timmy was like a big brother to me," Celeste starts, before pausing and clutching a black napkin to her face.

I'm impressed. Even their tissues are in mourning.

"He was a master of his craft."

I wonder if there's an edge to Celeste's voice, or if I'm imagining the tinge of sarcasm I can hear. Next to me Annie snorts at the word "craft."

"And he dedicated his life to it," Celeste continues, her voice warbling with emotion that must be put on. "He died doing what he loved . . . harassing women in bathrooms." She says this last bit as a whisper through her sobs, but it confirms my sarcasm suspicions.

A thrilled and inappropriate smile spreads across Annie's face at the comment. I look over at Joanna, who's torn her eyes from her screen long enough to shoot Celeste an angry look before resuming typing out what is presumably another shouty all-caps message.

"Timmy made me laugh every day, and he was so talented. I know that his legacy will live on forever in his fans, and the lives of those he touched," Celeste continues, somehow managing to remain straight-faced, which I think should earn her some sort of acting award nomination.

I look out at the crowd and see people clutching tissues to their faces as if moved by her words. There's a smattering of applause, and even from here I can hear comments like *"She's so brave"* and *"A beautiful tribute,"* confirming that Celeste has followed her brief closely enough even with the odd deviation. Joanna's face relaxes slightly but the grasp around her phone never falters.

"In memory of Timmy Eaton, may he rest in peace"—Celeste

does the sign of the cross—"Scaffolding Sports Bras—the only bra you can trust to keep your cleavage safe and sturdy while you exercise—is offering twenty percent off for the next forty-eight hours when you buy online and enter the code #TitsForTimmy at the checkout." She finishes completely deadpan, and while I once again fight the urge to snicker, the crowd responds with more murmurs of praise and sedate clapping. My jaw literally falls open.

At the bottom of the screen, below Winona's neutral face, the hashtag #TitsForTimmy joins the rolling procession of grief-tags. I can actually see people in the audience reaching for their phones, tapping away, and I wonder if they could possibly be ordering the sports bras. Would anyone really do that?

"It's so gross," I say, but when I look over at Annie, she doesn't seem to have heard me. She's staring in Celeste's direction, smiling at her, and running her fingers through her hair.

As Ethan rattles off some kind of speech about what a "truly great man" Timmy was, I stare down at the feed on my phone, watching with interest as the love hearts wane and then pick up pace again the moment Dougie starts to talk. The crowd mutters about how hot his grief is and I'm ashamed to have remembered my own sadboi horniness last night. At least it's not just me who appears to be a grief pervert, though.

I try not to look directly at him to keep myself in check as he talks about what a great guy Timmy was, such sadness in his kind eyes . . . Then I'm jarred as, like Celeste's, his message appears to have taken a turn.

"In memory of Timmy's passing and of what an absolute legend he was, BigBoy condoms is doing an exclusive offer on this never-seen-before product." Out of his back pocket he produces two condoms, holding them up to the audience. I peer closer, trying to see what's so special about them . . . Oh my god. Surely not.

"For a limited time only when you use the #RIPBigBoy code," says Dougie, "you will receive these special-edition condoms with Timmy's face on them. For your pleasure."

Quite outside of our control, Annie and I find ourselves laughing. I can feel Joanna's eyes on us as we try to contain ourselves, but the laughter's already started. The more I try to suppress it the more it comes out. I'm no longer controlling the laughter, the laughter's controlling me.

When I finally regain air in my lungs, I whisper, "Do you think Joanna knows how callous this looks?"

"I think Joanna just sees pound signs flashing and runs toward them at high speed," Annie says.

Sitting onstage in her death-card dress with her death-card earrings, her blond hair hanging loose around her shoulders, Mystic Millie closes her eyes and makes a gesture over her face as if she's centering herself, ready for an emotional upheaval.

"I don't need to say goodbye to Timmy, because I know that he's still here . . ." she says.

The whole crowd stops, and for a second I wonder what she means. I feel a sense of déjà vu wash over me, as if he might appear in a puff of smoke onstage again like yesterday.

The crowd waits, clearly wondering the same. Could she be about to raise him from the dead? Could all this have been another prank? If it is, I think there are several people who would now cheerfully actually kill him.

"Watching over us in the afterlife," Mystic Millie finishes. She sniffs, rubbing her black nails to her temples. "I have no doubt that his spiritual form is with us right now." She looks above her head dreamily, clutching a tissue to her face. The other influencers nod, while Ethan makes a peace sign. "And so, we'll be holding a live séance tonight. My hope is that if enough people tune in, we'll create a force so strong that we can contact Timmy and find out for sure how he died."

There's a gasp from the crowd, and when I look over to Joanna she's staring up from her phone, slack-jawed and as surprised as the rest of us.

"This definitely wasn't part of the plan," Annie whispers.

The other influencers look around, each one as confused as the last, while Joanna's eyes are lasered on to Mystic Millie so fiercely I'm surprised she isn't burning holes in her kaftan.

"I hope none of you will mind that we'll be doing this instead of the séances with audience members that we had planned in the schedule for tonight," Mystic Millie adds.

Joanna looks like she minds, a lot. So does Heather.

"I think we need to take a look into what else Mystic Millie might have been up to that wasn't part of the plan," Annie says out of the corner of her mouth.

"Especially in Timmy's yurt yesterday afternoon," I mumble back.

"We'll be doing the séance from a secret location outside of the festival ground to ensure that it's just Timmy's closest friends there in physical form, but you can join us on the spiritual plane! And on ReelLife Live. We've also put together a kit of everything you need if you want to experience the séance properly. Simply visit MysticMillie.com and place an order to receive your séance box by eight tonight. Make sure that you're part of the special effort to get to the bottom of such a terrible tragedy. And we'll see you at nine!"

Ethan starts clapping wildly next to her but stops when he realizes he's on his own. The rest of the influencers look, if anything, a bit pissed off.

"It's suddenly got very soap opera up in here," Annie observes.

"Uh-huh." I nod.

"We need to find out where that secret location is. We *have* to be at the séance," Annie whispers.

14

Annie and I stand outside of Mystic Millie's yurt in a pair of matching dalmatian onesies that she's stolen from the farm set. Hoods pulled up, long ears flopping around our faces. Despite me complaining to Annie that we shouldn't be screwing around with costumes and disguises, she told me it was essential so that no one recognizes us (she means because of her newfound fame obviously). Wearing a full-body fur costume on one of the hottest days of the year definitely wouldn't be my first choice, to be honest. If we must be in disguise, why can't it be something a bit more breathable?

We leave Herbie in the shade with some water because it's far too hot to be taking him into the oven-like yurts. But also since putting on these costumes, whenever one of us goes near Herbie he does a small growl and looks slightly traumatized, yet another reason why Annie's disguises are simply bad.

"I've only got limited pairs of gloves, and we might want to save them, so the great thing about this costume is that it has built-in mittens!" she declares, pulling the paw attached to the arms of the onesie over her hands and grinning at me as if she's a genius.

"Great, I didn't need my fingers anyway," I snark.

"Always so down about my costumes."

"This one actually makes us *more* conspicuous," I say. "And liable to get heatstroke."

"Get in and stop complaining." Annie holds open the yurt flap and glances over her shoulder.

"I love you, too," I say.

As I shuffle into the yurt, my fluffy dalmatian feet rustle against the grass and pad onto the smoothness of the yurt's ground sheet.

"So by my reckoning we've got at least ten minutes while Joanna tells them all off or whatever it is she's doing," Annie says.

Joanna called an emergency meeting after the panel event for Timmy, which looked like it was going to be incredibly serious. This of course is the perfect opportunity to break into Millie's yurt. Although it's hard to "break in" when there's no real door.

"Okay," Annie says, paws on hips, looking around the yurt. "You take over by the bed, and I'll take her suitcase."

"Got it," I say.

I head over to the bed, trying not to trip over my long spotty tail on the way. I start by looking under the covers, but there's nothing under there aside from a black lacy nightie that is incredibly sexy, and I feel a little bit embarrassed to be touching her things like this, even if I am doing it with my paws.

"You know I was quite surprised by Celeste in that panel," I whisper as we start looking around. "I think we misjudged her. She actually doesn't seem that shallow, she seems quite . . . aware."

"Never said she was shallow." Annie shrugs. "I always thought she was cool."

"You said she was vapid."

"Don't remember that."

"You definitely did." I blink at her.

"No way."

"You know this is the actual definition of gaslighting, right?" I ask. When Annie doesn't budge, I shake my head and move on because we only have a short amount of time to search. I can't waste it arguing with Annie.

I walk over to her bed, where there's a computer and a copy of a spicy-looking book on the bedside cabinet. The two characters on the cover give each other smoldering half-naked looks, and I feel myself blush. There's also another book underneath that called *Cherishing Your Inner Goddess*, which makes me cringe.

"Aha," Annie crows over by her bag.

"What's up?" I ask.

"Well, for someone so spiritual, it seems weird that she'd have two laptops." Annie holds up a computer in each paw.

"Can you get into either of them?" I ask as she goes down on all fours on the floor and opens the two laptops. I watch her tapping away for a while knowing that it's highly unlikely she'll be able to log in.

"No," she eventually sighs. Her long ears swing sadly on either side of her cheeks. "I wonder what she uses them for."

"Well, we know she has to update her website regularly," I say. "She sure got those séance kits up there quickly today, after all."

Annie stands up and heads over to the small coffee table, where a selection of crystals rest.

"This is weird." She holds up one of the crystals. "It's like the others but has a kind of . . . earbud attached to it?"

"Even her AirPods are spiritual," I say, going over to join her at the table.

"Why only one, though?" Annie asks, shifting the stone from hand to hand.

Out of the corner of my eye I see the screen on one of the laptops on the floor change, a message appearing in the right-hand corner of the lock screen.

"Look!" I say, pointing my paw to it.

The two of us rush over, Annie still holding the stone. "Are you starting a séance?" The screen reads. "To begin analyzing customer answers via earpiece, please click Yes."

Annie's eyes are suddenly alive. "Wait I know what it is!" She opens her phone, pawing down Mystic Millie's feed until she reaches some séance videos. "It's the crystal she uses in séances! Look!"

She's right: It's exactly the same crystal she's wearing like a cool ear cuff in the videos. She puts the earpiece in and clicks Yes on the message.

"We're wasting time," I say.

"It's fine. We're investigating." She points to the crystal in her ear.

"It's too hot for this. I think we should take Herbie back to yours so that your parents can look after him out of the sun.

I'm worried about him overheating."

"Oh yeah, I think that's probably a good—" But Annie stops talking and stares at me, pushing the crystal into her ear further. "So it's talking to me. It's telling me what to say about your lost loved one Herbie and analyzing the sound of your voice to let me know what you most want to hear about him. Not only that but now it's suggesting products from the Mystic Millie website that you'd be most likely to buy based on the level of grief it detects in your voice."

"WHAT?!" I ask, feeling disgusted and impressed at the same time.

"It's asking me for your name as a prompt," Annie says. "Kerry Adams."

There's silence as her eyes flit from side to side while she listens for a minute to what the app has to say to her.

"Oh my god, so it googles your name and then feeds all the information it can find about you from online into my ear," Annie says.

"That won't be much."

"It wasn't." Annie giggles. "But I guess the people Mystic Millie talks to are online more than you; they have social media profiles this thing can delve into. There's nothing on yours."

I squint at the screen of the laptop where the noise initially came from and note down the name at the top of the bubble: Sé-predict. I type "Sé-predict" into Google, but nothing comes up.

"Either way," Annie says. "She uses this app in her séances. She's not connecting with the dead; she's connecting with Sé-predict, and it's telling her everything about a person and what to say."

"Of course it doesn't prove she did it," I say, pulling up the picture of Timmy's prank list on my phone. "But it makes these notes under the prank for Millie make more sense, don't you think?"

App
Crystal
Speakers

"He was going to expose the app," Annie says, eyes going wide with sudden understanding. "Feed the audio through speakers before she could use it as her own."

"At ten o' clock tonight," I say, remembering his prank schedule. "When she was due to start doing live séances for specially selected festivalgoers."

"Yep, and she wanted to stop him," I say.

"So maybe she killed him before he had the chance." Annie jabs a finger to the time on the prank, just an hour after Timmy was killed. "Exposing this would have ruined everything her entire career is built on."

Something doesn't sit right with me, though. It all makes perfect sense, of course, and it all works out. I just don't feel quite as sure as Annie.

"Remember when we were investigating last year," I say slowly. "We realized that the first and most obvious suspect isn't always the right one?"

"You think we're being hasty?" Annie asks. "Even with all this evidence?"

"I just think, maybe we need something a bit more . . ." I suggest as Annie looks around before resting her eyes on a huge candle by the bed.

She walks over to it in its glass pot, standing on the floor. It's a big scented one with multiple wicks, of course branded Mystic Millie. She leans down and peers into it before standing up.

"If it wasn't her, then why's she burned the prank list?" Annie asks, holding scraps of burned paper up for me to see.

"What?" When I peer into the candle, I can immediately see she's right. The wick is surrounded by small scraps of charred paper, the leftover pieces of Timmy Eaton's handwritten list. But even with the majority of the paper missing, I can recognize his writing and the paper from the notebook. "Quick! Take pictures of the scraps. We might be able to figure something out from them!" I grab my phone, and Annie does the same.

I know we've been here awhile, we should really be getting out of here. Annie knows it, too; I can sense her tension as she tries to make sure she has every charred bit of paper captured. We're almost done when the noise of Joanna's voice cuts through the yurt. The two of us freeze. Annie's eyes dart around, searching for an escape while I wonder if we could get away with pretending we're real dogs if Joanna comes in here.

"That's probably the best time for him to come—the place will be deserted. Okay?" Joanna's voice gets closer, and our shoulders get higher. I start holding my breath and hear Annie struggling to keep hers in, too. The tiny rushes of air occasionally going in or out of our noses that threaten to rustle the yurt fabric and give us away scare the absolute crap out of me.

She's right outside now. I feel my heart in my throat as the tent flap starts moving and the tips of her fingers appear around the edge of it.

"What do we do?" Annie mouths, looking around the yurt for places to hide.

I shrug and crouch completely still trying to curl myself up into the smallest ball version of myself possible. As if that might somehow make me more invisible. My hands land on something hard and thin, a long wire with a kind of bulky ending, only a few inches long. I'd take a picture but I'm so afraid of Joanna catching us that I don't trust myself not to expose us by moving.

"I think you're being a little unreasonable," Joanna barks suddenly from the other side of the entrance as her hand withdraws. Her voice fades into the distance as she continues, "I'll have to go back to my yurt and check the contract on that. One second."

Annie is frozen on all fours like she's trying to do some sort of bad yoga pose; we must both look ridiculous.

"Quick, before she comes back!" Annie whispers, a wild look in her eye. "Go go go!"

For some reason, her idea of *going* is executing a really dramatic forward roll out of the yurt.

As I leave, walking on my hind legs like normal (which feels an odd thing to need to specify), I see her on the ground, slinking like she's doing an obstacle course, over to our yurt. I'm not sure what she's achieving because I get there much quicker, finally releasing all the breath in my body when I'm inside and flopping down onto my bed.

Two minutes later Annie sneaks in after me while I try to cool Herbie down. He's looking utterly fed up, and I think it really might be time to accept he's better off somewhere with proper shade and cool floors, like Annie's house.

"Well, that was enlightening," Annie says. "I think it's time we take Herbie home and find out where this séance is tonight. Don't you?"

I nod, but I'm still trying to process everything that's just happened. Who was Joanna telling to come here while the glamp site's deserted? What's she planning?

15

"Annie, come play!" Celeste shouts as a volleyball comes flying toward us.

Annie and I peer over our sunglasses as the ball lands at the foot of the loungers. We've been happily observing from a safe distance on these loungers, while the influencers do a meet-and-greet with fans on the beach set. But now Celeste bounces into our observation space to collect the wayward ball, and Annie jumps up, adjusting her pink visor.

"Sure!" she exclaims, having literally only just told me that she thinks it's inhumane that anyone could be voluntarily doing sports in this heat. The sacrifices we make for investigations.

At least Herbie's safely cooling down, out of this heat at Annie's house now. The festival life just wasn't for him. He's more of a home comforts kinda guy.

"Kerry?" Celeste asks.

"Not for me, thanks." I shake my head. Watching from the sidelines is quite a key skill actually. Plus in case I haven't already made it clear, I prefer to be as far away from anything

159

involving flying balls as possible.

"Fair, it's pretty hot out here! Some of us have to recharge in the sun to get ready for tonight." Celeste fans herself and gestures over to where Mystic Millie lies prone on the lounger in a black bikini. A matching Mystic Millie–branded T-shirt lies draped over her head, covering her face.

"Yeah, what's going on there?" Annie asks.

"She's resting. She told Joanna that she'd make an appearance here but she won't be talking to any fans because she needs to keep her pathways clear to reach the dead tonight," Celeste tells us with a respectable amount of sarcasm. "Hence the veil. She's protecting her vibes or something."

I've noticed that next to her, Ethan seems to be lying back, conserving his energy as well, although occasionally when he thinks no one's watching he'll dab his cheeks with water from the nearby wading pool so that he looks like he's crying under his sunglasses.

"About tonight, actually," Annie says quickly, and Celeste hangs back by us. "We thought we might come to the séance. Do you think that would be cool?"

"Oh yeah! Hundred percent." Celeste bats the volleyball over to the waiting fans.

"Sweet," Annie says. "Just wondering if you could . . . you know . . . tell us where it is? Because Mystic Millie said it was secret and everything."

"Of course. It's at the church tower in the village. You know it, right?"

We both nod, and Celeste carries on in a whisper, "Joanna's furious. It wasn't part of the plan and goes against all her instructions. But we have to do it now that Millie's announced it."

"Oh?" Annie says. She turns to me, eyes sparkling, clearly thrilled at getting so much information. Sadly it's at that moment that a ball comes flying over and smacks her in the cheek.

"I saw that coming," Mystic Millie alerts from under her veil.

Annie recovers swiftly, and after attempting and failing to spike the ball back, she throws it as far as she can—to Celeste next to her—and the two of them go off, to play a sport that Annie has just proved not to be her strong point.

Left alone, I try really hard to look like I'm concentrating on something on my phone, while I observe the scene around me. But the only things I seem to be observing really are Dougie's shirtless nipples that keep bobbing over the top of my phone screen and into view. They're just everywhere. All the time. His height means that I have to keep raising my phone up higher and higher to hide them from my view while he takes shirtless thirst traps with fans, which Heather and the Mini-Heathers seem to feel the need to police. Heather's already pushed some poor girl into the oversize blow-up pool, claiming she was too close to Dougie and it was a safety risk. I doubt that'll be the last casualty to Heather's jealousy.

I stare hard at my screen, Dougie's skin glistening in the sunshine around the edges of my vision. I think he's oiled himself up specifically so he glistens like that—it's like being dazzled by the actual sun. This is hopeless. I turn over and visit the band's profile on Instagram. My *boyfriend's* band, I remind myself. I scroll down, finally finding a distraction from Dougie's show of semi-nudity, because the band has posted new pictures of Scott, my hot, hot boyfriend. They've done an update from tour with some candid backstage and tour-bus shots. But I'm finding it hard to enjoy them because I keep thinking about the time stamps on the posts, and the fact that Scott hasn't replied to any of my texts since 6:00 a.m. I guess he's been too busy—these pictures certainly make it look that way anyway. But I just would have thought that he'd respond to *something*, especially because I messaged a few hours ago saying Annie and I were sure it was murder. Maybe he's just waiting to be alone so he can focus and message me properly? I try hard to convince myself. But then I reach a topless shot of him, fresh from stage and covered in sweat. The photo itself surprises me enough—he's not really a posing-topless kind of guy—but when I scroll to the next image he's still topless, just with the addition of Jen, draped over him in a smiling, post-gig hug.

I shake my head, trying to ignore a sinking feeling. This is what the patriarchy wants from me. It *wants* me to spend my time being jealous of other successful women instead of focusing on my own stuff. It's ridiculous. It's just a hug, and it's Jen. Nothing's happening. They must have just got offstage so he's probably hot and that's why he's got his shirt off. That's all. They're not making out or anything.

Of course as soon as I think of it, an image of Scott kissing Jen fills my brain, and I feel the punch of all my emotions gathering into a lump of anxiety, grief, and fear, like a horrible bowling ball in my chest. I should just call him—find out why he hasn't got back to me. Instead, I watch the messages, willing the word "typing" to appear at the top of the screen. Or for a message to appear that I've somehow managed to miss. But none of those things happen, no matter how hard I stare.

"OH SHIT!" I'm stirred by Dougie shouting, and when I look up from my phone I can't see anything except the volleyball flying toward me.

I move quickly sideways, jumping off my chair to try to avoid getting whacked in the face, but I stumble, landing on the edge of the lounger with force. It tips up, and I'm catapulted off like I've been riding a seesaw. Before I know what's happening, I've smacked against Dougie, taking us both down.

I feel my sunglasses cracking and the immediate sting of his shoulder hitting my cheek as the two of us land in a tangled heap in the sand. I lie there for a second, feeling winded and sore, too embarrassed to move, just taking time to appreciate resting on something solid and stable. I put a hand down trying to ground myself, the floor feeling smooth and warm and . . .

"You okay there?" Dougie asks, smiling at me, his head just above mine as I realize the surface I've been resting on is his abs.

I whip my hand away and force myself up into the seated position, untangling myself from him. To hide my burning cheeks, I lean down and pick up my sunglasses, the right arm on them slightly wonky and cracked but otherwise still okay I guess.

"Fuck, Kerry, your face!" Dougie's stooped over me, an expression of concern.

I reach up and touch my face, feeling the throb in my cheekbone from where it collided with his shoulder. My hand comes away clean, so at least I'm not bleeding on the Adorable Adonis.

"I'm so sorry! Are you okay?" Dougie's arm hovers around my shoulders, not making contact. "I've hurt you!"

"Oh, no, it's fine, honestly," I say, checking out my cheek in my phone camera. It's pink and swelling a little already. "It's just a bruise! I'm so clumsy!"

"No, I am!" he says, looking genuinely upset.

I wave him off and slump down on the lounger again, making sure all four legs of it stay on the floor this time just as Heather and the Mini-Heathers charge over to intervene. Of course it didn't take them long.

"Oh my god, Dougie are you okay?!" Heather screams. "Kerry's so clumsy!"

But Dougie ignores her. "Please, at least let me get you some ice," he says to me.

I nod silently, just wanting everyone to stop looking at me. "Sure."

"KERRYY!!!" Annie comes plowing through the sand like she's launching a *Baywatch* rescue and lands between the two of us. "ARE YOU OKAY?"

I look around, realizing that not only was my embarrassment seen by everyone here: people are now capturing it for ReelLife with their phones.

"I'm fine." I want to cover my face with a T-shirt like Mystic Millie right now.

No one takes this as the sign to stop filming me that I hoped they would, so I put my sunglasses back on and try to look as uninteresting to them as possible. But with Annie fussing around me that's hard. Dougie comes back over with some ice wrapped in a towel and one of the Mini-Heathers grabs it from him.

"We can take care of her now, thank you so much, Dougie," Mini-Heather Two says.

"Okay," Dougie says. But for some reason he looks back at me, unsure.

I give him a nod, and he goes back to the volleyball game while Annie holds the ice on my cheek. It's not like Dougie Trainor was about to play nurse with me. Right?

"You'd better not be about to sue me for that," Heather says out the corner of her mouth. "It's bad enough that I'll have to fill in an incident form for this."

"God, poor you." Annie rolls her eyes next to me.

With Dougie no longer in the picture, the people filming seem to have given up, thank god.

"I mean, actually yes, poor me," Heather whispers. "Someone literally died at my festival yesterday, and now you're getting floored by balls."

Annie and I snigger at this, and she shoots us both angry looks.

"It's no laughing matter, actually." Heather crosses her arms and stares down at the two of us.

Annie and I stop giggling, and I look up at her, my broken, wonky glasses keeping the ice on my face.

"Can't the two of you try to keep a lower profile? I'm still pissed at you from yesterday, Annie, when you were trying to convince DI Wallace it was *murder*."

"Errr, because it so definitely is," Annie replies.

Heather looks like she may commit her own murder as she leans in close to Annie's face. "We're barely breaking even as it is. If we have to finish earlier, people are going to want refunds. Please, promise me you're not going to 'investigate' this time. Please? Or if you must, at least just do it after the festival's over."

"Oh yeah," I say, crossing my fingers behind my back. "I hate all that murder-solving stuff anyway, you know I do."

"Same," Annie says.

"Okay," Heather says, still looking uneasy but tapping away at her phone just as mine and Annie's also chirp with notifications.

Les Populaires

Heather: Oh my god you guys, Dougie so definitely wants me. He just hit his volleyball over this way and nearly killed Kerry because he just wanted an excuse to come over here and talk to me.

Colin: Oh my god babe! THIS IS SO EXCITING! Are the two of you like bonding romantically in the throes of trauma?

Audrey: Have you kissed him yet?

Heather: Not yet, but nearly. SOON!

Annie and I sit looking from Heather to Dougie, who's miles away flirting with other girls.

"It's manifesting," Heather snaps to our confused faces. "I'm manifesting what I want by telling them it's happening in the group."

"It's lying," Annie says, her sunglasses slipping down her nose as she moves her head with aggressive judgment.

"Look, whatever, it's going to happen, okay?! He just needs to take his grief blinkers off and actually *see* me. Anyway, I have to get back. I'm a very busy woman." Heather stands up and adjusts the big straw hat. "Don't be dicks."

She turns on her heel and walks away, oversize straw hat wobbling on top of her head from all the stress contained within it. We watch her strut back toward Dougie with what I think is supposed to look like a sexy swagger but actually looks like she needs a poo.

"Where's the self-respect?" Annie shakes her head and opens her phone. "Right, let's see who ReelLife thinks is the chief suspect this afternoon."

I lean over, curious to see who they've moved on to now that Annie's out of the picture, but the first video is from Ethan and it's titled "Feminism 101." It was uploaded just minutes ago and begins with him talking about how feminism was invented by a woman called Emmeline Suffragette who was the only person who could achieve the vote because she had a powerful husband who helped her. Apparently we aren't the only people watching it; within seconds, Joanna's on the Instagram set.

"ETHAN!!" she shouts to him as he hides from her wrath under a beach towel.

Across the set there's a splashing noise as Heather pushes another poor victim into the pool for getting a little too close to Dougie.

"She's savage," I say. "If I didn't know her, I would have Heather down as the killer."

"Except she wouldn't sabotage her own festival like that," Annie says, readjusting the ice pack under my glasses before turning back to her phone.

"True," I say.

Annie suddenly sits bolt upright on the sun lounger. "OMG,

LOOK! A new video from Winona!"

She shoves her phone in between us and presses Play on the video. Winona sits in her usual pink crushed-velvet chair, around her stylishly decorated house with all its gold and pink and marble things. She looks glamorous in a casual cotton sundress, her blond hair pulled up into a bun and her tortoiseshell glasses perched on her nose.

"Good vulva, my loves! I hope you're all doing okay at this terribly sad time. I'm still at home with a bad foot and gutted to be missing you all in person at the Festival of Fame. I just wanted to let you all know that I'll be on the BBC News this evening at six, before the séance, discussing the sad events of yesterday and why it's so important for there to be better safety measures in place for influencers. That's six tonight, BBC News. GOOD VULVA!"

The video finishes on her face as she smiles into the camera, and next to me Annie's already fawning over it.

"She's just so gracious. Timmy was such a piece of shit, with opposing views to hers about pretty much everything, and yet she's still got time to go on the news and talk about the wider issue of safety, turning it into something that helps others," Annie says. "That's really classy."

"Really classy," I agree.

"She is *so* cool," Annie says. "You know Celeste was telling me earlier that she's been to her house and it's *so* nice."

"When were you talking to Celeste?" I ask, feeling a little weird that she's been hanging with one of the influencers without me.

"Oh, just around the firepit earlier when you were in the toilet." Annie shrugs it off. "We talked about feminism and

Winona's and Celeste's businesses."

I don't know why, but something about her chatting to one of the suspects without me unsettles me.

"Hey, Annie!" Celeste shouts over. "Could you come and take a video of Dougie and me playing volleyball? He keeps knocking the tripod over!" Annie gets up straightaway, ignoring the fact that she's mid-conversation with me.

Maybe it bothers me because she's not just talking to a suspect, she seems to be getting on well with her. And I know that the evidence is really stacking up against Mystic Millie, but that doesn't mean we should discount the others, does it? But maybe it's that I should be getting closer to them, like Annie is. Maybe I need to be a little braver.

"Hey, Dougie," I shout, feeling slightly out of body, as if my mouth's doing something quite against my will. "Actually I *am* in the mood for a bit of volleyball."

I've no idea what I'm doing as I plod over to him and Celeste, and Annie looks at me in shock. I've literally never played a game of volleyball in my life, but I've already hurt my face, how much worse can it get? As I sink my bare feet into the sand of the volleyball court, I jump at something sharp under my big toe. Looking down I see a small wire poking out of the sand, just like the ones I saw in Millie's yurt. Except this one's slightly charred and burned at the ends, and it lies next to an outer paper casing. I discreetly snap a picture of it on my phone. What is it? And why is it the second one I've seen today?

16

"So you're saying that these little wire things that we found in the beach set and in Millie's yurt are to set off programmed fireworks?" Annie asks in a whisper, stroking her chin as she paces the yurt.

"Yeah, they're e-matches," I say, turning the computer screen around to face Annie as she joins me on my bed. "You can design and program a fireworks display and these little guys are the thing that it all connects to. Like the kind that went off shortly after Timmy's death."

"And the one that went off after he faked his own death onstage," Annie says.

"Maybe, yeah," I say.

I'd assumed the Tim-sciples had set off the cock-and-balls fireworks, but maybe it was Millie? I wish I'd done a reverse image search of the wires sooner.

"What if she killed him, then she set up the fireworks to distract everyone from his death?" Annie says, scrolling Reel-Life as she talks.

"I just think that's a bit . . . I dunno. I don't think the

fireworks really distracted anyone from the actual death?"

"Maybe it was so she could hide a weapon or something while everyone watched?" Annie suggests.

"She was kinda next to us all the time," I say. "I guess she could have, though . . ."

"You are *so* negative today. Literally not accepting any of my theories," Annie tuts.

I hold back an eye roll because the reason I'm not accepting her theories is that I don't think she's thought them through enough. I feel like she's more focused on the glory at the end of solving the murder than the actual solving bit.

"I just don't know why she'd set the fireworks. And why she'd do the one onstage and help him specifically, if she had it in for him? It just doesn't add up. Not to mention the biggest question: How did she physically get in and out of there while it was filming without being noticed by Celeste or the livestream?"

"Look, he was going to expose her as a fraud and so she un-alived him. Dude, we've solved the crime; we just need to get proof and tell the police. Stop second-guessing yourself!" Annie sounds annoyed, as if I'm disrupting her precious Reel-Life time. But then she stops scrolling. "You want a motive for her?" Annie looks up from her phone. "Check it out."

Annie presses Play on a new ReelLife video from Mystic Millie posted in the past few minutes.

Mystic Millie stares into the camera. She's in her yurt with her legs crossed and an incense stick burning in front of her. "I've long believed in the power of spiritual connections, and there's no greater spiritual connection than the one that you share with your partner. So I'm thrilled to announce that following the sad death of Timmy Eaton, I'm the newest brand ambassador for BigBoy condoms."

I feel my jaw fall open. It feels like a giant leap to go from having Timmy Eaton as the BigBoy ambassador to Mystic Millie. There couldn't be anyone more the opposite of Timmy than Millie is. It's absolutely wild.

"There—she's got Timmy's most lucrative ambassadorship," Annie says. "She's directly benefitted from his death. So that's everything, means and motive. Done."

The video continues to play as I stare. Maybe Annie's right, maybe we have cracked it and I'm being overly critical.

"BigBoy has never had a woman as their brand ambassador before," Annie says. "I know she's like almost one hundred percent a killer and everything, but this is still pretty cool."

"Be cooler if she hadn't killed to get it," I whisper back to her. Suddenly I'm scared that Mystic Millie might hear us and then we'll be next on her list. "I just assumed Dougie or Ethan would get the role now Timmy's gone."

"Sexist," Annie chimes, bopping me on the nose like a naughty cat.

"*Boy* is in the name," I say, blinking at her. "And Dougie did do that whole BigBoy ad in the panel this morning."

"But maybe they're finally ready to exit the archaic old markcting ways and accept that people of all genders buy condoms," Annie says sagely.

"She's made so much money from his death. The kits? The ambassadorship? She'll be rolling in it," I say.

"She'll need that money for a good lawyer when we've proved what she's done," Annie says with a smirk.

"Ten pounds says that tonight she'll hear from 'Timmy' that

his death was an accident," I whisper back.

"I'm not willing to bet against you there," Annie says. "Plus, I don't have ten pounds. Speaking of, please will you buy me dinner later before the séance? I can't talk to the dead on an empty stomach."

17

"Ready to climb twenty flights of stairs?" Annie's voice booms cheerfully around the quiet graveyard.

I think she's pointing to the church tower, but since we're all following instructions from Millie that we were to wear black because apparently it makes you "less threatening to the dead," I'm actually struggling to see her. I look up at the tower and gulp. Its silhouette looks strikingly sinister in the twilight, and it's only made more menacing by the bats swooping and circling it.

"I'm convinced they'll be performing a séance for *me* before I can make it to the top," I reply, not entirely joking.

"Don't worry, I'll add some more about you to my ReelLife profile so she's got more to go on when Sé-predict does the Google search. I'm sure I can make it pretty interesting," Annie says mischievously.

I'd text Scott to let him know I'm about to die and it's been great knowing him, but he still hasn't replied to any of my texts. The longer I go without hearing from him, the harder it is to bat away the image of him topless, posing with his arm around Jen.

"Pretty cool and spooky being here at night, though, right?!" Annie says.

She forges ahead, oozing confidence and excitement as she weaves between the long shadows cast by gravestones. By contrast I tiptoe behind her, trying to avoid the huge old tree roots that I know are littered around here, ready and waiting to trip us up and break our necks. At the noise of footsteps, a whoosh of adrenaline fills my ears. The sounds of rustling leaves and snapping twigs echo as I swivel my head at top speed, ready to protect myself from whatever danger lurks behind us.

"I think Millie's already up there!" Celeste's voice comes out of the darkness.

My eyes finally focus, and I make out her, Dougie, and Ethan walking through the churchyard toward us. I wave alongside Annie, trying to pretend like I didn't just nearly pass out with fear.

"Hey! How are you guys doing?" Annie asks cheerfully.

I don't know why she's asking when, while I don't mean to be cynical, it's so clear to me that they're absolutely fine until a camera's on them, and then they're going to completely ham it up as much as they can.

"Yeah, bearing up," Celeste says earnestly.

"It's a loss," Dougie says, nodding and peaking his brows up in the way that guys do when they want to look serious but also cute. "I feel sad every day."

I don't point out to him that it's not even been twenty-four hours yet.

"A tricky time," Ethan says. "I've obviously been focusing on helping the women, especially my darling Millie, at this difficult time. Women are just far more emotional."

I don't know how more people don't hit him. I certainly don't know how anyone can believe that they're a couple, apart from that in pictures you can't quite tell what a massive dickhead he is.

"We would have been here sooner, but someone held us up," Celeste says, nodding to Ethan.

"I was creating a petition for better maternity pay for influencers actually." Ethan's superior tone makes me itch. "In this post-feministic world, we need to start supporting women. Only when we lift women up will they thrive rather than barely survive. I'm just making sure that the misogonycosm doesn't win. One day when you have a child, you'll thank me."

"Women don't *have* to have children. Have that for your next Feminism 101. You're doing a great job, pal," Celeste says, sarcastically patting his back. "Also here's a relationship tip I'll give you for free: When your girlfriend's hosting a séance, you show up on time."

"No time to bicker now, kids, we gotta go talk to Timmy," Dougie says, speaking to them like naughty children. "Don't disrespect my dude."

He forges ahead, leading our pack, and we all follow. Annie falls into step next to Celeste while I end up stuck at the back with Ethan. It's for the best unless I want to embarrass myself trying to keep up with Dougie on the stairs. Though it would be nice if, for once, Ethan decided to be quiet. Unfortunately I can hear him next to me, explaining Gloria Steinem as if I've never heard of her before. Except the more he talks, I'm realizing he's confused her with Barbra Streisand. Inside the church tower, I start to wonder exactly how much Mystic Millie really thought this through. It was built in the 1700s and because of this doesn't have any electricity. The stairwell is lit only with the occasional candle, and even these are being blown out gradually by the wind. Up front, Dougie turns his phone light on, illuminating the old bricks and the cold, uneven flagstone steps that wind up to the top of the tower. The smell of mildew intensifies the higher we climb, and while the occasional small window provides relief from it, the view of the village as we get higher gives me vertigo. I decide it's best if I try not to look. At least Ethan's so out of breath he's stopped mansplaining Barbra Streisand to me.

After what must be ten thousand million years we finally reach the top and I'm comforted that even Dougie seems a little out of breath. Ethan's practically bent double. There's no sign of Mystic Millie up here, but Celeste immediately starts a livestream, chatting away to her followers, showing them around the tower. Dougie briefly pokes his face into her shot before starting to film his own stream next to her, the two of them in friendly competition for the most viewers and likes, while I just try to regain my lung capacity.

I embrace the breeze on my face—a relief after the heat of the day, and the workout of the steps—and try not to look down at the tiny village below. I notice the long "protective crystals" (aka crystal dildos) have been strung up around the edges of the tower. It seems almost embarrassing now that we couldn't see what they were to begin with.

Annie catches my eye and nods toward a large circular table in the middle of the roof that's been draped in black velvet. In the center stands a gothic candelabra, but it's what surrounds it that's most concerning. There must be about a dozen life-size cardboard cutouts of Timmy Eaton.

"Good evening!" Mystic Millie's voice floats, ethereal, through the air, and everyone turns trying to work out where it's coming from.

Eventually she emerges from behind one of the Timmy Eaton cutouts wearing a black crushed-velvet flapper dress, a black choker with black stone in the center, and heavy black crystal rings and earrings. She's even donned some black lipstick for the occasion.

"Welcome." She slinks toward us, hands clasped. I notice she doesn't have one of her crystal earpieces in today, but then she wouldn't need one, would she? She knows exactly how this séance is going to go down because I imagine she's already planned every single word of it. Benefit of being the murderer and all.

"My darling," Ethan wheezes to her. She easily bats him away and flops a bit into one of the cardboard Timmys.

"I must conserve my energy for the spirits," she whispers.

There's a faint tinkling sound on the breeze as the crystal dildos knock together like wind chimes, creating a creepy tune. A small pinprick of light appears next to me, and I realize that Joanna's there with her phone, recording Mystic Millie's entrance from behind one of the other Timmy Eaton cutouts.

"Please, take a seat." Mystic Millie makes a sweeping gesture toward the table, her sleeves doing a lot of heavy lifting. "It is time to begin."

We move toward the table with caution, a chill stealing across the roof, making me wish that I'd worn my hoodie.

Ethan takes a seat next to Millie, the glimmer of a smirk visible on his face, which only makes me feel colder. Dougie sits next to him, propping his phone on the table, and I follow him, positioning myself between him and Annie, opposite Mystic Millie. Celeste takes the last seat next to Annie and we're all there, in position, ready to talk to the dead.

I glance across the table to our suspect and can't help wondering if being up a hundred-foot tower in the middle of the night with her—especially when we've found out the secrets she probably killed over—is the best idea. But when I look at Annie to see if she feels the same, she's far too enthralled by the whole thing to share my sentiments.

"Once you're seated, if you could put on the black cape from the back of the chair that would be really good for the atmos, please, loves." Mystic Millie says this bit quietly so people watching on Celeste's and Dougie's feeds don't know that we're just wearing the capes for the *atmos*. But I can't say I'm not glad of the extra warmth.

The Mystic Millie crystal ball and a similarly branded Ouija board spread out on the table in front of us would strike me as cliched and basic if I didn't already know Millie was a fraud. Aside from those and the candles, each place at the table is set with a mask of Timmy Eaton's face, and I have a terrible sinking feeling about what we're going to be asked to do with them.

"We're live with Winona," Joanna says, propping an iPad with Winona on the screen on the empty chair around the table.

I notice Annie giggling at something with Celeste rather than focusing solely on Winona Philips, which feels like an odd development.

"Good evening, loves! Our influencers are joining you live tonight from a secret location in Barbourough village where they're about to perform a séance to contact our dearly departed Timmy Eaton!" Winona announces from the screen. "I'm passing you over to Mystic Millie, who will lead this evening's proceedings."

Winona has always struck me as being incredibly sensible, so I wonder what she makes of the whole contacting-the-dead thing, let alone all the money that Millie's probably made from this today.

"I'd like to ask everyone around the table, and those watching, if you have one, to please put on your Timmy Eaton mask. This is so that the spirits know who we're trying to reach and so that Timmy knows where home is." Mystic Millie slides on her own mask.

I look down at the flimsy paper, reluctant to put it over my own face. It's giving me the ick—for *all* the reasons. Next to me, Dougie puts his on without even looking at it, as if this is all completely normal. I try to catch Annie's eye on my other side, but she's busy helping Celeste brush her long auburn hair out from behind Timmy's empty cardboard face. Grudgingly I place the dead guy's face over my own just like everyone else.

Millie nods from behind her Timmy face, catching the candlelight in a way that almost makes him look alive. "I'd like to ask everyone here to please join hands with the person next to you."

Dougie slides his large hand around my left one, eclipsing my fingers with his palm. His strong grip is reassuring, but I feel awkward. Like it shouldn't feel this comfortable. Part of my brain's telling me to pull away, that my hand shouldn't be in his hand. Oh god, I've just realized I'm wiggling my fingers. Will he think I'm trying to stroke his hand? I freeze, holding my fingers rigid in his palm. At least that's better than him thinking I'm some kind of weird petter. Isn't it?

I look up and see his eyes glistening down at me from behind the Timmy mask. It feels confusing that I find myself smiling up at him, when he's wearing the face of an utter dickhead. I look away, convinced that he might be able to tell what I'm thinking through my eyes.

"People watching online," says Millie, "if you've paid for the premium séance kit, I'd ask you to hold the black stone from Mystic Millie Minerals in your palm and warm it in your hand for a few seconds before pressing it to the back of your phone, iPad, or laptop screen. This helps connect you to the earth and makes the spiritual connection deeper. If you haven't paid for the premium package, please just hold your device with both hands. Whether you're here or watching at home: DON'T BREAK THE CIRCLE."

Out of shot, Joanna is holding up cards with lines written on, and Mystic Millie is reading from them—a portable ring light illuminating her face from behind her phone like she's telling ghost stories around a campfire.

"Your spiritual connection will be weaker if you're not a premium subscriber, but hopefully you can still feel it. Those that have paid will just be feeling something much more profound. If you'd like to subscribe to Mystic Millie's Minerals after the sho—séance you can use code #TalkToTimmy to save twenty percent on your first month. Offer does not include the daily horoscopes, or any crystals over the RRP of fifty pounds." Mystic Millie seems to say all of this in one breath, like she's reading the small print of a dodgy legal document. Next to her, Joanna simply throws the cue cards under the table now that they're finished with them. "Now please close your eyes and HMMMMMMMMMMMMMMM."

I jump a bit at the sudden noise as Mystic Millie hums into her crystal ball, doing the one thing she told everyone not to do, and breaking the circle to wave her hands around it. I guess the rules don't apply when you're the one with the "gift." I wonder at what point she's going to get us all to put our hands on the Ouija board pointer and have Timmy spell out "TE phone home" or something.

"I can sense that not everyone has closed their eyes," says Millie. She can sense it because her eyes are open and glaring at me. Against all my instincts, I do as she says, suddenly glad of Dougie's presence next to me, his hand enveloping mine. "Even if you're watching online, please watch through closed eyes or you'll weaken the force. We cannot see the dead with our eyes. Only our minds."

How convenient, I think.

Millie hums for a couple of minutes without saying anything and if I'm not mistaken what she's humming actually sounds a *lot* like "Unholy" by Sam Smith featuring Kim Petras. Next to me Annie squeezes my right hand in a way that I know means she's trying not to laugh.

"THE SPIRITS ARE AWAKENING!" Millie suddenly shouts, making us both jump and making Annie let out a smothered giggle that sounds like she choked a little bit. "It feels very warm! I can feel them joining us! Can you feel the warmth?"

I'm not entirely sure who she's asking, but I do feel much

warmer since putting on this massive thick cape to be fair. The worry that my palm might start to become sweaty in Dougie's creeps into my brain, and I bat it away. It doesn't matter. Dougie's a suspect. He's not Scott. Scott . . . Maybe I should get Millie to tell me what Scott's doing right now.

"My beloveds! The spirits are ready. The signs are aligned," Millie whispers. I can feel us all lean in to hear her when she screams out, "WE CALL ON YOU SPIRITS TO HELP US FIND OUR FRIEND TIMMY EATON! HERE TIMMY! HERE!!!"

I hear Annie lightly snort and just about manage to hold it in myself. It's as if she's trying to find a lost dog, not trying to contact the dead. But even so there's something unsettled in the air. The wind tickles the back of my neck, and I start imagining all the things that could be brushing past me: ghosts, birds, people lurking in shadows, murderers, bears . . . We're sitting ducks in a dark space that's already full of death . . .

"There's someone here . . . I'm getting something . . ." Mystic Millie's gasping and howling. She sounds like she's mid sexual encounter and I'm pleased not to be one of the people next to her. "We're streaming live to over one million people now . . . The more people that join, the stronger it gets."

How does she know how many people we're streaming to if she's got her eyes closed? She *must* have opened her eyes to check the figure unless she can see the figure on the livestream in her *mind*. Next to me, I can feel Annie's shoulders shaking with suppressed laughter.

"Tell your friends to join us, let's try to make it to two million . . . The numbers are rising, and it's working!" Mystic Millie's voice is becoming more frantic, louder. "We're at two million! Let's make it to three! THREE MILLION AND WE'LL

GET TO TIMMY!!! I CAN SEE SOMEONE COMING!"

I feel the pressure of Dougie's grip changing, holding me tighter. I'm hyperaware of every bit of his skin that's touching mine and the guilt, the feeling that it shouldn't be, despite the images of Scott's bare chest touching Jen, that flash through my mind constantly.

"Did you hear that, Timmy? There are nearly three million people here who want to find out what happened to you! COME TO ME, TIMMY, COME TO ME!!!"

The noise of a chair scraping back pierces the tension, and I simply can't keep my eyes shut any longer. I lift one eyelid enough to see that Mystic Millie is up and on her feet, swaying and making a noise like a haunted cat. She's broken the circle. Does that mean we can let go of each other's hands? . . . Do I want to?

"I can feel you, Timmy," she calls. "I know you're here. We're going to get justice for what happened to you, Timmy! You just have to tell us what happened!!!"

A gust of wind makes the flames of the candles flicker and extinguish. In the sudden darkness, the only light comes from the ring light Joanna's using to record Mille while she dances as if taken over by some mysterious spirit.

"Oh yes! DANCE WITH ME, TIMMY! DANCE WITH ME—OH, TIMMY, YOU *NAUGHTY* BOY!" She's screaming into the air as her movements become more erratic and she swings around. "But the people online can't hear you, Timmy, you need to speak up. You need to SHOUT so that everyone can hear you. We just want to find out what happened to you, Timmy. So, if you can, if you have the energy in your poor tired soul, knock once if you died at your own accidental hand

and knock twice if you died at the hands of another . . . KNOCK LOUDLY, TIMMY. THE WORLD IS WAITING!!!"

Annie and I stare at each other in recognition and amusement. The roof area is silent again apart from the wind and Millie's soft growling.

KNOCK.

Everyone's eyes fly open, and all the masks turn toward Millie. I'm sure that she must have just banged the table, but she's still standing up, dancing.

KNOCK. The second knock sounds louder.

"That confirms it. Timmy was murdered," Millie announces somberly.

I feel Dougie drop my left hand in shock, and Annie drops my right. On the other side of Annie, Celeste clings to her other hand as if for dear life.

There's a collective gasp around the roof, but no one's gasping louder than Annie and me. We weren't expecting this. Around the table I can only see people's eyes through the masks, but it seems to me that Dougie and Celeste definitely weren't expecting that. On the periphery of the circle, illuminated by her phone screen, Joanna's eyes give off a glint of anger. The only person with their eyes still closed is Ethan. He's either blissfully accepting that this is all very normal, or trying hard to prove that none of this bothers him, when surely it should?

"Good boy, Timmy," Millie says. "I know you must be tired, but we're nearly there and then we can help you find the light. Is this person, the one responsible for your death, are they here tonight? Knock once for yes and twice for . . . Ow!" Millie yelps. Her eyes fly open and I see Joanna in the dark periphery, just out of shot, retracting her leg from Millie's direction.

Millie rubs her shin under the table, scowling at Joanna while everyone else looks around in shock. Dougie and Celeste exchange panicked expressions. But behind her mask Joanna's eyes are steely and she performs a slicing action at her throat.

"Ah." Millie stops dancing, deflated. She stares down into the phone on the table. "He's left. Timmy has gone. I don't know what happened—the connection was so strong. I can only assume that those of you at home maybe didn't keep your eyes closed. I'd just like to thank you all for joining in with the séance and for your time and effort tonight. I'd especially like to thank those with premium subscriptions and remind those of you without a premium subscription to Mystic Millie Minerals that if you sign up now with the code #SoSadTimmy you can get twenty percent off. Good night."

Joanna stops the recording and looks at everyone with a solemn face. Her gaze eventually fixes on Annie and me.

"I think it's time you two head back to the camp. I'd like to talk to my clients alone, please," she says, her voice tight.

Annie and I stand and leave the table ready to walk down the millions of flights of stairs once more. Two things are for sure: no matter what we expected to happen tonight, it wasn't that. And we're not going anywhere just yet.

18

For the second time in my short life, I'm crouching behind gravestones, hiding from a murderer. Or at least trying to catch one, as we watch the influencers leave the tower one by one. All of them looked solemn as they walked through the graveyard, clearly having just had their heads chewed off by Joanna. All except Ethan that is, who was still wearing his cape and his Timmy Eaton mask propped on his head like he'd just been at a fun costume party. Now we just have to wait for Joanna and Millie herself.

"So maybe Millie didn't do it?" I whisper to Annie. "And she was about to reveal who did?"

"It could be a double bluff," Annie says. "A distraction? To stop people suspecting her when they do finally figure out it was murder. I just don't see who else it could have been. Everything adds up."

"Do you think any of the others knew she was going to do that?"

Annie thinks for a bit. "Nah, there's no way. They all looked as shocked as she did."

"Except for Ethan," I say. "He didn't even flinch."

"He could have known— Shit! Joanna!" Annie hisses suddenly, and curls up into a tight ball behind her stone.

I peer above the top of mine, then follow suit as Joanna comes stomping out of the tower and marches right past us in the darkness. Fortunately, she looks too angry to notice much around her, otherwise I think we'd be needing our own gravestones.

"That's everyone down except Millie," I whisper to Annie once I'm sure Joanna's far enough away.

"Maybe Joanna's told her she needs to clean up her own séance as punishment?" Annie quips, pulling out her phone. "Let's see what everyone's up to shall we?"

"If we must," I sigh. I'm starting to feel like ReelLife has become a third wheel in our friendship.

Annie's only been poking at her screen for a few seconds before she gasps and turns her phone to face me, a thrilled, scandalized expression on her face.

"She's started another livestream!" she hisses, pointing to her screen where Millie appears to be sat back at the table in front of the crystal ball. "Doing *another* séance. Ohhhh, Joanna's going to be so pissed!"

We watch the captions appearing as she speaks into the camera, so that we don't have to have the sound on.

"I think it's better for me to conduct the séance solo, to allow me to connect with Timmy on a deeper level, just the two of us. It became clear to me that he was nervous and found the amount of people here overwhelming."

She's gathered all the Timmy Eaton cutouts behind her in a

kind of gaggle of Timmys, like an audience of douchebags, that she sits in front of.

"Surely Joanna's going to be back here any minute when she sees this!" I say, looking around us nervously.

We stay crouched behind the gravestones—anticipating Joanna's furious return—watching the video in complete silence as the captions appear. After about three minutes of woo-woo chat from Millie, I get a bit bored and use the opportunity to take a quick peek at my own phone. I was hoping to have heard from Scott, but there's still no messages from him. I feel a twitch in my thumb wanting to look on the band's profile to see what he's up to, but I should probably focus on what we're doing now. After all, Millie's just closed her eyes, started swaying, and is claiming to feel a presence. I should probably pay attention to see what that is. I just can't believe he hasn't checked in.

On-screen Millie stands up, doing a pulling-down movement from the sky with her hands as if dragging Timmy's great spirit from the clouds. I wonder if she's going to pull something out from one of her capacious sleeves that she claims to be a gift from Timmy or something. But instead, the screen goes blank and fills with the message "Live Feed ended: try one of these other videos to keep the Reel Fun Times going!" Live feeds from Dougie and Celeste come up as suggested alternatives.

"What happened?" I ask.

"It got cut off," Annie says.

A loud, urgent scream rings out from the top of the tower and I leap into Annie's arms behind her grave. I look up, searching for the source of the noise with my heart thundering in my ears, dizzy with adrenaline. I hate this. I don't even want to be here. I clutch Annie as something small and rectangular floats from the top of the tower, watching as it falls through the air like a stone. It feels like it takes forever, but it could be only a couple of seconds before it lands with a crunch on the ground in front of the church.

Annie stands up, tentatively peering over her gravestone as I hold her wrist like a toddler who won't let go of their mum.

"It's her phone," Annie whispers. "It's Mystic Millie's phone."

"Maybe she just knocked it off?" I suggest hopefully, but I know I'm wrong.

Another scream echoes from the tower. It sounds more like words this time, but we're too far away to work them out. I squeeze Annie's arm even tighter.

"I think she's in danger. That someone's up there with her," Annie says. "And I don't think it's the ghost of Timmy Eaton. Come on; we have to go!"

My whole body thrums as I move to follow her. Every single organ in my body is telling me that this is a bad idea.

"We should call the police!" I suggest, yanking on her arm to hold her back.

"They'll take forever to get here! Come on!" Annie charges out from behind the gravestone.

I whirl around searching for anyone else who might be able to help, but something flies into my face. Immediately everything goes dark. I can't see, I just feel the flutter of wings battering my face, slapping against my cheeks and eyelashes and overwhelming my senses. I stumble back and try to put my hands up to push whatever it is away. I thought it was a bird, but it doesn't feel feathery against my skin. It feels smooth and leathery and soft, and there's definitely more than one.

I flap my arms, and the thunder of wings becomes more frantic. Next to me I can hear Annie swearing and trying to do the same. Trying to get my bearings, I make eye contact with something. Despite the panicked wings around my face, the world stills for a moment as I stare deep into the small, round, dark, terrified eyes of one of my assailants.

"BATS!" I scream, flapping my arms even harder.

"BATS?!" Annie's question's muffled by our winged attackers, she sounds far away—about ten bats away to be precise.

"BATS!" I confirm, trying to throw my arms over my face, to create some kind of shield.

"BAAATTTTSS!!!" Annie's scream is so high-pitched I think it'll break the sound barrier.

The thunder begins to die down to a patter. Are they leaving? Did Annie's scream scare them off? Or am I dying? I feel a strange kind of peace as the air around my face clears. Finally I open my eyes again and try to take deep breaths, in through my nose and out through my mouth. But it's at that point that Annie resumes screaming. This time louder, and more ear-piercing than before.

Not again. I turn to her slowly, expecting to see her swarmed by bats, and readying myself to go to battle with my winged nemeses. But there's not a single bat in sight—instead, she's pointing in the direction of the church. I look over and squint through the darkness, and finally I see what she's screaming about.

At the bottom of the tower, a crystal dildo clutched in her hand, lies the dead body of Mystic Millie.

191

* * *

"What happened after the livestream was shut off?" Annie asks. She's hurrying *toward* the very obvious dead body, which is completely the opposite of where I'd like to be going. "We could have got up there, if it wasn't for those bloody bats!"

"Wait," I whisper, stopping to stabilize myself on another gravestone, as a wave of nausea wracks through me. In the darkness I can sense Annie's impatience.

"She could still be alive!" Annie protests.

"She's fallen over two hundred feet," I whisper back, blinking. "And besides, that's why I called an ambulance!"

Annie was furious when I insisted that the first thing we did was phone an ambulance and the police.

"We need to get over there and look for clues before the police arrive and mess everything up. Maybe I should head up the tower? Take a look around? Someone must have been up there with her. She didn't just shut the stream off and fall." Her eyes are sparkling in the darkness, and the world starts to pixelate, like this is some kind of weird dream.

"Annie! No!" I do the shoutiest whisper I can muster. I agree with her that all signs point to there having been someone up there with Millie: the screams, the phone, the livestream shutting off suddenly, and now the dead body. "If there *was* someone up there, they could still be there! Then what are you going to do? End up at the bottom of the tower with Millie?"

"Or I could pin them down until the police get here?" Annie suggests hopefully, as if forgetting that she's about as physically intimidating as a mouse.

I sigh. "The police and ambulance will be here soon. They

told me not to touch anything. Let's just stay down here and keep *quiet*."

"You're behaving like you've never investigated before; this is so boring!" Annie moans.

"God, sorry for wanting to keep you alive," I mutter sarcastically.

The two of us stand there in the darkness for a while, keeping our distance from the body. Annie taps her foot on the ground impatiently. After a few minutes of projecting her dissatisfaction in my direction, she takes her phone out of her pocket.

"Now what are you doing?" I hiss. "Please don't be making a 'Come with me to find a dead body' video."

"Oh my god, Kerry, that's such a weird thing to suggest. No!" Annie looks at me like I'm a monster. "Actually just thought I'd see if Dougie and Celeste are still on livestreams."

"Feels like a weird time to be looking for makeup tips, but it's better than getting yourself killed I guess."

Annie rolls her eyes at me as Dougie appears on her screen talking about how hard today was, grieving Timmy, and how he thinks he's got a tan line in the shape of Timmy's face on his back. (It looks nothing like Timmy.)

"Actually I was thinking about suspects," she says. "If people are online, then they can't have been up the tower pushing Millie off. Can they?"

I have to admit it's a good point. She switches from Dougie to Celeste on her phone screen, and Celeste appears, taking off her makeup in another "Get un-ready with me" video, this time without a dead guy stalking her.

"What about Ethan?" I ask.

"Not online," Annie says. "Not on any of his profiles."

"Interesting," I say, prompting a smug smile from Annie. "We saw him leave, though. We saw all of them leave."

"But someone has to have been up there. She was screaming. What would she have been screaming at? And don't say Timmy Eaton's ghost, because I know neither of us believe in that. *And* how did her phone and then her end up on the ground here?" Annie's insistent but it's not me she has to convince.

No one else will have heard the screams we did, and no one else will have seen the phone fall first. And DI Wallace already thinks we're overdramatic.

"If someone was up there, though, how did they get up and back down again without us noticing?" I ask. "Assuming they *are* back down again."

"Either someone came back or there was someone else hiding on the roof. Someone we didn't know about," Annie says. I make a face showing I'm not sure I buy that.

"Who else is there though?" I ask, chewing on the side of my cheek in thought.

"I guess one of the influencers could have come around the back of the tower without us seeing and gone back up. Maybe when we were hiding from people coming out? We weren't watching as closely then."

"And then they got out when the . . . bats . . . ?" I shudder.

"Well, yeah, obviously," Annie says. "I guess. And if Dougie and Celeste are both on lives and have been this whole time, then it's just Ethan and Joanna who could have gone back up the tower."

"We know Joanna didn't kill Timmy, though, she wasn't here," I say.

"Do we know that? For sure?" Annie says. "She sent those pictures after all."

"We don't. But . . ." I scratch my head.

"I guess she wouldn't kill her own influencers, actually." Annie sighs.

"Which leaves *Ethan*," I say, just as he appears in front of us, walking into the graveyard as if he's been summoned by his name.

I reach over and clutch Annie's hand tightly next to me as he spots us.

"Hey," Ethan says, waving at us. "What are you guys doing here?"

"We're . . ." Annie starts talking but can't finish because the two of us are just staring at him, holding each other for safety. If he tries to hurt Annie, I reckon I could pull one of these gravestones out of the earth with my bare hands and fend him off. Such is the power of our Hulk-like friendship.

As he gets closer, Ethan stares past us at Millie and lets out a convincing gasp.

"WHAT HAPPENED?!" he cries, racing over to her body.

"You can't touch the body!" I shout as finally the sound of sirens and blue lights wash over us.

I wonder if Annie's thinking the same thing as I am. That if he killed her, he just wants us to witness his fingerprints and DNA on the body—then he has an explanation for them being there. But to my surprise he listens and backs away from Millie.

Annie releases my hand, and I think she might be toying with the idea of making a citizen's arrest, edging toward him slowly.

"Ethan—" she begins but she's cut off when he starts talking over her.

"I wanted to see if she was okay. I was watching her livestream, but then it just cut out. I was worried with her up there all alone . . ." His voice is dampened by an ambulance coming to a standstill on the path next to us.

DI Wallace's dark blue unmarked police car follows closely behind, its lights still flashing as he and DC Short step out of the car. He stands, rubbing his eyes, surveying the scene, looking every inch a man who's just been dragged out of bed against his will. By contrast, DC Short's wearing a full face of makeup with her hair sculpted perfectly into a beach wave—something that I know from personal experience takes well over an hour to do. How is this possible? At 11:00 p.m., when I think her colleague may actually be wearing a pajama top under his police-issued rain jacket. Is she just always ready?

DC Short goes over to talk to the paramedics but comes back very quickly.

"Dead, sir," she whispers to DI Wallace, but Annie, Ethan, and I can still hear.

Ethan collapses into me and Annie, almost pulling us down with him as he wails at the top of his lungs. The two of us shake him off, but DC Short stops to help him.

"Annie, Kerry, I presume you were the first to discover the body." DI Wallace pinches the bridge of his nose and sighs, like we are the cause of his constant personal headache.

We nod.

Annie pipes up. "She was up there recording a livestream. I think someone was up on the roof with her because the stream cut off and then—"

"You saw someone push her?" DI Wallace interrupts.

"No . . . but—" I say to defend Annie, but he also cuts me off.

"Don't GUESS, just tell people what you really saw. This is no time for dramatics and storytelling," DI Wallace snaps.

Annie's brows knot together before she continues talking with determination. "We didn't see exactly what happened, but there was a scream and then her phone fell down and then there was another scream and she was lying on the floor clutching the crystal dildo before we knew it. We were actually going to go up the tower and help when she was screaming, but the bats overwhelmed us, and we didn't see anything after that."

"The . . . ?" DI Wallace looks horrified.

"Bats," I say.

"No . . . before that . . . the?" DI Wallace's cheeks flush.

"Crystal dildo." Annie points to the phallus clutched in Mystic Millie's hands. "They're one of her key products, or they were before it was uncovered that they were actually really bad for vaginal health—they gave people thrush—so they were discontinued, but lately she seems to have been rebranding them as protection crystals that get sort of hung up like wind chimes to protect the energy of a space and stop the bad vibes from coming in." Annie seems to say this all in one breath, and DI Wallace looks like he might be about to lose his dinner before walking over to busy himself with the paramedics.

"Very resourceful," DC Short says. "Influencers really are so smart."

Ethan stops keening for a second and looks up at DC Short, chest puffed out. "Thanks," he says, before resuming shaking his fist in the direction of the tower and screaming. "CRUEL WORLD!"

DI Wallace stares at him. "And you are?"

Ethan stands back up. Composed, he reaches out to shake DI Wallace's hand.

"Ethan Woods, feminist, influencer, poet, and grime artist . . . and Mystic Millie's boyfriend." Ethan adds the last part in a whisper, wiping a nonexistent tear from his face and doing the driest sniff I've ever heard, as DI Wallace finally makes his way back to us.

"Can anyone explain what everyone was doing in a graveyard so late at night?"

"They've all been doing a séance on the roof, sir," DC Short says. "It ended a while ago, though. I was watching. It was incredible! She asked Timmy to knock if his death was murder . . . and he knocked!"

"DC SHORT!" DI Wallace chastises her.

"Sir, it was very compelling," DC Short whispers, looking at the ground. "I'll play you the video later."

"Please, if you would," he whispers back.

"She'd started another livestream. She was doing another séance by herself to try and find the truth! But it ended really suddenly," Ethan says. "I came to check she was okay. I was going to walk her back to camp."

I can't think of anything Millie would have liked less. Anne and I watch on, bemused, as Ethan seems to think for a moment, then drops back down to his knees. He pants and rubs his eyes, but it's really more of a poking gesture, that yields a frankly pitiful crop of tears.

"Don't suppose you'd be up for a selfie, would you?" DC Short asks him.

Ethan immediately stops fake crying, pops back up, and poses for the picture, pouting with his bottom lip out.

"Caption it: 'A grieving man,'" Ethan says with a rather dramatic sigh.

Murder Board Update
~~Mystic Millie~~

Mystic Millie has crossed over to the other side.

19

After walking through the eerie silence of the deserted festival ground, I'm a bit startled to find the remaining influencers gathered somberly around the firepit as we emerge into the glamp site. Annie had told me they would be, and it wasn't that I didn't believe her, I just don't understand why they'd still be here when the festival's been shut down and cleared out by the police.

"What's going on?" Annie asks, settling in next to Celeste, who's making some kind of video about her close friendship with Mystic Millie.

"Police closed down the festival, but Joanna's saying we can't leave," Dougie replies.

"Can't leave?" I try to avoid Ethan's eye and keep as far away from him as possible. The last thing I want is to encourage him going on about his "grief" again. I've already had three hours of that at the police station. I was actually relieved when the police let him go before us because it meant we didn't have to listen to him pretending to cry anymore.

When no one replies, I add, "And where is Joanna anyway?"

I'm a bit surprised she's not here. She didn't come to the police station when I'd have expected her to want to be with Ethan while he gave his statement. Where is she?

"Don't know. She says it's in our contracts, though. We have to do the whole weekend, or no one gets paid." Dougie rolls his eyes.

"But the festival's over?" I ask, perching next to him on his log. "What exactly does she think you're going to be doing here apart from hanging out in an abandoned festival site? That's already creepy enough!"

"Right?" Dougie looks sad and downtrodden, and I feel a bit heartbroken for the Adorable Adonis.

"How are you doing?" I ask.

"I'm pretty gutted," Dougie says, looking wounded. "She was cool, you know?"

My arm instinctively moves to hover behind him. I want to comfort him. I mean, the natural thing is to hug someone who's been through what he has, so of course I do. It's just normal behavior, right? It's not thirsty to hug a grieving man, is it?

But I feel like I'd be betraying Scott. The picture of him and Jen pops into my brain, like an unwanted visitor. I wonder if that's what they're doing right now and why he hasn't messaged me after Millie's death. The news is all over social media. It's not like he wouldn't know she's died, even if I hadn't caved and pathetically texted to tell him about it while we were waiting at the police station.

Screw it. "I'm sorry," I say to Dougie. I'm going to do it. I'm going to hug him.

"RIGHT!" Joanna emerges from the stage area, clapping her hands with purpose. I jump back away from the Adorable

Adonis just in time for Heather and the Mini-Heathers to appear, following close behind her.

"Please, can't we just go home?" Ethan pleads.

"No," Joanna says.

"But the festival's over?" Celeste asks.

"Not quite." Joanna turns to the Mini-Heathers, who have now changed from pink to black outfits, clearly as a mark of respect. "Video, please!"

Mini-Heather One takes out an iPad and presses Play while the other two stand on either side of her. A loud, tinny ballad booms from the screen as illustrations of white roses, thorns, and lilies creep across the screen. Black-and-white images of Mystic Millie and Timmy Eaton fade in and out with their dates of birth and death. Someone's thrown this together distastefully fast.

The music builds to a crescendo as the illustrations of flowers weave over the pictures. Huge white letters appear across the black screen reading: "The Festival of Fame is deceased: long live . . . THE FUNERAL OF FAME. #RIPFame." Mini-Heathers Two and Three unroll a black banner reading "Welcome to the Funeral of Fame!" with an illustration of an iPhone in a coffin on it. They throw black confetti in the air and strap on black party hats.

When the music finally cuts out, everyone is silent.

After what feels like an excruciatingly awkward eternity, Joanna finally nods to the Mini-Heathers. "You can go now," she says.

The Mini-Heathers walk back to the golf cart they use to get to and from Heather's house, but Heather stands firm.

"I said you can go now." Joanna glares at Heather, and Heather glares right back.

I've never seen anything like it. But then Heather cracks. She slinks off to join her mini-mes, her tail between her legs. We all watch as the golf cart trundles off into the distance with her on board.

Still, the influencers are silent. Celeste stares intensely into the flames of the firepit while Dougie cracks his knuckles next to me. I can tell that all of them are holding something in, apart from Ethan that is, who if anything appears the blankest he's ever been. He must be exhausted from all that "grief."

"We're going online!" Joanna announces again, trying to get a response. "All the panels will be virtual, and you'll be doing them from here together, but the audiences will be watching from their own homes."

"Cool," Ethan says.

"So if it's going online, why can't we go home, too, and do it from there?" Celeste asks, and I have to admit that I'm with her on this. "I have a green screen. I can make it look like I'm still here if you really need me to."

"Because people are going to want to tune in to see you guys *at* the Funeral of Fame and watch you all getting through this *together*," Joanna says sternly.

"This is gross," Celeste mutters.

"I'm just too sad, man," Dougie says, eyes locked on the fire.

"Do you want to be able to afford that expensive hair wax that you love so much, Dougie? Or do you want to give up and use a no-name brand? Because right now your engagement is going through the roof. Everyone's is, in fact." She points around the fire at the other influencers, even offering Annie a raise of her eyebrows to indicate she's kept an eye on hers as well. Great. Annie is going to be completely unbearable now. "And not only that, but you're getting a lot of requests for ads. Should I tell those sponsors to keep their money, Dougie? No one wants to be breaking contracts and having a legal battle right now do they?"

Around the circle the mood shifts. Ethan nods at her. But Celeste and Dougie stare at each other across the flames, as if having the kind of wordless conversation Annie and I are pro at. Eventually their faces turn resigned and grim.

"Whatever," Celeste sighs.

"Fine," Dougie mutters.

"Good." Joanna continues, "Celeste: Rave Graves want you to do an ad for their solar-powered neon headstones—'burial doesn't have to be boring' or something like that. Okay?"

"Yes, boss." Celeste salutes sarcastically before muttering, "Christ."

"Problem, Celeste?" Joanna asks.

"Nope." Celeste smiles falsely.

"I'm terrified," Ethan suddenly bursts out. "It'll be me next, won't it? From Millie? I'm the next logical step."

He makes a good point, if Timmy's dead, and Millie's dead, any one of them could be next. And something (experience) tells me we can't rely on DI Wallace and DC Short to figure out who it is before that happens. Especially as despite Annie's protestations, DI Wallace has already declared Mystic Millie's death to be a result of her "screwing around with her eyes closed at the top of a bloody tower." In his own words: "Of course she was going to fall, she wasn't looking where she was going." But she was miles away from the edge when she was doing her séance. Annie and I both know he's wrong. We just need to prove it. And fast.

"You're being ridiculous," Joanna snaps. "We're talking about two stupid accidents. There's no 'next.' You just all need to start being a bit more careful. My insurance can't take it."

"What about the fact that Kerry and I heard her screaming before she 'fell,'" Annie butts in, doing little bunny ear quotes.

I freeze. What's she doing? The killer might be here with us. Do we really want them to know that we're so sure she was pushed? Sure, Dougie and Celeste have alibis, but Joanna and Ethan don't.

The atmosphere around the fire's tense, with Joanna staring daggers right through Annie.

"What scream?" she asks eventually, her tone sharp. "No one heard a scream apart from you. No one on ReelLife heard one."

"Because the livestream had already ended when she screamed," Annie protests. "That's why it ended, because someone else was up there with her. Kerry and I were there. We heard it."

I feel like I could combust from the viciousness of Joanna's stare.

"That was probably because she was about to fall off the tower," Joanna says through gritted teeth. "This is your over-active imagination so you had better not repeat it to anyone else. The police say it was an accident, so it was an accident!"

There's silence around the firepit as the flames crackle and pop in the background. Dougie's the first one to respond.

"Yes, boss," he replies mournfully.

"Yes, boss," Celeste repeats, chewing her lip, her eyes shining in the flicker of the flames.

"If I die, I'll be furious," Ethan mutters to himself.

"Great, now don't forget to check your emails for your jobs from me." Joanna turns and walks toward her yurt. "Get to bed, get some sleep, and stop being dramatic. There's nothing to be afraid of."

She walks back to her yurt briskly in a cloud of vape smoke. I gulp. If this were a film, that would be exactly what a character says before becoming the next victim.

I look down at my phone and type a text to Annie.

> **Me:** Why is Joanna so intent on making these deaths look like accidents?

> **Me:** Surely she's not stupid. She knows it's no accident? Two influencers dying on consecutive days? No one's buying they're accidents . . . are they?

I glance up expecting to see Annie looking at her phone replying to me, but instead she's deep in conversation with Celeste. Their faces are just inches apart. She hasn't even noticed the message I've sent her.

"What are you doing now?" I hear her ask. "We should post some grief content, right?"

"Yeah, I actually need to start on something that Joanna's

sent over to me," Celeste says, a small smile flitting across her face. "Wanna come help?"

"Sure," Annie says, jumping up from her seat and following Celeste eagerly to her yurt.

Celeste turns and notices me staring at the two of them. "Will you come, too?" she asks kindly.

"Nah, Kerry's got to work on that blog I told you about that she's writing. Don't you, babe?" Annie answers for me. "Needs updating after tonight, that's for sure!"

"Oh yeah, sounds great!" Celeste says. I can't help feeling kind of betrayed by Annie. She told Celeste what I was writing? "I thought Joanna might have put you off writing about it with all her chat."

Are they actually going to let me get a word in edgewise?

"No," I say, relieved to finally be speaking for myself. "I just haven't published any of it yet. I don't like publishing things before they feel finished and perfect."

"She'll share things with her boyfriend before she publishes it, but she won't share it with me," Annie explains to Celeste, and my hackles rise at that again. Does she need to tell Celeste?

"I guess it's hard when you're writing. It's so personal," Dougie says, and I soften a bit at the warmth in his eyes. "It's really vulnerable, man."

I'm taken unawares by Dougie's comment because it's pretty intuitive. That's exactly it. I feel vulnerable sharing things that I've written. It's why I feel okay sharing things with Scott: because I trust him. But I shared a link with him to the blog's progress earlier, after I'd updated it with all the stuff we found out about Millie, and he hasn't said a single thing about it. I'm starting to wonder if he's even looked at it.

"What's it about?" Dougie asks.

"I'm just writing about this weekend," I say, trying to be vague.

"I always admire writers. You get to craft and build something. I just shove a filter on something and post it," Celeste says kindly.

"Well, better get on with it," I say, looking at the floor and shuffling toward our yurt. I find all this attention on me and my writing uncomfortable.

What I really want to do is delve into the videos that are bound to have built up on ReelLife by now with commentaries and dissections of what exactly happened. I want to see if there's anything in the live we could have missed. Maybe there was a reflection or something—some kind of hint or proof that someone else was up there. If there was, I know I can rely on the people of ReelLife to have picked up on it and be spreading theories by now. I'm surprised Annie doesn't want to do this, too, to be honest. I settle down on the small white sofa in the corner of our yurt. It's quiet—a little too quiet. I turn on a battery-powered lamp and pull a blanket across myself, shivering slightly.

I don't even need to search for Millie's name for the videos to start appearing. There are hundreds of them. But none of them seem to mention any theories about someone being up there with her. In fact, all of them are citing it as a tragic accident. Given how many people had theorized Timmy's murder within minutes on here, I'm shocked, but of course I realize, I shouldn't be. Joanna's powerful and she knows how to control a narrative. If she wants to spin a story to the advantage of her and her clients, she will. Joanna's smart . . . Maybe smart enough to commit murder? Except she has an alibi for the night Timmy died. So now I'm back at Ethan, but without any proof aside from his lack of alibi and him being first on the scene.

I feel like I've hit a wall. I need another opinion aside from mine and Annie's, and there's two people I know I can absolutely trust right now. So I start a new WhatsApp group and add Annie in just in case she's ready to start concentrating on the case again when she's finished making "grief content."

Big Secret Don't Tell Heather

Me: Hey guys, did you see what happened to Millie?

Colin: OH MY GOD WE JUST SAW SHE'S DEAD

Audrey: 💀

Me: Did you see the livestream she did?

Colin: Of course, we were gripped after the knocking. I can't believe she's gone 🪦

Audrey: She can talk to the dead all the time now 👻

Me: That's cool, yeah, anyway, did you see anything out of the ordinary on the livestream?

209

Audrey: No?

Colin: Not that I noticed.

Colin: Why?

Me: Annie and I were there when she fell . . . except we don't think she fell. We think someone was up there with her.

Audrey: You think she was murdered? 🗡️ 🧠 🪦 🫖

Colin: Oh my fucking god.

Audrey: OMG YOU HAVE TO INVESTIGATE

Me: Me and Annie are. But don't tell anyone. Heather would kill us.

Colin: We're telling no one. Can't believe the Tampon Two are back on the case again

Audrey: We're so discreet. SAYING NOTHING BABE.

Colin: 🫖 🫖

I message Annie because I think she'd probably want to know what I've discovered . . . which actually is next to nothing. It's weird, her not being here to talk through the case with. It feels kind of lonely, even though I can hear her laughing from Celeste's yurt. I close my messages, but my phone immediately lights up again. Scott's name beams out at me from the screen in the way I've hoped it would all day, and relief washes over me.

> **Scott:** Hey, I just saw the news about Mystic Millie. Are you ok?

> **Scott:** I'm so sorry I haven't messaged all day. I kept trying to but people are always interrupting, dragging me off for photo shoots or videos. I can't get a minute to myself.

> **Scott:** Are you all right?!

> > **Me:** Yeah. This whole thing just feels like déjà vu.

> **Scott:** The festivals over though right? You're leaving now? Jen just said that they've sent everyone home anyway. She said it's gone online.

> > **Me:** Yeah but the influencers are staying to do the online

bit from here so me and Annie
are too.

    Scott: Why? You can go home? It's safer
    there? Why are you keeping yourself in
    danger?

I don't like what he's saying. He's never told me what to do. Why's he suddenly starting now? And when he's all over the internet topless with Jen? It's not even about Jen, though. I thought he got me, so why isn't he understanding that I need to stay here and find out the truth? Doesn't he believe I can do it? Of course I want to go home, too. I'm scared, I know I'm in danger, but I'm being brave. I support him being on tour with the band; shouldn't he be supporting me? But of course I don't say any of that, instead I say:

    Me: So what are you guys up
    to?

    Scott: Been out after the gig but Jen and I
    are really tired, so we're just headed back
    to the bus now.

Jen. Again. And just the two of them? I'm trying hard not to let my mind race ahead but the picture of them from earlier constantly lingers in my brain, any excuse for it to rear its head. I can feel myself spiraling, and the world spins around me while I try to cling to its edges. It feels like there's a stone forming in my chest, and my breath's not strong enough to push past it.

I put my hand on my stomach and try to count breaths. After a few moments, my lungs start to steady.

"I told you! I'm next!!" Ethan suddenly shouts from outside in the camp, and I immediately feel my chest tense up again.

Dropping my phone, I race out of the tent to see what's going on. Dougie, Celeste, and Annie emerge from their yurts at the same time, looking as spooked as I am. We all stare at Ethan, sitting at the firepit, his head in his hands. I'm surprised to see that there isn't even so much as a stirring from Joanna's yurt.

"Ethan, dude, what's up?" Dougie asks, heading over to him.

Wordlessly, Ethan passes Dougie his phone while I move closer to Annie and Celeste. There's safety in numbers after all.

"What the fuck, man?" Dougie asks, staring at the screen.

"They tagged me in it!" Ethan cries.

"Ethan, it's not just you. They've tagged us all in it. You, me, and Dougie," Celeste says next to me, her voice shaky.

"Tagged you in what?" Annie asks, as Celeste turns her phone to face us.

On her screen is an Instagram post. A square picture with objects laid out against a black background: a Timmy Eaton mask, a crystal dildo, and one of Millie's tarot cards—the death card.

The post is from an account called @InfluenceSlayer with the bio #InfluencerCultureIsDead. The account only follows three people: Dougie, Celeste, and Ethan.

20

I wake up to the sound of Annie giggling to herself on her bed. The heat in the sun-drenched yurt feels suffocating, and I sit up, rubbing my eyes.

"What are you watching?" I ask, yawning.

Annie shoots me a mischievous grin. "Ethan's done this completely unhinged advert for Feminist Funerals. If I didn't know him, I'd think it was a spoof."

I get out of bed and stretch, heading over to her. The yurt feels weird without Herbie this morning, but I'm glad he's safe—which is more than can be said for Annie and me. I'm surprised I slept at all. I'm trying so hard to be the new intrepid Kerry, but sleeping in the middle of nowhere, in a bougie tent without a lock, when there's a murderer on the loose, does unfortunately still trouble me.

"I wanna see." I slide next to Annie on her bed, and she presses Play on the video.

"Especially in the light of my beloved's death, may she rest in peace"—Ethan looks up to the sky and makes the sign of the cross—"I worry about keeping hold of my feminist ideals after I die. For me, it's about ensuring that my funeral upholds the values that I like to keep in my day-to-day life, so that I can be one hundred percent sure that I'll go to feminist heaven."

"And what are those values, Ethan?" Annie asks, smirking. Clearly this isn't the first time she's watched this.

"Those values are that people of all genders should be equal, and that just because women may be biologically weaker doesn't mean we can pay them less," Ethan says.

"Mmmmm, biologically weaker . . ." Annie nods to me. "He really said that out loud, on film."

"Oh my god." I have my hand fully over my mouth now. I'm about to join Timmy Eaton and Mystic Millie in death.

"I don't think Joanna signed this off before he posted, do you?" Annie says, sniggering slightly.

I feel myself grin. "He's gonna be in trooooouble!"

Ethan suddenly turns his own volume up, making us jump. "I want to *know* that the person who conducts my funeral shares the same feminist idealism as I do, and I wanna be played out by 'Baby Got Back'—a song about body positivity, because what good feminist wouldn't?! And do you know who else wants this for me? . . . #FeministFunerals." In an ending more bizarre than the rest of the ad, he then starts rapping earnestly, eventually fading out his own voice to a whisper and ending with a somber stare to camera that goes on for an uncomfortably long time.

"Well, that was bizarre," I say.

Annie smirks. "I wonder how long it'll be before Joanna comes for him."

"It's gotta be any minute now I reckon."

The two of us sit in silence waiting for the inevitable moment that Joanna sees the video and loses it at him. We carry on waiting, checking the time on our phones.

"Surely she's seen it by now?" Annie asks.

"She's on her phone constantly," I agree.

"You don't think . . . something could have happened to her . . . ?" Annie trails off.

"She didn't say anything when the influence slayer account appeared last night," I point out. "And she was very sure of herself when she went to bed."

"Pride comes before a literal fall . . ." Annie whispers, gulping.

The two of us stare toward the yurt entrance, and then back at each other, almost daring the other to go and check. The air stills in our silent yurt and I hold my breath.

"ETHAN!" We hear Joanna shouting outside in the camp.

I exhale the breath I knew I was holding.

"No way I'm missing this!" Annie rushes up, and I join her, shoving on some shorts and a hoodie quickly.

We pop our heads out and see Joanna raging in the doorway to Ethan's yurt, waiting for him to emerge like a Venus flytrap about to snap. Celeste's already outside watching, so Annie and I feel safe enough to step into the open with her. She waves hello, and I notice Annie doing a little bob of a wave back. It's a sort of shy gesture and not at all the sort of thing Annie normally does. Just as I'm getting weirded out watching her twirling a strand of hair around her finger, I'm distracted by Dougie shuffling into view, shirtless in a pair of pajama trousers and scratching his head sleepily. I'm surprised there's no girl trailing out of the yurt behind him this morning. Is it possible he's spent a night alone? My body temperature rises at the sight of his bare chest and abs, because if there's one thing I've learned over the past couple of days, it's that I'm a massive pervert and I definitely need to be stopped.

"ETHAN! GET YOUR 'FEMINIST' ASS HERE NOW!" Joanna starts rattling his yurt.

If he won't appear of his own accord, she'll shake him out.

"Yes?" Ethan pops just his head through the canvas flaps, rubbing his eyes and blinking at Joanna innocently. He tentatively takes a step out into the open in a pair of pajamas covered in cartoons of the suffragists.

"CARE TO EXPLAIN THIS?!" Joanna thrusts her phone in his rapidly paling face.

I think watching Ethan about to be taken down is the closest thing to enjoyment I've felt in days. I expect to hear the video start to play but instead I hear nothing. Ethan reaches for her phone before hesitating.

"Please, may I finger your phone?" he asks her.

Joanna blinks at him for a second before her face turns red and she resumes shouting. "You've RUINED your career. What am I supposed to do with you now?"

Everyone immediately looks down at their phones, and Annie and I are no exception. I don't think she's actually talking about the video we just watched, so what *is* she talking about? I search Ethan's name on ReelLife, and the search results have barely loaded when Annie lets out a horrified gasp.

At the top of the feed there's a video posted by an anonymous account that features a woman explaining that Ethan had initially slid into her DMs as a feminist ally, offering to help get her career as an influencer off the ground. Within days he was asking her address because he wanted to send her something. She was initially excited, thinking it would be something to help her boost follower numbers. But what she received was a larger-than-average sausage, sent by courier. With an invitation from Ethan to send him pictures posed with said sausage. And it looks like this video's triggered a host of other videos, with more women coming forward to detail similar sausage-y experiences. The video's been up for ten minutes and there are already over fifty similar video commentaries from women sharing the evidence and receipts they have from such encounters, all from within the period when Ethan was with allegedly with Mystic Millie.

"He's the *wurst*," Annie whispers, and I let out a groan.

"It wasn't me," Ethan protests, red faced and sweaty. "Someone has used my name and impersonated me!"

"One of these girls has got you on video having a live webcam chat with them, in which you demonstrate several suggested poses with the sausage. Frankly it will haunt me in my nightmares, Ethan." Joanna narrows her eyes at him. "I'll never eat salami again."

Ethan's stumped. He looks around for someone to help him, but there's absolutely no one who's about to do that here. Celeste's tutting and shaking her head, and Annie joins in with her. They both seem to realize at the same time and exchange a smirk.

"All while you were with Millie, man? That's not cool."

Dougie shakes his head too.

Ethan looks like a lost puppy. I can't believe he wasn't even smart enough to realize that when he's in a high-profile relationship like he was with Millie at least one of these women was always going to expose him. I click on the @FauxFeminist account that posted the first video almost fifteen minutes ago. The account doesn't follow anyone but now has tens of thousands of followers and its only post is this video. It was obviously set up specifically for this purpose. I think back to the prank list and what was under Ethan's name:

Webcam
Log-in details
Chipolata

Catching Annie's eye, I know instantly that she's realized the same thing as me: this is Timmy Eaton's prank and someone else has carried it out after his death. Someone else who knew about the prank list.

I type in the name of the only other person I can be sure knew about that list into ReelLife and refresh their feed. There's nothing at first, but a couple of refreshes later, what I expected to see shows up, posted forty-seven seconds ago and timed to perfection.

"I didn't know they'd talk!!" Ethan wails. His defense is as pathetic as he is at this point. "I just thought they'd be so happy to talk to me and hear from me . . . and be so flattered . . . I've just lost my girlfriend . . . "

"We all know you weren't really together, Ethan," Joanna

says like she's talking to a toddler. "And it's disrespectful to use Millie's death to try to get out of this situation you've found yourself in."

This is it; I just need to have the courage to show them what I've found. I open my mouth and close it again, losing my nerve. But they all need to see this.

"I think she already knew!" The words spew out of me almost involuntarily. "Check her profile."

I click on the video I've been waiting to play at the top of Mystic Millie's feed and turn up my volume so everyone else can hear.

"My dear fans," Mystic Millie says to the camera. Her eyes are red from what I presume are fake tears, but I guess now we'll never know. "I am shocked and heartbroken at the news about my boyfriend, Ethan Woods, this morning. It's a betrayal that's left my heart shattered, and right now I don't know if it can ever heal. I just wanted you all to know that I'm here for the victims of his sausages and anyone else who's suffered. I also wanted to make it clear that I had no idea what he was doing. Please know that I am with you all in your betrayal and disappointment and that, as of this morning, Ethan Woods and I are no longer in a relationship."

The video finishes, freezing on the image of her sad face, with the message "Do you want more ReelLife from Mystic Millie?"

Joanna's face goes pale, and she drops her phone to the floor while a gasp travels around the camp in canon. As she picks up her phone, Joanna makes eye contact with me, holding it for what feels like hours but could only have been a terrifying few seconds.

Dougie's the first to puncture the silence: "Dude, you got dumped by a dead girl, like, from beyond the grave and shit."

Ethan's eyes widen. "She's been buried already? Did I miss it? Was it a Feminist Funeral?"

"The only thing that's buried, Ethan, is your career," Joanna says, composing herself again.

"SO SHE'S ALIVE???" Ethan shouts after her.

"Fuck's sake, Ethan!" Joanna sounds rattled for the first time since we've met her, her stress levels clearly at boiling point. "She's dead! She must have scheduled the video to go out before she died. She knew this was going to happen because she's the one who set you up. Your 'loving' girlfriend had had enough of you just like the rest of us!"

Dougie gasps, catching up with Annie, Celeste, Joanna, and me.

"What do I do?" Ethan throws his head into his hands dramatically.

"What every influencer does in disgrace, Ethan. An apology video, which you can figure out yourself. I've got ENOUGH going on this morning with all the death." Joanna marches away. "The rest of you need to be onstage for the live podcast episode of *SausageFest* with Dougie's new cohost in ONE HOUR!" she shouts over her shoulder, disappearing into the yurt.

"Am I *excluded* from the *SausageFest*?" Ethan cries after her in disbelief.

Joanna pops her head back out of the yurt. "Yes!"

Her head immediately disappears back inside and Ethan looks bereft, glancing around at everyone else for support. Celeste and Annie shake their heads with their arms crossed. I feel unsettled looking at how in sync they are with each other. Celeste is still technically a suspect, after all.

"Is no one going to help me?" Ethan pleads. "Dougie, you want me on the podcast, right? *SausageFest* bros?"

"I think you've had enough sausages, dude. I gotta do my morning workout." Dougie shrugs and heads back into his yurt.

As if she's heard all the way back at the house that Dougie will be sweating, Heather suddenly appears. She's practically skipping—all worries about the festival, police, and how much money she's lost by sending everyone home seemingly forgotten for a lusty moment.

"I can spot you, Dougie!" she says, following him toward his yurt. But when she reaches it, he simply shuts the flaps in her face.

"You're surely enough of a feminist to figure this out yourself, Ethan." Celeste smiles and walks off in the direction of the spa block. "I've got a 'Get ready with me to mourn' video to make . . . again. Annie, I'll see you in a minute, yeah?"

I turn to Annie, confused. They've got plans? Again?

"'Course, I'll practice now!" Annie starts dancing as Celeste walks away. "God, she's so funny."

I don't know what Annie's up to right now—apart from something that looks like The Robot—but at least one of us needs to stay on top of this investigation.

"I can help you, Ethan," I say.

I feel Annie's head snapping around in my direction immediately.

"Oh, thank god. Yes please!" Ethan says, as he races toward his yurt, tripping on his undone shoelaces. He spins back around suddenly. "Just to check, when you say you'll help . . .

do you mean it in a sexy way?"

"NO!" Annie and I shout at the same time.

"Okay, jeez, just checking." He holds his hands up like a surrender. "Just give me a minute to get decent, then." He gestures down at his suffragette pajamas.

"If only he'd thought of that when the camera was on him," Annie mutters before grabbing my arm and pulling me away and into our own yurt.

21

"What are you doing?" Annie hisses once we're inside. "I thought you said he was our chief suspect. Should you really be going into a yurt with him?"

"He *is* our chief suspect. Which is why I'm going to search his yurt," I whisper back.

I'm not sure why she asked, because she doesn't actually seem to be listening. She's setting up her phone on a tripod in front of her. Once apparently satisfied with the angle, she presses Record and, as music starts blasting from the phone, she begins dancing.

"Copy me," she says, slightly out of breath. "Okay, so fair enough. I mean good idea, but he's probably hiding the evidence as we speak."

"It's still worth a look, though. Hey, this isn't recording live, is it?" I point to her phone. I didn't intend to join in, but for some reason I have and now I hate myself for it. The last thing I want is for there to be any evidence of this someone else might see.

"No, this is just a practice. I'm doing this dance with Celeste in a minute. I just want to make sure I don't look silly," she says.

"Right, yeah." I narrow my eyes as I follow her and we both throw our arms out to the side. I don't think she's ever cared about either of us looking silly before. "I mean, you seem to be doing fine?"

"It's all a question of timing," Annie says. "You just have to match the timing up to the music."

"Do you think I should be worried?" I ask, as if suddenly realizing what the hell I'm about to do as I twirl around with my hands in the air. "I mean I really do think he's the most likely suspect. Should I really be going into his yurt alone?"

"Yeah, he seems most likely," Annie says, puffing through increasingly aggressive attempts at dance moves, her brow furrowing. "But I'll be in Celeste's yurt if you scream."

"You're spending a lot of time with Celeste," I say suspiciously, trying to attempt a full body roll. It's quite addictive, actually.

"She's cool. Pretty smart, and it's good to have a perspective from the inside, you know?" Annie says, bending her knees and wiggling down low to the ground.

"But should you be getting so close to a suspect?" I ask, trying to copy her but falling on my ass.

"She has alibis. Timmy died when he was pranking Celeste, and Millie died at ten last night, when Celeste was on a livestream. I'd say her alibi is ironclad," Annie says.

"Maybe—" I'm cut off by something clicking in my head as I process the timings that Annie's just said. "Ten p.m. was when Millie was supposed to be pranked by Timmy." I stop dancing and find the picture of Timmy's prank list on my phone, double-checking that I'm right.

Annie carries on dancing so I zoom in on the list so that she can see and hold it in front of her. She's staring at it and bobbing up and down and I wish she'd stop because it's actually starting to make me feel a bit sick.

"Look! The next prank was due to happen tonight . . ." I say. "What if it's a pattern? If it is, then there's going to be another death this evening!"

"Maybe," Annie says, not stopping her dance for my frankly world-shattering revelation. It's like she's barely heard me. "But Millie's already done that prank."

"That doesn't mean someone won't die. Millie died when she was supposed to be pranked, Timmy died when he was pranking Celeste. Besides, we know Millie set up Ethan being exposed and she can't be the killer. It's the timing, not the action."

Annie still doesn't seem convinced. "Maybe . . . "

It's like she's not even paying proper attention, and suddenly I feel my blood boil. I'm so sick of being ignored. I've been trying so hard to get Scott's attention, and now fighting ReelLife for a scrap of Annie's time is just too far. I wish she'd stop dancing and talk to me properly.

Decisively I reach out and cut off her recording. The music stops, and she blinks at me surprised.

"HEY!" she shouts.

"I'm just asking you to focus on the investigation for, like, five seconds," I hiss.

"God, sorry . . ." Annie says, half sarcastically before she realizes from my expression that I'm deadly serious and changes her tone. Her face softens and for once she actually looks at me and not the camera. "I'm sorry Kerry, I'm listening."

"I mean . . . I just think there could be another murder tonight and maybe . . . you know . . . we should try and stop it . . . that's all," I mumble.

"Okay," Annie says. "So if Ethan's our top suspect, we just need to keep an eye on the misogynist in suffragist pajamas over there." She nods in the direction of Ethan's yurt.

"Yes."

"It's a plan!" Clearly satisfied with this, Annie takes her eyes off me and reaches over for her phone, pressing Record again. "Hey, guys! Come with me backstage at the Festival of Fame to the VIP glamp site where two of the yurts are now empty because the inhabitants were murdered!" She makes a peace sign and flashes a winning and wholly inappropriate smile.

"Dude! You can't post that!"

"*Dude*, I have to give my followers what they want—constant content from the Funeral of Fame!" Annie clicks her fingers at me in an irritating way.

I wonder how many followers Annie even has now. Surely now Timmy's death has been overshadowed by Millie's, and since he was the only reason she had followers in the first place, the number's gone down. I open my phone and nearly choke on my own saliva when I see that she's reached eighty thousand. And not just that, but people are actually liking, sharing, and commenting on her videos. She's doing it. She's an influencer.

And I haven't even got a response from the texts I sent to my boyfriend before bed last night.

I open my laptop to update the murder board while I wait for Ethan and start adding in some notes about Ethan's DM scandal to my blog so that I can flesh it out a bit more later.

"Better go and meet Celeste and dance like eighty thousand people are watching!" Annie trumpets. She then skips joyfully out of the yurt.

Why is she screwing around with a dance when there's a killer to be caught? I stare at myself in the mirror. My reflection looks weak and scared, and not at all brave like I need to be. Oh god, I can't believe I'm about to go to the yurt of a probable killer to search for clues. What am I going to find? What if I . . . die?

I catch myself and blink back at my reflection. I need to be brave. Everyone's here, in the camp. It'll be okay. People would hear if anything went wrong. Somehow, my body carries me outside, toward what is probably certain death.

"You ready, Ethan?" I shout standing outside his yurt.

"Ready!" Ethan shouts back.

I take a deep breath, push my shoulders back, and head inside.

22

Still alive. Found absolutely nothing.

After thirty minutes in a tent with Ethan, I think the only thing that could have killed me was the boredom. He talked *at* me, rattling off reasons why people should feel sorry for him and how it wasn't his fault for so long I thought *I* might murder *him*, though. Thankfully, after half an hour, he was summoned by Joanna for something obviously terribly important, so when he left—still ranting away—I, of course, used the opportunity to snoop. Sadly (very sadly) all I found was a jumbo box of the special BigBoy condoms with Timmy Eaton's face on it and a huge amount of black T-shirts and marker pens.

Now, standing at the side of the stage waiting for the *SausageFest* podcast recording to start, I feel thoroughly defeated. My phone vibrates, and for a second I think I've imagined it when I see Scott's name. I've spent all morning willing a text from him, and now that I finally have one I feel immediately lighter. Maybe he's actually looked at the link to the unpublished blog I sent him and now that he's seen what I'm working

229

on and how far I've come with it he understands why I have to stay. Maybe that's why he's messaging me? To apologize?

> **Scott:** Just woke up, I'm so tired!

> **Scott:** Poor Ethan, how's he doing? I can't imagine what it's like to have your girlfriend just die like that.

My stomach drops because this confirms that he hasn't looked at the blog. If he had, he'd know that Millie and Ethan weren't a real couple. I get a sinking feeling while I try to type my response quickly before he disappears again, every fumble of my fingers and typo making me more impatient and frustrated with myself. I need to reply while he's still paying attention, before he gets distracted.

> **Me:** They wern't a real couple. They were jst doing it for socal media.

> **Scott:** Why would anyone do that man?

My fingers hover over the screen. I want to ask about Jen, if those hugs and pictures are just for social media, or if they're something more real. But I don't. How can it be that I write hundreds of words every single day but when it comes to the person I most want to express myself to in the world, I can't seem to say anything I need to? Eventually I manage to type out a message, but it's not what I really want to say to him, and I know it's taken me too long.

> **Me:** Yeah I don't really know.
> But this morning loads of
> girls have come forward to
> say that Ethan's been DM-ing
> them trying to get pictures of
> them posing with sausages
> and flirting with them. I
> don't really have that much
> sympathy for him I guess.

I watch the note turn from delivered to read and stare at the screen waiting for a reply, but deep down I already know none's coming.

> **Me:** Anyway what are you
> guys up to today?

I'm trying so hard to keep hold of the conversation, but deep down I know it's already over. I'm left staring sadly at his small avatar picture of the face I miss so much.

I can't help myself, despite knowing that last time this was a bad idea. I open ReelLife. There's a new reel from the band themselves and some pictures from fans. I click on the reel and a video of the band on space hoppers, racing each other across a field starts. Scott and Jen are far in the lead compared to the rest of the band. I watch them duke it out as they head toward the finish line, exchanging a look, the start of a smile. I hate myself for being this person, and yet I feel the jealousy eating away at me while I watch the two of them bouncing. As they cross the finish line, they both go tumbling, landing almost on top of each other and the video ends.

It was posted earlier today. He said he was asleep. Was that a lie? Was this what he was doing when he wasn't replying to my messages after everything that happened? My guts twist as I try to remind myself how much Scott loved me when he left, and attempt to bat the feeling of unease out. But it's no use.

"Hey, guys." Celeste's voice startles me out of my trance, and I lock my phone as she comes to stand with me and Annie. "How's it going?"

"Good! Who do you think the new cohost is going to be?" Annie asks. "I guess we know it's not you."

"Oh yeah, a woman would *never* be asked on there, let alone as a host! But they *have* been super secretive, and Joanna says they're taking a new direction. So maybe it'll be a more interesting unveil than we think," Celeste says, scrolling her feed for comments from people who are consoling her on her great loss. A loss that actually she doesn't look that gutted about.

"Yeah, I'm surprised Winona's even introducing *Sausage-Fest*," Annie says. "It doesn't really fit her brand."

"Part of her contract," Celeste says. "She has to introduce everything at the festival. Even the bits she doesn't agree with. Or she doesn't get paid."

"That's gotta suck, but I would have thought she had more . . . integrity?" Annie screws her face up.

"Honestly we're at Joanna's say-so. If she says jump, we all say how high. It's not great, but it's just how it is. Also, did you know that *SausageFest* has over three million subscribers?" Celeste says. "And Winona's *Feminist Fandom* podcast only has one million."

"Urgh, patriarchy!" Annie and I say in unison. But the comment about Joanna controlling their commitments and work still sticks.

I look over at where she's sitting on one of the black inflatable sofas, tapping away on her phone. Of course Joanna's still frantically trying to pull the strings and control a situation that's resulted in the deaths of two of her clients.

The Mini-Heathers appear, but Heather isn't with them, which feels weird. Mini-Heather One nods at something Joanna says, before muttering into her headset and within seconds the same ballad that was used on the Funeral of Fame video's booming out of the speakers. The stage lights go up, illuminating the black inflatable sofas and a set draped with black velvet, black roses, and lilies. Poor Jessica looks a bit exhausted and I wouldn't be surprised if she's been spray painting those flowers black all night.

Two people with cameras whip into action, just as Winona's saddened face appears on the big screen. There's a second screen that we can see at our side of the stage displaying the live feed with its rolling comments and likes from the people watching at home, so that Joanna and her newfound minis can keep an eye on engagement.

"Good morning and welcome to the Funeral of Fame! How's everyone doing?" Winona shouts into the camera leaving a short pause, as hearts, tears, and messages of grief float up the other half of the screen. "All of the influencers here wanted to let you know how much we appreciate your continued support at this difficult time. It's such an honor to see over a million of you have tuned in today to celebrate the lives of those that we've lost as well as showing love to those of us left behind in the wake of such tragedy."

I want to say something about how this whole thing is just using other people's deaths for likes and clicks, but I don't know if I can say that in front of Celeste. And it feels like Celeste is *always* here.

"As influencers we strive to be real, to talk about the difficult issues and to face things head on," Winona says. "So, without further ado, I'd like to introduce a very special live recording of *SausageFest*. In honor of his dearly departed cohost, Timmy Eaton, please welcome to the stage Dougie Trainor!"

Silent clapping emojis fill the left side of the screen onstage following the livestream as Dougie walks on take a seat. You can see that Dougie's not used to walking out to eerie silence, the vibe's all off. The atmosphere died with the influencers, and being here certainly feels more like a funeral than a festival.

"Hey, guys." He throws a hand up to his head and brushes his hair back, flexing a muscle or three at the same time. "Thank you so much for watching along. I know I speak for all the influencers here when I say how much we appreciate your love." His brow furrows in a way that looks sad, serious, and sexy all in one as he looks into the camera. "Timmy was such a huge part of *SausageFest* that without him it almost feels impossible to go on. But I know he'd want me to; he'd want his legacy to be immortalized, our own SausageBoy. And so it gives me great pleasure to introduce my new cohost! Everyone please welcome to the stage . . . Tommy Grover!" Dougie gestures toward the other side of the stage to where the late Timmy Eaton appears to step out . . . or at least, someone who looks exactly like him.

I do a double take, and I'm able to see a few slight differences, but he's wearing the same clothes, has the same haircut and fake tan. Tommy is Timmy 2.0.

"How is it honoring his legacy to replace him with someone completely identical?" Annie mutters to me.

"Right?" Celeste says before I can speak. "It's like you were saying earlier, they're trying to pretend it's a new exciting thing that's different to get people's attention but now they've just gone for the same old misogynistic mold."

What's going on here? Annie and Celeste are behaving like some kind of double act, sharing observations and thoughts with each other like detectives or something.

"And apparently misogynism gets likes." Annie gestures at the feed screen where hearts and thirsty emojis fly up the side in droves.

I google Tommy Grover and nudge Annie in the ribs, showing her the search results. Tommy Grover's picture is displayed above a short bio about this newcomer to the scene. A newcomer that Joanna has just signed to Talentz Management company.

"She's replaced Timmy with Tommy," I whisper.

"Callous," Annie mutters.

"I guess she still has to make bank," Celeste says bluntly. "It's a cutthroat business."

Next to me, Annie and Celeste have been watching intently as Tommy talks onstage about what big shoes he has to step into, while making some kind of joke about penis size that provokes a stream of laughing emojis on the feed.

"It's a sad time for all of us," Dougie goes on to say. "But I know that we will all be using the rest of this festival to share tributes and memories of Timmy and, of course, Millie. Everyone here really feels for their friends and families."

"Exactly that," Tommy says. "And now I believe we have one other, serious matter to attend to before we finish the podcast."

"Yes!" Dougie blurts out cheerfully. "I know that this morning everyone was hit hard by the news about our friend and the late Mystic Millie's boyfriend, Ethan Woods, and his . . . indiscretions. At *SausageFest*, we believe in letting people have their say—"

"As long as they're men," Annie, Celeste, and I mutter at the same time.

"So here to talk about the scandal around the DMs he was sending frankly hundreds of women, pathetically begging for pictures with his sausage . . . it's the man himself . . . Ethan Woods!" Tommy finishes.

The screen onstage flickers, and Ethan appears, the word "live" in the lefthand corner next to a flashing green dot. I don't get it—if he's doing it live, why isn't he onstage?

I sneak a look at Joanna but as the Mini-Heathers buzz around, it's as if a calm has washed over her. Maybe she's just waiting for him to screw it up and sign his own death warrant, and stick the final nail in the coffin of his career?

Ethan's in his yurt, wearing one of his turtlenecked vests in black. In his hands he holds a piece of paper that simply says, "Apols." He looks somber as he takes his glasses off, and his eyes seem damp but knowing him it's more likely he threw a glass of water at his face than he's actually crying.

"I'm so . . ." Ethan swallows. "I'm so *glad* to have this opportunity to give my version of events. I know that a lot of people are disappointed in me and the way I have conducted myself." He pauses, taking some deep breaths, as if summoning courage. "I cannot make excuses apart from to say that I have an addiction to sending sexy messages." He puts his head in his hands and sits like that for a while.

The uncomfortable silence around the festival ground deepens while we all wait to hear what his next words will be. Mostly I'm wondering if it's possible for him to make things any worse.

"I could never have anticipated when I DMed the first girl that it would become such a huge and uncontrollable part of my life," he continues, giving what I think is supposed to be a "brave" smile to camera. "But now I have accepted my addiction, and I'm seeking help. It's going to be hard, but I'm ready to face my demons."

He lowers his head as if in shame. After a few minutes when it feels like he's definitely finished, Celeste removes her hands from over her eyes, where she's been hiding from the spectacle. Sadly though, we were wrong, and he raises his head to speak again.

"I would also just like to clarify that obviously the pictures circulating that purport to be of my penis are not my penis. My penis is obviously, in fact, much bigger. Thank you."

"Oh, fuck that," Celeste whispers.

"Oh my god," Annie breathes.

I gag slightly as the screen goes blank. On the *SausageFest* live feed I'm disappointed to see hearts and clapping emojis flying up the lefthand side. People are actually commending him for his apology when I didn't hear him utter the word "sorry" once. And 'Apols' written on a scrap of paper doesn't count. Not a single person seems to have picked up on that, though; they're just congratulating him on his bravery and honesty. I stare at the stage, hot with rage, clenching my fists.

Tommy and Dougie end the podcast, and I'm left blinking in disbelief at the continued influx of positive response to Ethan, as more and more messages of support for him 'facing his demons' fly up the feed. Is that it? Has he got away with it? Will his career be fine now?

"Well, I guess if we got angry about all the men who were never truly held accountable for the things they've done, we'd never know peace," Celeste says.

"Amen and namaste." Annie puts her hands together in prayer pose, as I sputter silently. How can they be so calm?

Celeste opens her phone, and the two of them crowd around it, moving onto the next thing.

"I love that," I hear Annie say, pointing at the screen. "You look so cool there."

Celeste looks up at Annie. "I could totally do your makeup like that for you later if you like. You've got such good cheekbones, you know." She brushes Annie's cheek with a finger.

Is Annie seriously talking about cheekbones rather than working out how to stop Ethan from getting away with being a total shit and probably an actual murderer? It's truly terrifying to see how being an influencer's changed her in such a short space of time.

"Hey." Celeste suddenly looks to me as if she's only just noticed I'm there again. "I've got to go and do a police interview but we're having a pool party later—it's an ad thing for Timmy's Tan that was supposed to launch today. Joanna's convinced it'll sell even better than it was going to now he's dead. Do you guys wanna come?"

"Oh god, yes, please!" Annie answers for me. "I think I lost some followers this morning and I don't know why, so it'd be good to replenish! That sounds like great content!"

"Fab," Celeste says, and it's like I don't exist again. "We're doing it this evening, in the beach zone. We can hang and have fun by the fake pool! I can help you get ready!"

"Cool," Annie says, looking all at once overwhelmed and excited.

Don't bother waiting to see if I want to go, Annie . . . She's behaving so weirdly, so un-Annie like right now. Celeste leaves and she starts filming again.

"Here we are at the deserted Funeral of Fame site," Annie says. "@AnnieTamponTwo here just giving you a glimpse of life after the party. We, the influencers, are still here providing content for you after these terrible losses."

With nothing else to do, I find myself on ReelLife just like everyone else here. I type in Mystic Millie's name, dying to see what people think of her message from beyond the grave, but the first post that comes up isn't about that. It's from someone called @KosmicKween and it's the "unlucky thirteen things that the universe sent to warn us about Mystic Millie's death." All of the things she's found are really tenuous and ridiculous and I nearly stop watching before I get to thing number ten. "There were thirteen Timmy Eaton cutouts on that roof with her!"

There were twelve cutouts, because there were six of us

around the table and we each had two behind our chairs. Obviously thirteen fits her list better. But then I count them on KosmicKween's video, and she's right. There actually *are* thirteen.

"Annie?" I tap her on the arm. "How many Timmy Eaton cutouts were there on the roof with us all the other night?"

"What?" she asks scrolling through comments.

"At the séance, how many Timmy Eaton cut outs were there?" I ask again.

"Twelve," Annie says. "There were two behind each of us. I remember because it was like being flanked by the twat twins."

"Okay, but in these videos of Millie's solo séance there are thirteen," I say.

Annie looks up, her attention finally drawn away from her own profile. "Let me look." She takes the phone out of my hand. "Shit, you're right. Was there one we missed . . . or?"

I look at the gaggle of cutouts, the thirteen faces of Timmy Eaton beaming out at me from the screen. They're packed so tightly together so that they all fit into the screen that you can't see all the bodies. It's possible . . .

"What if one of them wasn't a cutout?" I think out loud. "What if it was someone wearing a Timmy Eaton mask and blending in?"

I quickly scroll other videos of Millie's mini séance, counting the Timmy cutouts and double-checking that there are definitely thirteen in the background. I scan their faces, trying to see if any of them look a little different to the others, searching for anything that makes one of them in particular stand out.

"I KNEW IT!" Annie shouts, eliciting the attention of the

Mini-Heathers. She puts her hand over her mouth and continues in a whisper. "There was someone up there with Millie! I said it, didn't I?! Take that, DI Wallace! There's proof for you!"

"Wait," I whisper back. "I dunno, can we really be sure? There might have been an extra one we didn't see?"

"I'm sure," Annie says, with a bold confidence. "Shit!"

"What's up?" I ask.

She spins her phone around slowly to me. On screen is another post from @InfluenceSlayer. It's a simple black square with red words written across it saying: "Tick Tock Tick Tock: it's the sound of the influencer clock. Which one is time running out for today?"

"DO NOT FEED THE TROLLS!" Joanna bellows across the backstage area. "THERE'S NO MURDERER HERE! THIS IS JUST SOMEONE TRYING TO GET ATTENTION!"

"I think you were right earlier when you said you thought there was going to be another murder today," Annie whispers. "We need to do something to prove that these aren't just accidents, and fast."

I catch sight of the costume stall in the main festival ground, offering costumes for every kind of influencer photoshoot, and I think I've thought of a way that we can be one hundred percent sure how many cutouts there were on that roof. And it's going to pull Annie back in the investigation and out of Reel-Life world, too. Because if there's one thing that Annie finds completely irresistible, it's covert missions in disguise.

23

"Wait," Annie hisses to me across the graveyard, her star-shaped sunglasses glinting in the sunshine. "I'm stuck on something."

There's a tearing sound as she yanks the bottom of her nun's habit from some brambles, before continuing into a kind of fast shuffle momentum. I have to say that nun's habits aren't as roomy or airy as they look. They're actually quite restrictive when you're trying to run through a graveyard toward a church tower that's also a taped-off murder scene while remaining completely undetected by the police who are watching it. And, despite being holy, they're hotter than hell, actually. Unless this is just some kind of burning in eternal damnation style comeuppance for disrespectfully imitating a nun.

Despite the heat and discomfort there's something quite freeing about being dressed like this, though. Everyone thinks I'm this sweet old lady. And although the massive faux gold crosses on big chains that make us look like we're auditioning for a part in *The Exorcist* were maybe a stretch too far, I've done a good job of making us unrecognizable.

"We just need to tell the police guard we're on official business to see the priest or vicar or whatever," I whisper to Annie, looking over to the officer standing out the front of the tower. "Then once we're through the tape, we run up the tower instead of going in the church. And then we count the cutouts."

"Genius," Annie says over the top of her sunglasses.

The two of us shuffle toward the tower, the afternoon sunlight making it far less sinister than it felt last night.

"What kind of official business?" Annie asks.

"The archbishop has sent us to pay our respects," I offer. "People are always going to trust a nun. We could say anything."

Annie eyeballs me with admiration. "When did you get so devious?"

"I think it's the habit, it's really brought something out in me. Ready?" I ask, pointing my first two fingers to my eyes and then to the police officer. "Eyes on the target. Look holy."

"Ready," Annie confirms, clutching her cross to her chest as if this piece of gold painted plastic can save us now.

Our habits trailing along the ground, we approach the police officer standing on guard in front of the taped-off church. For good measure, I give myself the vibe of someone who's been blessed by a higher being and is incredibly pure by raising my nose in the air.

"Good after*noon*, Officer," Annie says, startling the policeman who had been squinting into the sun.

"Good afternoon . . . ma'am." He breaks off to complete a small kind of bow/curtsy. You can tell that he wasn't expecting to encounter a pair of nuns today and he doesn't know how to behave.

It's fascinating that despite us both being just under the age of eighteen, the police officer calls us ma'am. He really thinks we're old ladies, despite the sunglasses. The disguises are working and I'm living for it.

"We've been sent by the Archbishop of Manchester for an appointment with the vicar to discuss the tragic events of last night, may their influencer souls be blessed," I say as Annie and I both do the sign of the cross.

I don't even think there is an Archbishop of Manchester. Fortunately, though, I must have said it with such confidence the officer doesn't question it. He lets us through, pulling the police tape up over our heads.

"Of course, sisters," he says.

"Thank you, young man, so kind," I say to the man who is at least eight years older than me.

"God bless you, child." Annie bobs to him.

The two of us move toward the door to the church at a glacial pace befitting for two nuns before turning around to check the police officer isn't watching us. Relieved that his attention seems to be very much directed at his phone, we share a brief moment of eye contact before nodding to each other, opening the door to the tower, and disappearing behind it.

At the top of the tower, everything from last night's still exactly as it was. I'm even panting with exhaustion just like I was then, too. We catch our breath and survey the scene. The crystal ball's still on the black velvet adorned table, the chairs still slightly pulled out around it, and the crystal dildos still hang—minus one—tinkling and sparkling in the sunlight.

The life-size Timmy Eaton cutouts have faded slightly in the sun and are a little wind beaten, but they're also still in the same position as they were in Millie's video.

"There's definitely only twelve!" I announce.

I feel triumphant, but when I look over at Annie, she's staring down at her phone already. Maybe I haven't got her attention back quite as well as I thought I had.

"Yup," Annie says, tapping away. "Exactly like we said."

"So there was definitely someone up here, and the question is who?" I say.

"Ethan was wearing his mask when he came down from the tower, wasn't he?" Annie says, looking up from her phone for a precious second. "And he was still wearing his cape."

"Yep. But he didn't have them when he came back later. So maybe he went back up and then left them up here? You count the capes, and I'll count the masks?"

I head over to the table where there's a pile of masks, and Annie heads over to the chairs to count the capes that have been left on them.

"Six capes," Annie says, putting her hands on her hips.

"And six masks," I say. "There were seven including Joanna's, so that means there's still one missing."

I take off my sunglasses and crouch next to the table, scanning the floor, and Annie joins me. "So we know there was definitely someone up here with her and that they were wearing a Timmy mask to blend in with the Timmy cutouts. There must be something else up here we're missing," I say.

"Maybe the police have already taken some stuff away?" Annie suggests, looking defeated.

I'm not ready to give up and go back down just yet, though. Crawling along the floor, I scour each and every flagstone with my fingers, and the gaps in between them, trying to find clues that aren't visible to the naked eye. Finding nothing, I stand up again to take another look at the table, and the crystals.

"We just need to be thorough, that's all, the two of us together will find something in no time!" I say cheerfully.

But when I look over at her, Annie's on her phone again, half-heartedly gazing around her, while she taps away, smirking occasionally. As I rub my reddened knees, sore from crawling on the flagstones, I can't help being more than a little annoyed with her for the second time today. I slump down against the wall of the tower and, feeling a sharp prick in my bum, immediately leap back up.

"What was that?" I mutter, glaring at the ground.

I crouch back down and run my finger along the same piece of stone until I feel the sharpness again and lower my face to take a closer look. Staring at it sideways I see the faintest sparkle between the flagstones, where a shiny gold post sticks out. I grab my keys from my pocket and jiggle them between the flagstones, trying to pry it free, until it eventually jumps out: a small gold stud earring, with shining black stone. Gold posts clutch the stone, like sinister claws.

"Annie," I say, from my crouched position at the side of the tower. "I've found something."

Reluctantly tearing her eyes from her screen, Annie comes over and stares at the earring on the stones before peering over the side of the tower and realizing the same thing I have, that this is the exact point Mystic Millie fell from. I can even see the gravestone that we hid behind from here. I look back over to the table where we were all sitting, which is several meters away. I don't think anyone aside from Millie would have had the time to come over this way.

"Take pictures of it. We need to document it and leave it here for the police to find so they can do probably absolutely nothing with it," Annie says.

I'm a bit irked by her tone, like she's suddenly in charge of the investigation when she's been nowhere today until now. "It could be Millie's, but it could also be the murderer's."

I try to remember the earrings that Millie was wearing last night. She had multiple piercings in each ear, but from what I remember most of the earrings apart from the first ones were gold hoops. It's still possible it's hers, though, I guess.

I take pictures from every angle, zoomed in, making sure I capture all the details of the stud and then stand up to get a longer shot, making sure it's clear exactly where we found the earring and just how relevant it is.

"Oh crap," Annie says, ducking down below the wall.

I duck down next to her but briefly take a small peek above the level of the wall as I go. Out in front of the church, a police car has pulled up and DI Wallace and DC Short are getting out.

We crouch on the flagstones, our hearts thumping, backs pressed against the wall.

Annie clutches my hand and I squeeze hard back. "Maybe they won't come up here?" I suggest. "Maybe they're just visiting the church?"

"What for? To visit confession? Beg for forgiveness for being such shit police officers?" Annie quips.

247

I peer over the edge again and see our worst fears confirmed. "Now isn't the time for sarcasm. They're on their way up!" I whisper.

A good investigative journalist uncovers things that others can't. They have determination, fearlessness, and guts. I can do this; I can hide and not get caught. I'm a fearless nun and there's . . . a table. We can hide under a table.

"Annie, under there." I point toward the tablecloth.

We can hear the detectives talking down below, so I cup my ear, hoping the rumbling will resolve into words. Next to me, a light comes on, and I realize Annie's on her phone. Again. She types out a message quickly and sends it before closing the screen again. I could have sworn I saw Celeste's name.

"She's really pushing for this to be declared accidental death publicly," DI Wallace is saying. His voice echoes up the steps, growing louder and louder as he nears us. "She's been on the phone to the commissioner almost nonstop. It's ruining his holiday and riling him right up. The last thing we need is him on our backs."

"It's sad, obviously, but influencers do die doing stunts," DC Short says. "But if we need to investigate more thoroughly, the offer still stands, sir. I'm happy to put on a wig and some color contacts and go undercover as an influencer."

"I still think that isn't necessary . . . at all." DI Wallace is firm despite being out of breath, his footsteps slowing. "The commissioner thinks it's accidental, too, he just doesn't want us to be bullied into making a call by some jumped-up talent agent."

They're talking about Joanna—they must be. Annie clutches

my hand under the table, clearly finally paying attention and hearing what I'm hearing.

"Don't you think it's a little weird that she lied about where she was to her clients on the night of Timmy's murder?" DC Short says.

"She explained where she was, though. I hardly think she'd be lying to us about it. And I can see why she'd want some privacy from her clients. She just wants this cleared up as quickly as possible for her business," DI Wallace replies.

If Joanna wasn't at a meeting in the US the night Timmy died, then where was she? And what secrets are they talking about? My face screws up in annoyance as I will them both to say more. I feel like I'm close to eavesdropping my way to a breakthrough.

"We'll just do one last sweep," DI Wallace says, his voice sounding almost directly overhead.

"Right," DC Short says, the trot of her feet getting closer as they reach the top of the stairs.

Annie's hand becomes increasingly hot and sweaty in mine as the two of us lock eyes. There's a wheezing noise from DI Wallace that sounds worryingly close, inevitably followed by the sound of their shoes against the flagstone roof. Their voices are now so close that I'm sure they can hear me breathing. I feel like I might pass out but I don't know if it's fear, the heat, or the fact I might be accidentally suffocating myself in an effort to not make any sound that'll do it. I'm trying to channel my inner fearless nun, but the tips of DI Wallace's shoes dart underneath the table.

"You should come to HIIT class with me, Sarge," DC Short

says perkily. "Get your fitness up a bit."

"I'm fine . . . thank . . . you . . ." DI Wallace continues wheezing and spluttering. "Let's just get on with it, shall we."

"Gotcha," DC Short says.

There are a series of umming and aahing noises before DI Wallace lets out a big sigh.

"Well, I can't see anything else, can you?" DI Wallace declares.

"No, sir," DC Short concurs.

I feel Annie loosen her grip, and I'm torn between being relieved that they haven't found us and annoyed that they're not taking this case seriously.

"Let's head back to the station and feed back to the commissioner. He said he wanted a report before happy hour, which is apparently in thirty minutes in Mauritius," DI Wallace says. "All right for some."

Annie and I try to hold our crouched positions, listening to the sound of their shoes disappearing back down the tower steps. Once we're sure they're far enough away, we climb out. Annie's habit's wonky around her face, and her hair sticks to her cheeks with sweat. The sunglasses perched on top of her covered head wobble as she attempts to right herself. Her phone vibrates, and this time I definitely see Celeste's name on the screen.

"You and Celeste exchanged numbers? When did that happen?" I don't even try to pretend I'm not looking at her phone.

"Oh, the other day, after Timmy died, but before Mystic Millie," Annie says casually.

"Nice use of deaths to mark out a timeline there."

As she texts Celeste back, clearly more invested in that than our actual active evidence hunt, something clicks into place in my head, and I can't believe it's taken me this long.

"You fancy her!"

"What? No way!" Annie says. "She's fun and way smarter than she appears, but she's definitely not my type."

"You've gone from calling her shallow and vapid to smirking while you text her and spending loads of time with her. So something's going on."

"Well, someone's jealous . . ." Annie mutters. "What's the issue?"

"She's a bloody suspect!" I hiss loudly in her face. "Just because you fancy her doesn't mean we can trust her. I seem to remember you saying the same thing to me about Scott once."

"I can't believe I keep having to remind you that she was on a livestream when Millie's murder happened. And annnyy-waaayyy, I don't fancy her, so that's not an issue," Annie says. "She's just asking where we are. Think she finished giving her statement and had some free time."

She presses Play on a ReelLife video of Celeste walking through Barbourough.

"Hey, guys! Come with me to give a statement to the police about Mystic Millie's tragic death last night!"

"Jesus Christ," I say, flapping my arms in disbelief.

"I've told her we're on our way back," Annie says.

"Anything else you haven't told me yet?" I mutter.

"You're being so dramatic," Annie says, flouncing down the stairs ahead of me.

I can't believe that suddenly *she's* the one calling *me* dramatic. Everyone knows that's her role in this friendship, not mine. I don't know what's going on, but she needs to snap out of it. I feel like I've entered some kind of parallel universe via ReelLife.

When we reach the bottom of the stairs, the bright sunlight burning through my costume combines with my irritation at Annie and I'm so ready to get back to camp and get out of this habit. At least it's been worth us wearing them, though. No one figured out it was us. Our most successful disguise yet, if you ask me.

"Annie! Kerry!" DI Wallace's voice makes us both jump.

We look up and come face-to-face with him and DC Short leaning against their police car. Annie quickly pushes her sunglasses back over her face.

"Ohh, hello, Officer . . . what a nice young man . . ." Annie hunches over and puts on her best old lady voice, despite the fact that we've definitely been busted. I'm sweating nervous sweat on top of my I-just-hiked-a-tower sweat.

"Annie, give it up. We know it's you," DI Wallace says.

"Who's Annie, dear?" Annie feigns ignorance, but DI Wallace just keeps staring at her. "FINE!" She straightens up. "But did you know that there are only twelve cutouts up there and there were thirteen in Mystic Millie's solo séance video right before she died?"

"I don't see what—" DI Wallace starts, but Annie cuts him off.

"SHE WASN'T ALONE UP THERE! SHE WAS PUSHED!!" Annie shouts.

"This again . . ." DI Wallace rolls his eyes.

"I can show you!" Annie says, getting out her phone.

"That won't be necessary, Annie. We need you to come down to the station with us." DI Wallace ignores her and continues talking, while I feel slightly faint. I didn't think it was possible to get hotter, but somehow I have. My vision blurs as I try to process what's going on here. Are we being arrested?

"Wha—" I start to say, but the words don't come out. The best I can do is attempt to swallow all the saliva that appears to have built up in my mouth blocking anything else. "Both of us?"

"No, just Annie," DI Wallace says to me.

Why just Annie? What's going on?

"Why?" Annie asks him, eyes wide.

"Now, Annie." DI Wallace stares at her.

"But . . ." I protest, but Annie takes my hands in hers.

"Go on without me. Go back to the camp, do what we need to do. I'll call you." Her eyes glisten with emotion. "I GET ONE PHONE CALL, RIGHT?"

"I mean you're not under arrest . . ." DI Wallace mutters.

"You can come and visit," Annie blurts out. "Maybe I'll get one of those jumpsuits." She starts to walk away from me, her fingers sliding out of my grasp, and I hate it. I feel like someone's stealing part of me.

"Godspeed, tiny queen," I whisper to her as our hands finally part.

"CALL MY LAWYER!!" she shouts back.

"Your mum can meet us at the station," DI Wallace says holding the car door open for her. "You're not under arrest. We just need to talk about your meddling, young lady. I assume after last time you're the ringleader here, anyway."

He's got it wrong, and if he knew the truth, would I be being arrested instead? Maybe it's a good thing I'm not, though, if this is what they're going to spend their time doing instead of doing their actual job. Someone needs to find the killer.

I stare as DI Wallace closes the passenger door and him and DC Short climb into the front seats. They drive off at normal speed, no blue lights, no fanfare, just Annie in the back seat mouthing words to me through the window, her sweaty hands pressed against the glass.

24

Kerry's phone notes—transfer to murder board as soon as you're back at camp!!!

Joanna lied about where she was on Friday night. Why? Where was she that she didn't want them to know about?

Unless she was at the camp . . . secretly???

She doesn't have an alibi anymore.

She was really annoyed with Mystic Millie when she stopped the séance. Really annoyed . . . And Timmy can't have been a piece of cake to manage, either.

What if Joanna's not just killing their careers when they act up—she's killing them?

If Joanna's getting rid of the influencers who are causing her problems, is Ethan next? Maybe Ethan isn't the killer after all.

I can definitely do this without Annie. I just need to be strong and brave. I need to be the new bolder Kerry who I found when I was wearing the nun's habit. Just because I thought I was actually going to faint from heatstroke so I had to take it off doesn't mean I can't still be that person. Get back in the habit, Kerry.

I stand in the middle of our yurt trying to work out what I'm supposed to do next. What would Annie do? Whatever she did, she'd launch herself into it straightaway and get going!

There was someone up there with Millie. I know that for sure now—I just need to work out who. Did I see anything before the bats came? All I can remember is their wings smacking me in the face over and over again. Bloody bats.

Hang on . . . the bats . . . there's something there. Something to do with the bats that can help. I can't believe I didn't think of it before.

THE BATCAM!

I grab my phone and text my coworker Doris from the newspaper internship.

> **Me:** Hey Doris, I need a favor.
> Do you have access to the
> BatCam footage? I think one
> might have flown into my
> face the other night. I want to
> check it flew off ok after.

Doris is in her sixties and always struck me as incredibly cautious, so I doubt she'd agree with me investigating. But surely a small white lie so she doesn't realize what I'm doing won't hurt.

Doris: You want to know who was around when that influencer fell off the tower don't you? Roger! I'll head to the office now. Should be no one around. I'll send you what I find.

Safe to say I was *not* expecting that response from Doris. But maybe she can be more helpful than I thought.

Me: Thanks Doris. I owe you.

Me: Just wondering if maybe if there's anything from Friday night too?

Me: Oh and please could this just be our secret.

Doris: Roger roger. And Mum's the word!

Thank Taylor Swift for Doris. I feel bad for being kind of shocked that she's so eager to help. I'd sort of underestimated her, I guess. I didn't realize old ladies could be cool and devious. Well, apart from me when I'm wearing a nun costume anyway.

The killer could be plotting another murder right this minute, so I need to kick into high gear and update the murder board so I can make as much progress as possible while I wait for Doris to get back to me. I reach into my backpack to grab my laptop, but my hand just scrabbles around. There's nothing there. I open the backpack wider and try to look, but I can't see it. I start pulling everything out, turning my clothes, baby wipes, deodorant out onto the bed. The backpack's completely empty.

"SHIT!" I throw the bag down. When was the last time I had it? This morning before the panel? But I put it back in my bag—I'm sure I did. It's definitely not there now, though,

I put my head in my hands. How could I have been so stupid? I never should have left it there. Of course it's gone. There's no lock on the yurt. I know myself how easy it is to get in and out of those yurts without anyone knowing. And now the festival is shut down, there aren't many people who it could be—and one of those people is likely to be the murderer.

Surely they can't get into it without my fingerprint or my password, though, right?

I walk out into the camp, but there's no one else here, not even any Mini-Heathers. I walk up to the final security guard who Heather has kept on to watch over the camp, hoping that they might be able to help me. But it looks like even he's packing up to leave now.

"Excuse me," I say, trying not to look as frantic as I feel. "Do you know if anyone's been in here aside from the usual? Just my laptop's gone missing."

"No one's been in here aside from Joanna and the influencers," he says to me. "I'm under strict instructions."

I stare helplessly at his empathy-less face because that's it. I'm totally fucked. I'm not going to get my laptop back and it's got all my notes on it. The entire investigation's on there. Not to mention my parents are going to absolutely kill me for losing it.

"Okay, thanks," I say, feeling more than slightly defeated.

I walk back into the camp and slump on one of the logs around the firepit. What am I going to do? Think, Kerry. THINK.

But my head's too scrambled to focus. What if the killer took it and they've got into it and now they know everything about the investigation? Suddenly the camp feels smaller, like the yurts are closing in on me. It really is just me here with a bunch of strangers, and at least one of them is a murderer. I open my phone and immediately stop sharing to my laptop. At least I can stop sharing all my thoughts from my Notes app with them.

For the first time since Annie came back from London, I feel completely hopeless and alone. I'm already doing a terrible job at being the "New Kerry" and it's only been ten minutes. I don't know where the influencers I'm supposed to be investigating even are right now. I need Annie back.

The loneliness washes over me and I can't help it. Before I realize what I'm doing I'm on the band's profile again. I just want to see Scott's face. But the first reel that pops up is one made by a fan. Far from comforting me, it's a reel made from pictures of Jen and Scott. Picture after picture of them looking at each other while a schmaltzy song plays over the top about love. I swipe to the next video but that one's pretty much the same, and the next reel and the next one. I click on the comments on one and feel the earth growing unsteady underneath me.

> OMG LOVE these guys. Please tell me
> they're together IRL
> 🫶🫶🫶 WOULD DIE FOR THEIR LOVE

**THE WAY HE LOOKS AT HER!!! They HAVE
to be together right?
OMG I'm calling it! It's Jott! The greatest
love of our time!**

My heart starts thumping in my chest, and a queasiness sweeps over me. I want to scream at the screen that they're not a couple, WE ARE. But instead, my hands shake as I gasp for breath. I think I might vomit.

I open my text messages to Scott, but I don't have a clue what I'm planning to say. It feels like there's a wave of hurt crashing back and forth over me, slapping me again and again. My chest's so tight that I don't even have the air to cry. What if the last time I saw him was the last time I'm ever going to kiss him? What if the last time I saw him was the last time we were us? I feel like my insides are about to burst out of my chest. Tears start falling in wet salty trails down my cheeks.

"Hey, are you okay?" I hear Dougie's gentle voice in front of me and look up. He moves closer, his shape blurred by my tears.

I wipe my eyes on the back of my hand and sniff. "Yeah, just a bad day."

He looks over at my phone, where my texts from Scott are up. The last one, where I asked what he was doing today, sits unanswered.

"Boy trouble?" he asks, crouching down onto the log next to me.

"You could say that, yeah." I decide it's best not to mention the laptop. Dougie's the least suspect of all the suspects, what with him definitely being in his yurt with a girl when Timmy was murdered and on a livestream when Millie was killed. But I know I still shouldn't trust him totally.

"I'm sorry. That's the worst." Dougie, a man who I have seen with more women than I can count on my fingers these past two days, sympathizing with me on my love life does actually make me almost laugh.

"Thanks," I say.

"What's his name?"

"Scott."

"Solid name." Dougie nods to himself. "I'm sure it'll be okay soon, man."

"Yeah," I say. "I just . . . it's really distracting me, I guess."

"Yeah, matters of the heart always do." At this, he points to his chest, as if to show that he knows where his heart is. "What's going on? Might be good to get a guy's perspective?"

I look at him and think for a second. I mean, he has a point. A guy's perspective probably couldn't hurt right now.

"He's away on tour, and we don't get to talk a lot. I know he says he's just really busy, but it's starting to feel like maybe he just doesn't *want* to talk to me," I start.

"But you guys are tight, though," Dougie says. "Your friend was saying how great you are together the other day. I heard her."

"Yeah, except he hasn't replied to any of my messages for hours, he's been really distant, and he hasn't actually read that blog draft I sent him. It's not just that, either, there's just, all these . . ." When my voice starts to shake, I stop to show him the band's profile and scroll through the fan videos of him and Jen so he can see.

"Oh, bro," he says. "That's tough."

He leans over, placing an arm around my shoulder and pulling me in. It's the first time anyone's hugged me for days, and I feel myself sink into it, letting myself be enveloped by his big strong arms. I feel guilty, like I'm betraying Scott or something, but actually, at least I've got all my clothes on, which is more than he and Jen managed. Besides, this is fine, totally nonromantic, there's nothing sexy about a hug from a guy who just called me bro, right?

Oh I just accidentally rubbed his leg.

I move my hand away, but then it's just hovering weirdly so I put it back down. Now I'm patting him. Like a dog. WHAT IS WRONG WITH ME? STOP TOUCHING HIM!

I stop still like a statue, rigid in his arms and start to peel myself out of his strong, safe embrace.

"You know, that might just all be internet stuff," he says as I pull away. "Besides, why would he let a girl like you go? You're awesome."

I blush furiously as he keeps his arm around my shoulder. I find my gaze drifting over his jaw, his full lips, and his brown eyes . . . oh god he's staring right at me, smirking slightly. He's caught me perving on him, hasn't he? This is excruciating. I stare down at the ground, cheeks burning.

"How are you doing anyway? After everything?" I ask, trying to regain my composure.

"Just really sad dude, I dunno," Dougie says. "I know Joanna keeps telling us this was all a coincidence and it was just two accidents, but it doesn't feel right. Something feels off, and now we're just here in this camp by ourselves. It's kinda creepy, you know? I just worry, and then I feel like, am I the only person who, like, actually thinks this is weird? You know?

I mean I know you do. I feel like you're the only person who really gets it. And it all just feels so . . . heavy. Like all this bad stuff's happened and now it's like we're on an island of death or something?"

I almost laugh at "island of death" because it sounds like the world's worst reality TV show. But it's actually not far from what this abandoned festival feels like.

"I keep thinking, if I could just find out what happened to them, maybe it'll help me deal with things. Like maybe then I can start grieving them properly. You know?" Dougie swallows back tears but one still manages to roll down his cheek.

Now it's my turn to put an arm around him. I hadn't realized. I knew he was sad, but he seemed to be carrying on with things. I guess you never really know what's going on behind the thirst trap.

"God, sorry, I'm a mess," Dougie says. "Just really wish I could figure out who did it. I'm just not that guy. But you can, can't you? You're super smart. Way smarter than anyone I know. You can figure it out, Kerry. Please?"

He's looking at me with such a pleading expression I don't want to say no, so I just nod, my eyes locked with his.

"Of course," I say.

"I knew you were a good person," Dougie says with such sincerity that I actually feel nervous about letting him down.

At least I know a good place to start that he might be able to help me with. I open the photos on my phone and pull up the picture of the earring.

"Have you seen any earring like this before? Someone wearing them perhaps?"

"Oh yeah, I bought those as gifts for all my best girls on

263

International Women's Day last year," Dougie says. "I was dating this girl that did PR for the jewelry brand. I don't remember what happened to her actually . . ."

"Who exactly did you get them for?" I press.

"Mystic Millie, Celeste, Winona, and Joanna. Why?" He asks.

"No reason," I say. I'm still not giving him all the details. "They're super pretty."

Great, so the earring could have come from Celeste, Joanna, or Millie herself. I guess I'll need to rewatch the séance recording later and see if I can clock who was wearing them on the night. They're so small, though—that's going to be a lot of zooming in. Just hope my tired eyes can take it.

"Was there anything you noticed about Millie on the day she died?" I ask, my Notes app now open.

"Just that I heard her fighting with Ethan. She told him she wanted to end the whole farce of their relationship and that she wasn't afraid to expose him if she had to, and then he said something about how he'd tell everyone everything if she did that," Dougie says.

"What did he mean?" I ask. I think we all know what she meant by exposing *him* by now anyway.

Dougie hesitates, looking unsure as he chews on a fingernail.

"The more I know, the quicker I can figure it out."

"And this doesn't go any further?" he whispers, looking around him as if he's scared of something. "I can trust you, right?"

"Cross my heart," I say, and then realize I shouldn't finish that sentence given my current predicament.

"Mystic Millie was really good at tech stuff; she could code and program. She'd programmed an app to help her with the séances and churn out daily horoscopes."

I try to look surprised, like this is new information to me.

"He was threatening to tell everyone *she* was a fake if she ended their fake relationship because he knew she was the only reason he was getting followers now."

"Gross." It's not new information, I mean we all were thinking it, but hearing it is extra repulsive. I blink, trying to fight off a full-body retch.

"Right?" he whispers. "When I saw that video this morning, I realized she must have found a way to get out. She would have been free if she'd have lived."

What if Ethan knew that she was going to ruin his career and so to stop her, he pushed her? But equally, Joanna could have done the same, to protect him, I guess? Although I can't see her putting herself out in any way for Ethan.

"That's so sad," I whisper, and he nods somberly.

"She was the best—she deserved so much more. She was always thinking of ways to make everyone's lives easier. There's this thing she did, it's so cool, but I don't know if I should tell you because it's like an insider secret. Joanna would actually kill me—" He stops whispering and stares over at Mystic Millie's yurt. "Did you see that?"

"What?" I whisper.

"I think there's someone in there," he hisses, and gets up just as I hear a rustling sound and the wall of Millie's yurt ripples.

"You're right," I mouth.

There's another, louder sound from inside the yurt, and

there's no mistaking it this time. The fabric walls start moving even more, shaking as if someone's on the other side of them trying to work out their escape.

Old Kerry would have run away, scuttled off and hidden. But I'm not her anymore, I'm being more Annie, so I stand up, ready to find out who it is.

"What are you doing?" Dougie asks, placing his hand on my shoulder, near enough to my collarbone to make my knees go a little weak. "What if it's the killer? Stay behind me!"

Dougie shoves himself in front of me, so close and tall that I can't see much around him. With the confidence of New Kerry, I grab myself a half-charred log from the firepit for protection. I pretend I'm ready to defend myself but honestly I don't really think I've got a good swing in me, and I also don't want to hurt someone. I'd feel really bad about that. So I follow close to Dougie, cradling my charred log weapon like a baby.

I tell myself off, muttering under my breath, "You've gotta be a killer. If it's you or them, and it's gotta be you. Be a killer, Kerry. Be a killer."

Dougie turns around. "You okay?"

"Oh, yeah, fine, why?" I say. I have never looked less fine in my life, sweating away, clutching my log.

"Cool, thought you said something that's all."

I offer him a weak smile, but the second he faces front again my grip on the log intensifies.

Of course I don't *need* a man to protect me, but I'm so relieved he's protecting me I could cry with gratitude.

We reach the yurt and Dougie looks back at me, nods, and then shouts. "YO! Who's there?"

When there's no response, I try, "Hello?" My voice is shaky.

The walls of the yurt ripple again and I hold in a scream. The entrance flaps rustle open, and the face of Tommy Grover, the new cohost of *SausageFest*, appears in the gap, prompting me to let out the scream involuntarily and drop the log on my foot. I try to pretend that I'm not in agony as a second head appears, and although I don't recognize her, she's smiling at me rather than brandishing any kind of killer condom or crystal dildo. So maybe we're safe?

"Oh no! We didn't mean to scare you!" the girl says, her head below Tommy's. "Joanna told us to make sure no one saw me. We're going to be in so much trouble! I'm Spiritual Sarah."

I look at her, taking in her dark hair with purple streaks and glowing green eyes.

"I'm new here," Spiritual Sarah says. "I just signed with Joanna's management company."

No shit, I think.

"Ah, I'm Kerry," I say and then can't figure out how to describe myself, so I leave it at that and hope no one asks.

"I'm Dougie." Dougie holds out his hand and gives her the kind of dreamy-eyed look I've seen him give countless women this weekend. He doesn't need to explain who he is.

"And who the fuck are these?" Behind me I hear Celeste's voice. I hadn't noticed her even arriving, but when I turn she's glaring at Joanna, who's standing next to her not even slightly sheepish about it.

"New friends." Joanna shrugs.

"Tommy was one thing, but you've replaced Millie?" Celeste asks as Dougie stands scratching his head and yawning, clearly recovered from the fear. "It's sick!"

"I'm Sarah, Spiritual Sarah." Sarah offers a hand to Celeste before looking back at Dougie and touching his arm. "You have a very nice aura, Dougie."

I've never seen someone diagnose an aura by feeling up arm muscles before. Spiritual Sarah must be really talented. I narrow my eyes.

"I need you all by the stage in five minutes for the 'Grief Online' panel," Joanna says, ignoring Celeste. "We're teaching people how to construct the perfect memorial post on social media. Winona's going to be there, too. I want EVERYONE in this one. No exceptions."

I do the math in my head. She must have already had Spiritual Sarah ready and waiting as some kind of replacement? That's the only way I can think she's got her here so quickly. Mystic Millie died less than twenty-four hours ago.

"What's going on?" Ethan pops up as if on cue. "Why are you in my beloved's yurt?"

"Spiritual Sarah," Spiritual Sarah repeats for the millionth time.

"Ethan," he says, offering her his hand with a great affected sadness. "Mystic Millie's widow."

I blink at Ethan, wondering if he even takes himself seriously anymore.

"How are the dirty DMs going, pal?" Tommy interrupts his grief play.

"Honestly, that feels a little aggressive and unnecessary at this stage in my widowhood," Ethan tuts, narrowing his eyes.

My phone vibrates just as Spiritual Sarah's about to go back over to Dougie to predict his future by listening to his crotch or something.

Annie: OMG I have been released but I am not free.

Annie: I'm being put under house arrest!!!

Me: WHAT? WHY?

Annie: DI Wallace just told my parents that I'm meddling in investigations and causing him trouble and now I've been grounded until the festival's over.

Annie: GROUNDED?! I'm nearly eighteen FFS!

Me: OMG! #FREEANNIE! I'm so glad you're not in actual jail though!

Annie: IKR? But thanks to DI Dickhead I'm being held captive by my parents instead.

I'm so relieved. Annie might be under house arrest but at least she's not in actual prison, and she can still help me with the investigation. Like a remote detective. I've already got so much to catch her up on.

Investigation Phone Notes—in lieu of laptop murder board (RIP)

Who had the opportunity to murder Timmy?

Celeste: Was on a livestream because she was being pranked.

Joanna: We now know she was not where she said she was. So where was she?

Dougie: He was indisposed in his yurt at the time of death. We all heard the sex noises.

Ethan: No alibi

Who had the opportunity to murder Millie?

Dougie: On a livestream

Ethan: No alibi—again

Celeste: Was on a livestream.

Joanna: No alibi—again

Who had the biggest motive?

All suspects had a motive to kill Timmy—he was exposing their insider secrets to fans and ruining careers.

Joanna—Was she getting rid of influencers who pissed her off? She seems to have replaced them quickly enough.

Ethan had the biggest motive to kill Millie because she was going to end their "relationship" and she'd threaten to expose him to everyone. But if he was going to expose her, were they in a stalemate situation?

Top Suspect = I can't decide if it's Ethan or Joanna.

25

Oh god, what have I done? I can't believe I've just sent Scott a sext. Maybe I can blame stress and say I had some kind of out of body experience? Maybe it's because I'm surrounded by half-naked people? Maybe the sexiness of the influencers is doing something to me? I just wanted to get Scott's attention, but now I've sent the sext, I feel it was a grave error.

It wasn't just any old sext, either. It was a Regency-style sext: heaving bosoms, lust, bodices, the full *Bridgeton*. In horror, I watch the stamp turn from "delivered" to "read." Maybe it's not so bad, maybe it's actually good? Maybe he's going to sext back? I watch through my fingers, as Scott's status changes to offline.

NOOOOooooooo.

I put my head in my hands. I can't even take it back because he's seen it now. This shame will kill me. At the time I sent it I was even deluded enough to think it was pretty good. Nearly had to get the smelling salts out on myself. I was sure it was going to elicit at least some kind of response. How bad can it be? I reread it through my fingers and get half a line in before cringing so hard at the word "ravish" that I want to swallow my own face.

I try to distract myself with what I'm supposed to be doing, watching the influencers as they film their ad for Timmy's Tan, particularly Joanna and Ethan. Although Ethan doesn't actually seem to be here. Everyone else is, though, so at least I know he's not off killing one of them.

Celeste's floating around the oversize kiddie pool on an inflatable flamingo in a bikini while I watch from the sidelines on a lounger, pulling my knees up to my chest and yanking down the oversize T-shirt so I disappear entirely inside of it. I wish I had her confidence. Unless she's a killer, I don't want *that* kind of confidence. I look away just as she reaches over to Dougie on his inflatable unicorn and starts rubbing Timmy's Tan into his muscles with a branded mitt. My hormones don't need that kind of rampant encouragement. They've already misbehaved enough today.

Heather appears for the first time since being so savagely dismissed by Joanna last night, wearing a huge straw hat. It's as if she's been summoned by someone touching Dougie, and now she's here to slap that mitt right out of Celeste's hand. Although she does look a little different from usual—slightly less imposing? More kind of demure maybe? She's hanging back a bit. It takes me a while to realize it, but she's not flanked by her usual mini-mes. Instead, the Mini-Heathers are buzzing around Joanna, dressed in matching black trouser suits. Interesting. It seems there's been some kind of coup. The Mini-Heathers are now Mini-Joannas.

"AHA!" Ethan appears in a surprise mankini underneath

the massive neon "Empower Women" sign hanging on the wall of the beach set.

As soon as I see him with just two tiny strings of swimsuit material protecting his modesty—or lack of—I spin back around, hugging my knees even tighter toward myself. No one needs to see *anyone* in a mankini. Everyone else stops what they're doing and stares as he stands by the entrance to the set posed, with his hand on his hip.

"Well, well, well, BETRAYAL!" He points to Joanna.

"What are you wearing?" Joanna asks. "A cry for help?"

I sit up, trying to capture the scene on my regretfully still message-less phone for Annie without making it too obvious that I'm filming. At the very least, if I have to see the mankini, so does she. Not that she even seems interested in how I'm doing without her. She's not responded to any of the stuff I told her about the investigation. She's in isolation for fuck's sake. What could she be doing right now that's more important than texting me back? Especially when she knows I'm out here alone on—as Dougie called it—"this island of death."

"I knew you were leaving me out of something!" Ethan screams across the set. "Is this it? Are you trying to phase me out now? Am I about to get replaced just like Timmy and Millie were? WELL, I'VE GOT NEWS FOR YOU JOANNA, I'M NOT DEAD YET!"

Barely anyone bats an eyelid.

Nice cover up, Ethan, talking about not being dead yet when you're probably the one doing the killing, I think.

"We're filming an ad for Timmy's Tan," Joanna says, in hushed but very measured tones as if talking to a toddler. "I've already explained to you that it's better for you keep a low

273

profile right now. You've done an apology, but it looks super bad if you're out here the day after your girlfriend's death playing by the pool."

"Right okay," Ethan says. "In that case though I should probably just tell these guys something before I head off. Something really important that I found out recently, and I know they'll find really interesting. I'm sure you won't mind if I just take a moment of their time. It really is im—"

"FINE, ETHAN!" Joanna roars, cutting him off. "For god's sake. You can be in the ad. But you have to be on your own. I've got no one for you to partner with anyway, and it's a really insensitive time for you to be out here rubbing other women."

What was that? What was Ethan going to tell us? Does he have something on her? Is that why she hasn't just dropped him after this scandal?

"I can be in a throuple." Ethan stares at her, his head tilted as if challenging her.

"Oh god, do whatever you want," Joanna sighs, chucking him a fake tan mitt.

"Ew, not with us," Celeste says, before smirking in Heather's direction. "We already seem to have a third."

"Fine." Ethan goes over to Spiritual Sarah and Tommy with his grubby little mitt. "I really respect you. And I will *be* very respectful to you, throughout this advert. Am I okay to mitt you?"

"No." Sarah starts attempting to paddle away furiously on her phone-shaped inflatable in the tiny pool, but there really isn't much room. They're packed tight in there.

Dougie and Celeste seem to decide instead of engaging with Ethan any further, they're just going to use the downtime between takes to check their notifications and scroll ReelLife. Ethan's follower count had gone down by over a million when I checked earlier. He's a desperate man—God knows what that desperation might lead him to do if he's the killer. I feel like I should be more afraid but when I look at him, armed purely with a fake tan mitt, in a mankini, I wonder if this could really be the guy that's killed two people?

"Okay, let's go again!!!" Joanna shouts and the influencers continue with their awkward rubbing of each other and paddling around the pool with mitts.

Joanna, on the other hand, scares the absolute shit out of me. It's less of a stretch to believe she could be the killer. But then maybe that's what Ethan wants me to think . . . But then . . . when he's wearing that mankini it just feels impossible to consider him as a serious suspect.

After Dougie and Celeste have applied their tan, they start posing for pictures and trying to ram each other off their inflatables. They seem to know instinctively what makes good content and start batting one of the brightly colored beach-balls at each other. I watch as the golden evening sunset shines on Dougie's toned muscles, his skin glistening, a few splashed water droplets settling on his back . . .

"Hey! Kerry! Why don't you join in!" Dougie shouts, gesturing to me. I realize I've been staring at him, licking my lips. I'm an animal.

"YEAH JUMP IN!" Celeste says.

But I screw up my nose. "Nah, I'm okay, thanks! I prefer to watch!"

That sounded worse. What I mean is I'd prefer not to take my T-shirt off or go anywhere near any of that fake tan. My phone beeps, and I grab it so frantically I nearly send it flying across the set. Maybe all my romantic troubles are over and I'm about to get into a Regency sext exchange with Scott! But when I look the name on the screen is Doris. And she's talking BatCams rather than a damp, see-through puff sleeved shirt.

Still exciting I guess, just in a very different way.

> **Doris:** These pictures are from the Saturday around the time that that poor girl fell.

> **Doris:** I think the camera probably wasn't pointed in the right direction to capture it all.

I open about twenty pictures, all varying degrees of utterly horrifying. Every single one of them depicts Annie and me being attacked by the bats. It's even managed to capture some of our facial expressions through the bats, which I really wish I hadn't. I'll be deleting these pictures and hoping that no one else ever sees them. I also wonder about breaking into the office and destroying the BatCam entirely. I'd break the law to ensure no one ever saw me like that.

> **Doris:** But here's something interesting from the Friday night. Taken about an hour before that Timmy lad died.

She sends through another ten pictures from the graveyard on Friday night, all of them showing a woman walking through the graveyard with purpose in the direction of the festival site. I zoom in on the screen and see her face as clear as I can see it now across the pool. It's Joanna. So she was here.

"Okay guys! I think we got it!" Joanna shouts, and I jump.

I stare at her. If she was here on Friday night, what was she up to? Why wasn't she honest? Do the police know she was here? Is that what she told them? Or did she tell them something else?

> **Me:** I think you should probably send these to the police.

> **Me:** Just the ones from the night Timmy died though, definitely do not send the other ones.

Doris: Gotcha.

"Okay, everyone, out of the water and let's get ready for the final panel in one hour!" Joanna shouts, barely even looking at her clients.

"ONE HOUR, EVERYONE!" Mini-Joanna One echoes.

Immediately Dougie and Celeste dunk themselves in the pool to wash off the fake tan, with Tommy and Spiritual Sarah following suit, before the four of them get back out.

"Ethan!" Joanna shouts. "I can't believe I'm saying this, but BigBoy have just been in touch. They want *you* as the next ambassador for BigBoy condoms. Apparently your whole redemption arc has made you appealing to them. God knows why. They're calling it a fresh new angle!"

"I knew it!" Ethan doesn't move, just continues floating around the pool on his inflatable looking smug.

"Contract coming your way later." Joanna sounds reluctant, bitter even.

"I'VE MADE IT! YOU ALL THOUGHT I WAS DONE, BUT I'VE MADE IT!" Ethan starts singing along to the latest Reel-Life banger and waving his mitted hand in the air.

"Going to head to the spa block and wash this off properly," Celeste says to Dougie.

"Good idea," Dougie says, the two of them ignoring Ethan entirely.

They head off to the camp while I sit on the lounge chair working out what to do next. Should I stay and watch Joanna? Or should I go back to the camp with Celeste and Dougie? I forward Annie the pictures of Joanna in the graveyard and start typing out a message to go with them, explaining the BatCam. As my fingers tap away at the screen, I feel strange though, like someone's walking over my grave. I shudder and look up and make immediate eye contact with Joanna, giving me a stare that turns my blood to ice. She doesn't blink, just keeps glaring at me, flanked by the Mini-Joannas, all in black. Like an angel of death with her disciples.

"The stage needs to be ready for the last panel," she suddenly snaps at Mini-Joanna One.

Turning on her heel to leave, she shoots me a final savage look and storms out of the set. I shiver in the wake of her stare and think it might be time I leave, too. I walk out of the set in the direction of the camp, leaving Ethan on his floatie rapping along to the music, with a smug grin.

* * *

I forwarded Annie the pictures of Joanna about fifteen minutes ago and still haven't heard anything back, so I'm not waiting anymore. I'm taking matters into my own hands. If Joanna's the killer and she's got my laptop, she's seriously smart and seriously scary. I could be in big trouble. I'm not about to hang around to find out what she's going to decide to do with me. That look she gave me felt like a warning. It's been fun being brave Kerry and everything, but actual Kerry wants to survive to see her eighteenth birthday.

I start stuffing everything into my backpack as fast as I can. I'll go via Annie's house on the way home. Maybe I can stay there for the night in her nice safe bedroom with her and Herbie, and her parents in the room next door. Scott was right. I don't need to be here anymore. It's not worth losing my life over a blog.

I'm about to text him when my phone lights up, and I see his name. He's replied! I feel my heart soar and my face break into a smile. It's all going to be okay. I'm going to tell him I'm going home to safety and we're going to be okay. I open his message.

> **Scott:** I'm really sorry, I can't do this
> anymore. I think I'm in love with someone
> else. I just wanted to be honest. I'm so
> sorry Kerry x.

The phone drops out of my hands and onto the bed. The screen still displaying the message glows up at me. My fingers and toes tingle, and I feel my chest getting smaller, like all the air's being crushed out of me. I look around the yurt as its

279

fabric walls start to spin. How is it possible for it to be over? Just like that? In a second. Nearly a year together and he ends it with a text?

"Knock, knock! Hey! Wanna hang out?" Dougie stands in the doorway to the yurt, shirtless yet again, in just his frayed jean shorts. His forehead crinkled with concern. His words barely break through my shocked fog. "Wait . . . what's . . . are you going? What's going on? Are you okay?"

I want to reply but I feel like I'm choking every time I try to speak. He comes over to me and I point at the phone on the bed. As he picks it up and reads the message, I focus on trying to get some air into my lungs while my eyes fill with tears.

"Shit, Kerry! Man, that's rough! I'm so sorry." He stoops down to my eye level, taking my hands in his. "You're having a panic attack aren't you?"

I nod.

"Okay. It's okay. Breathe with me."

He keeps eye contact with me, breathing in and out. I feel his hand rest on my back as he counts breaths until I'm breathing more easily again, despite the world still spinning into freefall around me.

"Look, you can't go like this. You're so upset. Why don't you stay? Just one more night? I can protect you if you're scared. And maybe I can cheer you up."

He looks so happy, and hopeful, like golden retriever. But the tears keep coming. He reaches down and puts his arms around me, resting his chin on my head as I soak his bare chest in my tears.

"You'll be okay," he says into my hair, stroking it gently. "You'll be okay."

There's a vibration in his shorts, and he pulls away, reaching down and taking out his phone. In an instant as he looks at the screen his face changes.

"What's up?" I ask.

"The influence slayer," Dougie says, turning his screen to face me. "I think Ethan's in trouble."

On the screen there's a new post from the influence slayer: a video of Ethan lying on his pool float, with the caption "That reel feeling when your time's up, in ReelLife and real life."

"Is he on his own?" I ask.

"Shit!" Without hesitation, Dougie runs out of the yurt, and I chase after him.

"What are you going to do?" I ask, already out of breath but trying my hardest to keep up.

"Just stay with me! You're safe with me! I'll protect you!" Dougie yells back, pressing buttons on his phone and holding it up to his ear. "Shit, where's Celeste? Why isn't she answering? I need to know she's safe."

I open ReelLife to see if there are any hints about where she might be and see that she's on a livestream.

"She's on a live!" I say. "She's safe in her yurt."

I turn my screen around, but Dougie shakes his head.

"She recorded that earlier. It's a prerecord. This is what I was going to tell you before we got interrupted by Spiritual Sarah. Mystic Millie set up this app that means we can pre-record lives and schedule them. They behave just like normal lives, but you can tell because we never interact with any of the questions people ask."

I look back down at the screen. There are people asking questions, some of them repeating their questions in block

281

capitals, but she just carries on.

"She did it the other night, too, when Millie was killed. She said she had something to do, but I didn't know where she was. I was so worried the killer would get her then, too."

Around us the fairy lights flicker, and as we race through the flower arches the camp's electricity goes out completely.

I feel Dougie's reassuring grasp around my fingers. "Stay close. I'll make sure nothing happens to you," he says with determination.

But from the depths of the festival ground, an ear-piercing scream slices through the darkness. Dougie's grip tightens, safe, sure and secure as he leads the two of us racing faster through the camp in the direction of the noise.

More screams echo as we run, and by the time we reach the beach set I've already got the sinking feeling that I know what we'll find. Around the pool Celeste, Tommy, and Spiritual Sarah have gathered, their shock now silent as they stare straight ahead into the water.

"Guys! Where's Ethan?" Dougie shouts, but no one moves.

He pushes his way through and lets out a strangled gasp. There in front of us, lying face down in the pool, next to the submerged neon "Empower Women" light that was once hung all the way across the other side of the set, is Ethan Woods. He floats, unmoving, across the water to the sound of "Baby Got Back" playing out of his phone.

26

"He never did finish *The Feminine Mystique*," Dougie says, wiping away a small tear.

"Someone needs to check his pulse," Spiritual Sarah says.

"NO! He's been electrocuted!" I shout, surprising us all.

I point to the light, floating in the water with its long cable dragging from a power point in the faux wall.

"No one touch him! The current travels through water. It'll be why the power's out."

"You're so smart," Dougie whispers into my ear.

"I'll call the police," Celeste says.

"What the fuck?!" Joanna's voice travels from across the set where she stands alone, no Mini-Joannas with her.

She cuts a sinister figure in her black suit, and I watch her with narrowed eyes. She was here when Timmy died. The footage proves it. She was here. Where was she just now? And what's she done with the Mini-Joannas?

"Any of you going to explain to me how the 'Empower Women' light went from hanging on the wall over there"—she points to the wall of the beach set—"to being in the pool? It didn't jump itself twenty feet, did it?" She scans from face to face like an angry teacher asking whose phone rang in class.

"Joanna?!" I'm relieved to hear the voice of Mini-Joanna One as the three of them rush onto the set. For a second, I thought she'd got rid of them just like she's clearly got rid of Ethan. They might be annoying, but they don't deserve to die.

I do the only thing I can think of to do. I need backup, even if she hasn't replied to me for hours. I message Annie.

> **Me:** Annie, Ethan's dead. It
> wasn't him. It has to have
> been Joanna. Right?

Annie's reply comes instantly and I'm surprised to receive it.

> **Annie:** It's okay Kerry, I know who did it.
> I'm going to FaceTime you in a second, is
> everyone there?

> **Me:** Yeah why?

> **Annie:** Good, just make sure no one
> leaves. I'd like to address the group.

Is Annie about to do a Miss Marple and start accusing the gathered suspects, via FaceTime? There's no time for me to question it because my phone rings straightaway, and when I answer it, I quickly realize that yes, she *is* doing a Miss Marple. She's even dug out some tweed for the occasion despite the heat. I turn the phone around so everyone can see Annie's face displayed proudly on the screen, beaming out at them.

"Good evening," she says, but people are talking among themselves, terrified, freaking out about what might have happened to Ethan, how the light could have ended up in the pool from so far away.

"GOOD EVENING!" Annie shouts it this time and everyone stops talking and turns around. It takes a little while for them to focus fully and notice where she actually is.

"I've gathered you all here this evening—" she starts.

"We were already gathered here," Mini-Joanna One butts in.

"IT DOESN'T MATTER!" Annie shouts. "I KNOW WHO THE KILLER IS! IT'S JOANNA!"

Everyone turns slowly, wide-eyed and inquisitive, to stare at Joanna.

"Joanna?" Tommy and Spiritual Sarah say in unison.

"Joanna?" Celeste asks.

"Joanna?" Dougie's the last one, his face like a wounded puppy. "We trusted you."

Joanna looks absolutely furious. "Of course it wasn't me," she snaps, huffing aggressively on her vape.

"Oh reallllly?" Annie starts stroking her chin. "Then riddle me this, why did you pretend that you weren't here on the Friday night, that you had some kind of important business meeting or something? And then earlier when Kerry's colleague checked the tapes for the village BatCam—"

There's a confused look on everyone's faces at the word "BatCam."

"Barbourough's big on village wildlife watch," I explain.

"WHEN KERRY'S COLLEAGUE CHECKED THE BATCAM TAPES," Annie shouts over me. "She found there you were, bold as brass, walking through the churchyard on the way to the festival ON FRIDAY NIGHT!"

There's a gasp around the group, and everyone turns once again to Joanna, looking unmoved in her cloud of vape smoke.

"If you're not the killer, then what were you doing here and why did you lie about it?!" Annie shouts. "And it's not JUST that, either. We found your earring, up the tower where Millie fell. This IS yours, right?" She holds up a printout of a picture of the earring we found, lying on the flagstones. "You dropped it when you were busy murdering Millie!"

"You mean these earrings?" Joanna says, pointing to two small black studs, one in each of her ears.

"Oh," Annie mouths before looking away from the camera.

"Well, Ethan clearly had something on you earlier," I say. My friend needs backup. "Or else why wouldn't you drop him after the sausage scandal? Did you kill him because he had something on you? You couldn't break his contract, so you killed him instead?"

"Why would I do that? That just doesn't make business sense." Joanna rolls her eyes. "There's a clause in everyone's contracts that says I can terminate representation when they do something that brings me or themselves into disrepute. I'm not stupid. Ethan did know a secret, but it wasn't worth killing him over. He knew where I was on Friday night. But I may as well just tell you all, it's not worth all this. I was delivering Timmy his pajamas because he was worried he was going to get cold overnight."

"You what?" Dougie scrunches up his face. "You said you were out of the country at a meeting for something? How come you were able to deliver his pajamas?"

286

"Yeah!" Celeste asks.

Joanna looks cornered. "I lied. I didn't have a meeting in the US. I was at home recovering from surgery. I had an ingrown toenail fixed and I didn't want anyone to know that something so small could take me out of action."

"To be fair, those bad boys are painful." Tommy nods solemnly.

Joanna looks suddenly a lot smaller to me, puffs of vape smoke disintegrating around her.

"Timmy was always threatening to leave me for another management company. He knew how big he was and how important his money was to me; at points, he was all that was keeping my business afloat. No one else ever really brought in anywhere close to the amount he did. No offense, guys." She shrugs. "He found me out. He called to tell me he needed pajamas, and he heard my neighbor's dog in the background. That fucking dog barks through all my calls when I'm at home, so he knew it. He knew I'd lied. I had to rush the pajamas over here. I couldn't risk losing him. But I didn't want you guys finding out as well."

"That's where you sent the picture from? *You* were watching us all?" Celeste asks disgusted.

"This is too much," Dougie puts his head in his hands and squats on the ground. "I always suspected he was your favorite, but to hear it laid out like that man . . . it's a stab to the heart."

"EVERYONE, STEP AWAY FROM THE BODY!!!" DI Wallace shouts, stomping across the set toward us. "I'm locking this whole place down. No one leaves and no one comes in. UNDERSTAND?"

DC Short and a team of paramedics follow him onto the scene, heading for the pool.

"It's the influence slayer," Spiritual Sarah says, her voice ethereal.

"I'll be the judge of that," DI Wallace says.

"No, look!" Spiritual Sarah turns her phone around to face DI Wallace.

On the screen there's a new post from @InfluenceSlayer, with a picture of the neon sign hanging on the wall, as it was before it ended up in the water with Ethan. The caption reads "Before his light went out."

"What does that even mean?" Tommy asks, scratching his head.

"It's the account taking responsibility for Ethan's death. It's them!" Joanna shouts at DI Wallace but he's standing firm.

"I won't be told how to do my job. We're investigating the scene. Please step aside and let us work. We'll talk to you all when we're ready to take statements. This is why kids don't run festivals."

If we wait for DI Wallace to finish, then we'll all be dead. Surely Heather should be here by now, with another death happening on festival ground? What if the killer's got her, too?

I try to ignore my shaking fingers and put a message on the Les Populaires group asking if anyone's heard from Heather and if she's okay. The response is instantaneous.

Les Populaires

Heather: Although Heather Stevens was
the founder of the Festival of Fame, she
is no longer attached to or CEO of the
Festival of Fame. Any information to the

contrary is slanderous. Heather Stevens
has no further links with the Festival/
Funeral of Fame or any events resulting
in the death or injury of any influencers at
said festival. Heather Stevens would like
it to be known that she does not condone
the ongoing nature of the festival and
that she is saddened that something
that started in her name has become so
devastating.

> **Me:** Are you ok? Do you know
> what happened to Ethan? I
> think you should get up here,
> the police want to talk to you!

Heather: Although Heather Stevens was
the founder of the Festival of Fame she
is no longer attached to or CEO of the
Festival of Fame. Any information to the
contrary is slanderous. Heather Stevens
has no further links with the Festival/
Funeral of Fame or any events resulting
in the death or injury of any influencers at
said festival. Heather Stevens would like
it to be known that she does not condone
the ongoing nature of the festival and
that she is saddened that something
that started in her name has become so
devastating.

Me: Colin, Audrey, what's going on? Is Heather ok??

Colin: Although Heather Stevens was the founder of the Festival of Fame she is no longer attached to or CEO of the Festival of Fame. Any information to the contrary is slanderous. Heather Stevens has no further links with the Festival/Funeral of Fame or any events resulting in the death or injury of any influencers at said festival. Heather Stevens would like it to be known that she does not condone the ongoing nature of the festival and that she is saddened that something that started in her name has become so devastating.

Audrey: Although Heather Stevens was the founder of the Festival of Fame she is no longer attached to or CEO of the Festival of Fame. Any information to the contrary is slanderous. Heather Stevens has no further links with the Festival/Funeral of Fame or any events resulting in the death or injury of any influencers at said festival. Heather Stevens would like it to be known that she does not condone the ongoing nature of the festival and that she is saddened that something

that started in her name has become so
devastating.

Colin: She's fine babe she's just taken
legal action to distance herself from it all.
She's exhausted.

Well that's nice for Heather, to be able to distance herself.
I look around surveying the damage as the paramedics and
police deal with the body. Dougie is tending to Joanna, who's
now crying and clinging to him. And Spiritual Sarah is looking
after Tommy. Where's Celeste, though? I spin around, things
becoming more visible in blue-tinged light coming from the
police cars and ambulances. But I don't see her anywhere.

"Where's Celeste?" I ask the others.

Dougie's head snaps up from Joanna's weeping and spins
around, his panic-stricken face searching the scene for her, the
same way I just did.

"She was right here. She wouldn't have gone anywhere without telling us!" He drops Joanna, and she slumps to the floor.

"Maybe she's gone back to the camp?" I suggest hopefully.

"I'll go and take a look," Dougie says, and he takes off running in the direction of the glamp site.

I race after him, because if it wasn't Ethan who was the
killer, and it wasn't Joanna . . . the killer's still out there.

27

Dougie's quick, but it turns out that I can also run pretty fast when I'm on a mission. Away from the police lights, the sun's going down, the deserted camp steadily falling into darkness. I follow as he keeps calling for Celeste, becoming increasingly flushed and panicked when she doesn't answer.

Dougie makes a beeline for Celeste's yurt. "Celeste!" he shouts, sweeping through the yurt flaps.

We stand in the doorway shining our phone flashlights and inspecting every inch of the tent. But, as I suspected, it's empty.

He walks across the tent and drops down onto her bed among all her stuff that's still there, another sign that wherever she's gone she was in a hurry. He tries to call and text her again, but I can tell it's of no use. Giving up, he drops his head into his hands.

"What if they've got her?" He sounds so devastated, it's hard to know what to say.

I perch next to him on the bed and lean into him, putting my arm around his shoulders.

"It's okay, we'll find her," I say, looking into his sad brown eyes, just like he did when I was upset earlier. "I'm sure she's okay. I'll text Annie. She might have heard from her."

"You think?" His eyebrows peak up in hope as I fire off a text to Annie. "I don't know what I'd do without her. She's been here every step of the way—we've done everything together. Life without her . . . it just wouldn't make sense."

The way he loves and cares for Celeste is just about the sweetest thing I've ever seen in my life. I put an arm around him and he slumps down, craning his neck to rest his head on my shoulder, his breath tickling my ear as he speaks again.

"I'm just so scared." For a moment, he pulls away to look up at me. His eyes glistening, he looks vulnerable and I feel like I'm seeing the real him. Not the person everyone else sees online with all the bravado. I'm seeing his real personality, nuanced and fragile.

Without thinking, I brush a tear from his cheek. His eyelashes flutter and he reaches out to me, cupping my chin, his thumb brushing across my cheekbone delicately. My skin tingles at his touch.

"I've never met anyone like you before," he whispers, searching my eyes and leaning toward me. My heart's pounding so hard I nearly don't hear him.

But I know deep down this isn't what I want. Dougie's sexy and he really is an adorable Adonis, but I want Scott. It's Scott I want to kiss right now, and watch the smile spread across his face, little dimples popping. I know we're over and I know what he's done is shitty, but I can't help it. I pull back and he looks hurt.

"Have I done something wrong?" he asks.

I'm about to respond when I see something behind him on Celeste's nightstand that makes my blood run cold. A small single stud, black earring with gold claw grasping the stone. Exactly the same as we found on the roof, and there's only one.

What he said earlier about how she faked the livestream last night pops into my head. She doesn't have an alibi for Millie's murder. And if she can fake one livestream, she can fake two. Could she have manipulated the livestreams around Timmy's killing? He could have been dead before they even started. We never heard his real voice in it; it was all typed, and she was being streamed the whole time, so no one would suspect her. What if she played Timmy's victim when she was his killer all along?

My phone beeps with a reply from Annie that makes my heart leap to my throat.

> **Annie:** Yeah she just arrived here. She's freaked about Ethan. Said she had to get away.

I jump up and start running out of the yurt.

"Kerry?" Dougie looks so confused. He starts to follow me.

"I'm sorry!" I shout behind me. "It's Celeste. She's with Annie. And I think she's the killer!"

"Celeste? No way?" Dougie stops, and scratches his head. He looks entirely lost.

"I'm sorry! I have to go!" I shout back. "I have to save Annie!"

"You can't leave!" Dougie shouts after me. "The detective said no one can leave!"

"I'd like to see him try and stop me!"

28

In Annie's front garden, still panting from having run through the village at top speed, I can see the light from her bedroom window beaming out across the dark street like a beacon of hope. Despite my sweat and not being able to breathe, I head straight up the trellis and onto the extension roof under her window.

I don't have time to think about the fact that I'm about to confront someone who might have actually suffocated a person with a condom, thrown someone else off a church tower, and electrocuted another person in a kiddie pool with a neon "Empower Women" sign. I'm too busy needing to stop her doing any of those things to Annie. I guess if I were to think about it though, it's quite the body of work for a serial killer, especially at such a young age.

I reach the top of the trellis more by determination than skill. My legs feel like jelly after the run and I practically fall through the window, dizzy and full of adrenaline, ready to fight Celeste and save my friend. But when I land on the pink carpet of Annie's bedroom, the sight ahead stops me in my tracks.

Over on the bed, Annie and Celeste are in a somewhat compromising position that is both confusing and impressive. I turn away immediately before glancing back. Maybe I've misunderstood the situation? But no, I haven't because my best friend is getting it on with a serial killer.

"OH MY GOD MY EYES!" I finally shriek.

The two of them turn to me, lips still locked, eyes wide. We're all too shocked to move, the three of us trapped in the world's most awkward three-way eye contact. Eventually I slap my hand over my eyes, hoping to end this mortifying moment, and as Herbie runs over to greet me, I lean down to cover his as well. I think I realize why Annie hates me and Scott kissing in front of her so much now.

"Oh shit! Kerry!" Annie shouts.

I hear a rustling, which I'm hoping is her covering herself up. But I'm keeping my eyes firmly shielded. Under normal circumstances obviously I'd be happy for her, apologize, and leave. But I kind of need to save her from the person she's sort of . . . under? I think? No matter how complex that position might be for them to get out of.

"You can look now," Annie finally says.

I slowly remove my hand from my face but keep the other one over Herbie's eyes. He's far too young for this, and he's already dealt with another trauma in his life without seeing one of his dog mums in flagrante.

"Um, hi . . ." Celeste gives me a wave and I find myself pathetically waving back at her, which is not the kickass way I assumed I'd be doing this whole thing. To be honest, I imagined myself flying through the air and knocking her to the ground.

"Hi," I say, waving back at her, again.

"Sorry, I thought you'd be a bit longer than that," Annie says.

"Yeah, I ran." I'm still waving. When will I stop waving?

"Are you okay? Did you need to get out of there, too?" Celeste asks.

I feel like I'm giving her a hard stare that indicates that I need to speak to my friend ALONE, and she needs to get out of here, but she doesn't seem to be taking the hint. But then I am still waving. Maybe if I stop waving, she'll get it?

I finally reclaim control of my hand, and she still doesn't move. I guess I wouldn't, either, if I was planning on killing us both, though. I look around the room, wondering what Annie's got that can serve as a weapon against a murderer and curse her for having such a safe bedroom.

"Are you feeling gassy? Your face looks funny," Annie says. "Want me to rub your tummy like I did when you ate too many strawberry laces that time?"

"What? No, I think it's the pollen," I say, trying to sniff my face back into some kind of normality but in reality probably only succeeding in making it look worse.

"At night?" Celeste asks.

"Pollen's actually peak at nighttime. I know that because Annie has terrible hay fever," I snap. For some reason I'm petulantly playing a game of one-upmanship with a serial killer over my best friend rather than like, trying to save our lives.

"Right, but she said pollen count's low today, right?" Celeste looks at Annie confused and then back at me when Annie nods in agreement.

I can't believe Celeste has the audacity to look at me like I'm weird right now, when she's the one that's been smothering people with prophylactics. I really need to focus on getting her out of here and away from my best friend's bed ASAP.

"I need to talk to you," I say, giving Annie another, hopefully less gassy, meaningful stare.

If we did have some kind of best friend telepathy going on she'd be able to hear me literally screaming out to her "GET AWAY FROM HER! DO NOT TOUCH THE SERIAL KILLER'S BOOBS, PAL!" But instead, she's just gazing at Celeste in a really moony way. I need to do something. It's us or her and I don't have a proper plan but at least it's two of us against one, right? Three if you count Herbie.

This will take subtly, delicate planning. Stealth.

"ANNIE, YOU NEED TO GET AWAY FROM HER—SHE'S THE KILLER!" I shout at the top of my lungs.

"Dude, don't shout, do you want my parents to hear?" Annie says before doing a double take. "Sorry, what?"

"What?" Celeste echoes.

I notice that Annie doesn't jump away from Celeste and Celeste doesn't look like she's going to jump up and kill me to silence me so I'm a bit stumped. Even Herbie's looking at me like I'm being unhinged.

"You think that I . . . ? You think it was me?" Celeste asks, indignant.

"Well, yeah," I say. "Dougie told me that you didn't come back with him after the séance and that you can do these fake livestreams where you record them earlier and then schedule them so people think that you're live but you're not, which is exactly what you did with Mystic Millie *and* I bet that's how you killed Timmy, too!"

"I mean the prerecorded livestream's definitely how who-ever killed Timmy did it. No question," Celeste says. "But it wasn't me. FYI everyone does those prerecorded livestreams. Also, how do you think I got the condom on Timmy's head? You think I had the strength to hold him down? I'm, like, way smaller than him. I'm, like, this tiny girl."

I stare from Annie to Celeste wondering how this whole weaker-woman thing sits with Annie's feminism, but she's too overwhelmed by lust for Celeste to call it out by the looks of things.

"I saw the earring in your yurt!" I swing back and forth between the two, settling on Annie. "She had the other ear-ring to the one that we found on the church tower! It was in her yurt!" My accusing finger wags between the two of them.

But Celeste points to her left ear where a small black stone sparkles from her tragus.

"It's the pair to this one?" she says.

"Oh," I say.

Annie stares at me like she thinks I'm being weird and ruin-ing her hookup.

"But where were you when Mystic Millie died?" I ask. "If you didn't go back to the camp with Dougie?"

"I was waiting for Annie," Celeste says. "We were going to go for a walk, try and get some time alone."

"It's true," Annie says. "She was waiting outside the grave-yard. Then everything happened."

"Right," I say, and stare at them both.

"Annie texted me to go back to camp and wait for her there when it all kicked off. So I wouldn't get caught up in it," Celeste says. "She knew I'd be upset. Millie was a friend."

"She's not the killer," Annie says.

I shrink against the wall and slide all the way down to the floor. "Sorry," I say because I think I actually might believe them both. I suddenly feel exhausted, my legs heavy and aching.

"But I can tell you some things that you might not know about Timmy's death, if you like?" Celeste offers.

"Please!" Annie says, apparently enthralled in the case again now that Celeste's involved.

I try not to be offended.

"So on Friday when we arrived, Mystic Millie got a call from Winona. She tipped her off that she'd found out Timmy was going to be pranking everyone. It's why Winona decided not to come but to stay at home. She made up an excuse about why she couldn't make it. So Millie went into Timmy's yurt, and she found he had these really detailed plans in his notebook. She tore them out and stole them so that she could try to stop him."

"He was such a total snake," Annie says.

"A real piece of shit," I agree. "Not to speak ill of the dead."

"Millie got ahead of him," Annie notes, her face smug, even though this is all stuff we've already worked out.

Celeste nods, and Annie nods with her. "He was going to set her up so that the software she uses for seances played out loud on Saturday night when she was supposed to be doing her live seances. She stole his plans and was working out how to intercept him. The fireworks on Friday night were her doing. She programmed them to let him know what we all thought of him. Give him a hint that we knew what he was up to."

"And he would have known the fireworks were from her?" I ask.

"Yeah, he knew she could program them digitally. She helped him set off the firework that went off on stage earlier that day when he 'came back from the dead.' She couldn't believe he had the audacity to ask, considering he was planning on ruining her career. She wanted him to know she was onto him, and that she knew he was trying to fuck her career. So she set off the fireworks, calling him a penis. He'd have known they couldn't have been done by anyone else there."

I remember Millie showing up late to the panel now that she mentions it.

"Wow," Annie says. Honestly, I don't know why Annie's praising her so much for telling us all this, though. The only thing we hadn't fully worked out ourselves was the fireworks.

"Right," Celeste says. "She didn't think to warn me before Timmy did his prank on me, though, did she? And I don't get why Winona didn't tell me. Millie only told me all of this because she was worried it all made her look suspicious after Timmy died and she freaked out."

"Really shitty of her not to tell you before." Annie nods.

"I think she knew I wanted out of influencing," Celeste says. "I mean if it weren't for Joanna keeping me locked in contracts, I'd chuck it all off and go work as a makeup artist. I'm so sick of all this."

"See, this is why I thought Joanna could have been the killer! She's so savage it would have made sense," Annie says.

"Anyway, Millie burned the plans in her yurt so no one would find them. But I guess she obviously went ahead with the plans for Ethan because she wanted rid of him. Just a shame she died before she got to see him cancelled."

I'm not sure I'm entirely sold on Celeste's explanation but

I'm willing to accept I might have got it wrong.

"If it's not you, then, you're saying someone else must have known about the pranks, too? Because whoever it was has to have killed Timmy before the prank on you even started," I say. "There's no way they'd get in or out without being seen otherwise. They must have killed Timmy, set him up behind the mirror, then triggered the stream to start remotely. Then it looked like he was pulling his prank on you and it went wrong."

"Could Winona have told someone else? Someone who saw the perfect opportunity to get rid of someone who was annoying him?" Annie asks.

"I guess," Celeste says. "I could call and ask her?"

"Yes! Let's phone Winona!" Annie grins at the suggestion. "You know, I think we should FaceTime her so that we can all talk to her!"

"Good thought," Celeste says, not realizing that Annie's only suggested this so she can fangirl. I shake my head at her. She used to be so professional. How things have changed.

Celeste holds her phone out in front of her, pressing on Winona Philip's name to FaceTime her as Annie shuffles around trying to contain her excitement.

"Celeste, darling, are you okay?" Winona answers, sitting in the comfort of her own home away from the murders and the festival. She looks quite relaxed compared to our stressed faces staring back at her in the corner of the screen. "I heard about Ethan! Are you okay?!"

I feel comforted just listening to her. She looks so classy, in a jumpsuit sitting on her cozy pink chair.

"We're okay, we're just . . . I wondered if you'd told anyone apart from Millie about Timmy's prank list?" Celeste says, while Annie squashes her head into the shot.

"Oh, darling, didn't you hear?" Winona gives Celeste a sympathetic look. "They've arrested Joanna. It's all over. Check the news."

What? The three of us stare at Winona on the screen for a second, processing what she's just said. I open ReelLife on my phone and the very first video is a recording of DI Wallace outside Barbourough's tiny police station giving a statement to the press saying that he's arrested Joanna for the murders. He looks in his element.

"But we already know she has alibis," Annie butts in. "She didn't do it. I accused her earlier, and she was able to explain where she was each time."

"Sorry, who are you?" Winona asks.

"I'm Annie! @AnnieTamponTwo?" Annie says but Winona just looks puzzled. "We solved the menstrual murders!"

"Who?" Winona doesn't even wait for an answer to that question though. "Apparently they had some new evidence, darling. There's pictures of her in the graveyard, and it turns out that the influence slayer account was set up with her email address."

"What?" Celeste blinks at her in disbelief. "Why would Joanna do that? She explained why she was here on Friday night. It doesn't make sense."

Celeste's right: it doesn't make sense. Joanna's massively intelligent. She'd never do something as easily traceable as that. Surely? Something doesn't add up. In the background of the call, something flickers behind Winona and there's a crashing noise. Winona turns around and part of her head disappears on the screen and is replaced by something brown-looking; I catch a glimpse of something in that patch that I recognize but I can't place. When she turns back around, the screen takes a while to go back to normal and she looks confused.

"Gosh, darling my signal's bad, I should really go. Go home now and chill out, darling, I'll call you tomorrow," Winona says. "Love you!"

"Bye, Winnie," Celeste says.

She hangs up the call and Annie looks starstruck. Am I the only person here that thinks the way her surroundings warped just then was weird? And then I remember something else.

"Her necklace!" I blurt out. "I don't think Winona's where she says she is."

Celeste looks angry. "First me, now Winona?"

"What are you talking about?" Now Annie looks angry, too.

I'm pretty sure I'm onto something. I scroll Winona's Reel-Life feed until I see what I'm looking for. I take a screenshot from one of her videos at the festival and another from before the festival, when I can be sure she's in her house.

"I can prove it. Look." I show them the picture of her in her house before the festival. "This is her normally. See this green necklace?"

I point to the necklace that Winona's wearing. The one I noticed the first night we were at the festival as I watched her lives in the disco set.

"Yeah, it's emerald. Joanna got it for her years ago to celebrate her winning her first Innie award," Celeste says, scowling at me. "She wears it every day, barely takes it off."

"What's your point?" Annie's furious with me for suggesting that there might be something fishy about her hero. She doesn't seem to realize that this is as difficult for me as it is for her.

"But it's not green in any of the videos while she's here this weekend," I say, ignoring her and persevering. I show them the picture I screenshotted from her videos this weekend and then go onto her feed to demonstrate even more, where the necklace shows as a light spot. It looks clear or white rather than green. I scroll down again to prove my point, showing reams and reams of videos all with Winona wearing the same necklace.

"I mean maybe she has an identical one in a different color?" Annie suggests but I can see her starting to grasp what I'm saying. She's stopped fidgeting with impatience and is frowning with concern instead.

"What does that even prove anyway?" Celeste shouts at me, frantic. "Does it really matter if a necklace is green or not? People have DIED."

"You shouldn't have green on when you're using green screen. It can't detect it," I say, feeling my confidence build. The more I talk, the more I know I'm right. "The emerald on her necklace looks funny because she's on green screen."

"And she's on green screen because she's not at home . . ." Annie sighs reluctantly.

"Where is she, then?" Celeste asks, hands on her hips.

"I think she's here, in Barbourough. I think it was her on top of the tower who pushed Millie, and I think it was her who killed Timmy." Annie's face lights up as I talk, and I can tell it's at the thought that she's been so close to her hero all this time, even if it is completely inappropriate. "And I think it was her who threw the feminist light into the pool and killed Ethan."

"Why? Just why?" Celeste looks lost, but I can tell I'm

starting to get through to her.

"Call her again," Annie says gently. "See if you can get her to move around more, leave the chair."

"Fine," Celeste says.

She presses the Call button and Winona answers immediately.

"You okay, darling?" she asks sincerely.

"Yeah, just wondering," Celeste says. "You know that sweater that I gave you ages ago? Do you remember where it was from? Would you be able to take a look for me? A brand's just got in touch about a partnership, and I think it might be them but I can't be sure. Might be more your thing than mine, and I'm happy to pass it over to you if you're interested."

"Oh, I'm not sure, darling, it's upstairs. I can let you know in a bit if you like?" Winona says.

"Sure, that's fine," Celeste says. "Is that something moving behind you? Like a bird or something?"

Winona turns behind her quickly, and finally I have my proof. The picture around her head breaks and a lamp behind Winona seems to jump in front of her face, half obscuring it. It flickers and disappears, again, a space appearing behind her showing a small smooth patch of green and something else against the green space that I recognize, because it's very unique. My laptop, with the picture of me and Scott stuck to it. Annie sees it immediately, her jaw dropping. Winona's got my laptop, and she's not where she says she is. Winona turns back to face the camera, and the image is restored, but it's too late. The illusion's cracked and Celeste's face falls.

"Winona," Celeste says, but Annie puts a hand on her arm.

"You okay, darling?" Winona says. "You look like you've seen a ghost."

"No," Celeste says flustered. "I mean yes, totally fine. Have to go."

Celeste hangs up before Winona can say anything else, and the three of us sit taking in what we've just learned.

"I can't believe it," Annie says. "I'm so sorry, Celeste."

Celeste starts crying, and Annie puts an arm around her, bringing her in for a hug.

I immediately phone DI Wallace at the station, but I'm told that he's too busy interviewing the suspect to talk to me, so I have to leave a message for him. The moment I've hung up, though, Annie's already holding up her phone with something else for me to worry about on the screen: a post from @InfluenceSlayer. There are three pictures of Dougie, in the dark at the deserted festival ground. One in the backstage area, one in the camp, and one outside the spa block. All of them taken from above and showing him completely alone. The caption reads, "Let's play a little game. #Where'sDougie. 30 mins till kick off IYKYK."

"It's nine thirty. What time was Dougie due to be pranked?" Annie asks.

"Ten p.m. today," I say.

"He'll be okay, right?" Celeste asks, so shocked that she's stopped crying.

I race for the window. There's no time to waste waiting for DI Wallace to get back to us. Because the influence slayer account only seems to post about people when they're going to die.

29

"We've got fifteen minutes," Annie says, checking her watch. "And three separate locations to check."

Annie, Celeste, and I arrive at the "Welcome to the Festival of Fame" sign, its once sparkling Hollywood bulbs now dark and dusty. The power doesn't seem to have been restored to the site in the hours since Ethan's death. And now after nine thirty it's even harder to see. Having arrested his suspect, DI Wallace also appears not to have even left so much as a police guard at the entrance.

"We need to check out the three locations they posted him in. The spa, the camp, and the farm set," Annie instructs.

"We can split up and take a location each," Celeste says. She alternates on refreshing @InfluenceSlayer's feed and calling Dougie, as she has the whole way here.

"But surely that's why they've done it. They want us to split up," I say. "We need to stay together."

"Okay, but how do we know which one to go to first?" Annie asks. "Because we're kind of on a deadline here."

"I don't know!" I shout.

"We're just wasting time!" Celeste says breathlessly. "I'll take the farm set; Annie, you take the spa; and Kerry, you take the camp."

She's right, we need to do something, and I don't have a better suggestion.

"Right," Annie says, making eye contact with me as Celeste runs off.

"Right," I say.

She reaches over and grabs me in a fierce hug. "Be careful, Velma."

"You too, Daphne," I say. "Love you."

"Love you, too." Annie says.

We carry on holding hands as we move apart, stretching so that the tips of our fingers still touch right up to the last second as we run in opposite directions.

The firepit in the VIP glamp site has burned out, and unlit fairy lights hang between the abandoned yurts. I stand in the middle, spinning around in the darkness with my phone flashlight, looking for any sign that Dougie could still be here. But it's completely deserted. A faint buzzing noise comes from above, getting louder as I scan the sky looking to see what it could be. As if appearing from behind a cloud, two pinpricks of light suddenly careen toward my head, forcing me to duck before they swerve away again. I straighten up and take a stabilizing deep breath. What was that?

The buzzing's got quieter but it hasn't disappeared completely and I study the sky, trying to find the pinpricks of light, but suddenly there it is again, right by my face, as if having approached by stealth. It's aiming straight for me. What the hell? I duck and drop to the ground, my pulse racing as I fall in front of what used to be Timmy's yurt, feeling every blade of grass prickling against my skin.

I direct my phone light toward the buzzing and immediately realize what it is. It's a drone, and it's chasing me. I turn around and go to grab it. I can break it—it's just bits of plastic and batteries. But it swings around and goes back up higher into the sky, hovering above my head at an annoying height so I can't reach it, but I can't stop it either.

"HAHAHAHHAHAHHAHAHAHA!"

I jump, dropping my phone as a laugh comes from the inside of Timmy's yurt.

Adrenaline shoots through me and I fumble in the grass for my phone, my hand no longer cooperating with my head fast enough. I finally feel its firm plastic casing under my shaking fingers but accidentally turn off the light. Jabbing at my screen wildly in the darkness, I try to turn it back on.

"Dougie?" I call. It has to be him. No one else is here.

"HAHAHAHHAHAHHAHAHAHA!" It comes again from behind me in the yurt. I can hear the blood rushing in my ears as my head spins.

Finally I get the flashlight on through my frantic prodding, and I shine it around me.

"HAHAHAHHAHAHHAHAHAHA!" The laugh sounds again.

"Dougie?" I shout, clambering up and heading into the yurt. If he's laughing, he must be okay right? "Dougie? Is that you?!"

I race through the flimsy fabric flaps of the yurt eager to be with Dougie, to feel safety again.

The beam from my phone exposes every inch of the yurt

while I spin around, getting dizzy. But I don't see him anywhere.

"HAHAHAHHAHAHHAHAHAHA!"

My heart drops, and the world dips under me, fight or flight
kicking back in because I see where it's coming from.

There's a phone sitting on the bed, its screen lit up. I walk
over to it tentatively, scared of what the phone could represent,
or who put it there. I stand over the bed as the laughter comes
again, on the screen a video of Timmy plays on loop. His mouth
open like a gaping black hole as the sound echoes, sinister and
smug. I reach down with shaking fingers and turn it off.

"HAHAHAHAHAHAHAH!" Another laugh sounds from
one of the yurts behind me.

I head back outside, and the buzzing's back, the pinpricks of
light high up in the air hovering above me as I go and stand by
the firepit to text Annie and Celeste.

I spin around just as—

"HAHAHAHAHAHHAHA!" Another laugh sounds, this
time from a yurt the other side of the camp.

"HAHAHAHAHAHAHAHA!" And another.

The laughter continues from the yurts, more joining in as
the seconds pass. I spin, trying to keep track of all the laughter,
the buzzing over my head now louder and constant. There's too
much going on. I make a snap decision and run into the nearest
yurt. Each yurt must have a phone in that the laughter's coming from, I just need to turn them off. In the darkness of the
first one I find the phone easily and switch it off before racing
out to the second yurt.

My own phone lights up in the dark with messages from
Annie while I'm between tents, and I look down.

Annie: Not in the spa and Celeste says
he's not in the farm set.

Annie: Oh my god Kerry! We're coming!

Underneath the message there's a link to a ReelLife Live. I click on it and am confronted with an image of myself, running across the camp. I stop, and so does the figure on the screen, I look up at the buzzing drone and so does the figure on the screen. It's as if the temperature drops ten degrees in one second, a chill settling in my bones. But I can't give in to any of this—I need to find Dougie and save him.

"WHAT DO YOU WANT???" I shout up to the sky. "WHERE IS HE??"

I'm sick of this, I'm sick of being watched. I do something I swore I'd never do. I take out my phone and start my own ReelLife livestream. If something's watching me, I'm going to be watching it back with all three of my followers: Annie, Colin, and Audrey as witnesses.

My screen lights up again with another notification from Annie, this time it's a screenshot of a message from @InfluenceSlayer.

@InfluenceSlayer: This was a fun
distraction. I've actually got Dougie
exactly where I want him. Eight minutes
to go.

30

I feel the air being knocked out of me as I read and reread those words. Where could they be? I crouch down with my head in my hands, like I can force the thoughts in my brain, but my mind just reruns all the discussions Dougie and I have had today. How kind he was to me. I can't let him down now.

The laughter tracks are still sounding around me on loop. I put my hands over my ears, trying to block it out so I can think.

"KERRY!!" Annie's voice booms into the camp like a beacon of safety, as she dashes in with Celeste.

"ANNIE!?" I'm shouting back at her when she appears from behind the yurt.

"OH MY GOD, YOU'RE SAFE!" Annie shouts, before stopping in her tracks, her eyes widening. "What's that noise? It sounds like my worst nightmare?"

"There's phones in the yurts, playing a clip of Timmy Eaton laughing on loop. At first I thought it was Dougie, but then I saw the video they were playing," I say.

"This is just Winona messing with us," Celeste says. "She's

trying to distract us so that we don't find him. We need to ignore all of this and work out where he is! We've only got five minutes left!"

"It's okay," Annie says, enveloping her in a hug and rubbing her back. "We can find him."

I hear the throb of my pulse in my ears while I scan the festival ground, trying to work out where else he can be. Annie's phone vibrates with another message from @InfluenceSlayer and this time we all read it together.

> **@InfluenceSlayer:** He's made so many people thirsty in his time, but it's his own thirst that's killer.

Underneath the message is a picture of Dougie in the backstage area, a drink perched in front of him.

"The green room!" Annie and Celeste shout together, but I'm already running.

We run back through the flower arches toward backstage. There are only two minutes left. I try to push my legs to move faster but it feels like I'm racing through Jell-O. Prickles creep up the back of my neck when the outside of the small pink mobile green room comes into view. And, despite the rest of the festival still being in darkness, there's light coming from inside.

I run faster, feeling the familiar burn of a stitch in my side. But I push through any pain, adrenaline propelling me forward.

"DOUGIE!" I shout as the three of us vault through the green room's doors.

He turns to me slowly from where he's sitting at one of the dressing tables in front of a mirror. His eyes are red from all the crying. I run to him, my heart beating so fast with the physical effort that I worry it might explode.

"DOUGIE, DON'T DRINK THAT!!!" I shout, panting between each word.

"A toast to the fallen," he says over me, taking a swig as if in slow motion.

"NO! IT'S POISONED!" I shout as his Adam's apple bobs, the poisoned liquid traveling down this throat.

Annie, Celeste, and I watch wordlessly as he puts the glass back down and wipes his mouth.

"What's up?" he asks, adorably clueless.

"It's okay. We just need to get you to the hospital!" Celeste wails, jumping out of the trailer and running to him. "They can reverse whatever she put in there. You'll be okay. We can save you!"

"Whatever who put in there?" Dougie asks, confused. Maybe it's already working. What if confusion is one of the symptoms?

Celeste starts tapping at her phone but the battery's dead.

"Where is she?" Annie asks. "Where's Winona?"

"Looking for me?" Winona's voice comes from the doorway as it slams shut behind her. She turns and locks the door, tossing the keys to Dougie and approaches us. "Actually quite thirsty myself, can I get a sip of that, Dougie?"

"Sure." Dougie hands her over the drink.

Annie, Celeste, and I stand open-mouthed as she drinks from the glass. I can tell that Annie's first thought is that she can't believe Winona and her are locked in a room together.

"But . . . isn't?" Annie asks, the words escaping from her in puff of overwhelmed air.

"Poisoned?" Winona asks. "No. After all, why would I poison my partner in crime? We've killed three people together this weekend. Really bonds you, you know?"

I look from Winona to Dougie, and back again. But this doesn't make sense. They're in it together? How?

"Phones to me! NOW!" Winona holds out her hand but we all stare at her, so she pulls out one of Mystic Millie's crystal dildos from her pocket and drops it, snapping it into two sharp shards.

"Gifted product," she says, kicking one of the sharp shards over to Dougie and keeping the other for herself. "Never liked it. Always found the whole crystals thing a bit far-fetched, let alone putting them in your vagina."

"Everyone behave and we'll get this straightened out fast," Dougie says, waving the crystal dildo at us before gesturing over to the inflatable sofa. "Over there!"

"PHONES." Winona holds her hand out again.

Reluctantly I take my phone out of my pocket and press the lock key, handing it over. I guess now I just pray someone saw my livestream before it cut off. The other two add their phones on top of mine and the three of us do as we're told and sit on the sofa, Celeste between Annie and me.

"Oh man, Kerry, I was hoping you wouldn't come. I actually liked you." Dougie gives me his best puppy dog eyes.

"Rein it in, Casanova," Winona snaps.

"Dougie?" Celeste asks in a small, tearful voice. "What's going on?"

"Sorry, sis," Dougie says. "Had to be done. Your friends know way too much.."

"We can't let them leave," Winona says.

The two of them smile to each other for a sickening minute before Celeste speaks.

"We've been friends our whole lives. I know you better than anyone. You wouldn't do this. You wouldn't hurt people. This isn't you." Celeste's eyes shine with tears that threaten to spill as she pleads with him.

Dougie just stands, smiling at her, but it's not the smile of the Adorable Adonis. There's no glimmer of the man who comforted me back in the camp behind his eyes. The man who was helping me with the investigation and consoling me about Scott is gone. Or maybe he never existed. A wave of shame washes over me as I realize how much information I fed him; I was so naive. I practically helped him to get away with it. My shaking fists clench, fury building, but it's only with myself.

"It's a shame because obviously I'm all about women supporting other women, but we're going to have to get rid of you all," Winona says, as if she's just told us she's running a workshop in self-defense.

"We know everything, Winona," Annie says. "If we can figure it out, the police will get there soon enough."

"You know as well as I do that they won't. You're far smarter than either of them," she says to Annie.

Annie blushes. "Oh, thank you, that's a huge compliment coming fro—"

"ANNIE!" I snap.

Dougie paces the green room as I search around for a way out.

There has to be something. Surely someone saw my livestream. But I know I'm putting a lot of faith in Colin and Audrey, who aren't even in the country.

"You know I've been here all weekend, locked in a little abandoned shed just off the festival grounds. I swear to God, I didn't spend three days pissing in a bucket, without running water, for you pipsqueaks to ruin it for us now." Winona turns the crystal in her hands.

"Why are you doing this?" Celeste asks, tears streaming down her face as Annie puts her arm around her, pulling her in close, protectively.

A pang of loneliness hits me while I sit, clasping my knees to my chest again, trying to ball myself up as small as possible. My limbs feel heavy and tired and I want to be at home in bed, watching something silly with Herbie, and eating strawberry laces. That's all I've wanted this whole time.

"We were sick of everyone else getting the contracts and glory we deserved," Dougie says. "Fucking Timmy's been influencing for five seconds and gets the BigBoy contract. I froze my ass off in the Welsh countryside, and they still gave it to him!"

"Without the others for competition, Dougie'll get the Big-Boy contract now, and I've already got far more publicity and followers than I ever dreamed of. It turns out that every time an influencer dies, I get more money and more fame. Isn't that wild?!" Winona claps. "For a while there it really felt like my career was over and people preferred the likes of you, Celeste, with your shallow bullshit. It felt like Joanna wasn't even trying to get me work. I only hosted this festival because Clara Gregory, who does all the online takedowns of celebs, behaving badly was busy."

"Clara Gregory is really hot, though," Dougie says.

Winona glares at him. "Finished?" she asks, and he shrinks back.

Next to me Celeste and Annie shuffle, the sofa squeaking under them as they hug tighter. I wish I had someone to hug right now.

"Timmy had to go; he was a little weasel. Trying to take everyone down so he could get more work. I was doing a favor for the whole influencing scene there. And Dougie *really* needed him gone." Winona gives Dougie a pitying look. "After all, he was about to expose Dougie's whole thing about—"

"WINONA, NO!" Dougie shouts, cutting her off desperately. A vein pops in his neck as he speaks. "You said if I told you, it would go no further!"

I think back to the prank list but all I remember under Dougie's name was the word "pants." I'm both curious and convinced that actually I don't want to know.

"Aren't you worse than Timmy now, though? Taking people down to get more work?" I ask. I need to buy us time, keep them talking while we figure a way out of here. "Except you haven't just sabotaged people, you've killed them."

I stare particularly at Dougie. I can't believe I thought he was a nice guy. I've wept in his fucking muscley biceps, for god's sake.

"We wouldn't have had to if people just respected their elder influencers," Winona snaps, glaring at me.

I try really hard to stand my ground despite wanting to sink back into the sofa.

"It was embarrassing being second best to that dick," Dougie says, flexing as he talks. I try not to look. I cannot be thirsting over a serial killer. "But I was definitely always better-looking. And it felt really smart killing him the way we did. We killed him and set him up behind the mirror with his phone. Winona started the stream remotely and typed in everything he was saying."

"I just modified Millie's software," Winona brags gleefully, as I look around the room. There must be *something* we can use to get us out of here.

"And it was great because then I got to hook up with a hottie while we waited." Dougie grins.

"What about Millie?" Annie asks. "Why Millie?"

"We knew she was onto us, with that whole séance thing. The knocking just proved it," Winona says, staring at herself in the mirror and smiling as Annie and Celeste shuffle again.

I think they might be up to something, but I can't be sure.

"It was harder to orchestrate but also really funny because Dougie made Kerry suspect Celeste by saying she used the software to do a fake livestream, and actually that's exactly how I managed to do it." Winona laughs. "I wasn't really live at the séance. I was fake live. In fact I was hiding behind the Timmy Eaton cutouts the whole time. I snuck out when you were being attacked by bats. Really embarrassing for you."

"So who killed Ethan?" I ask, clocking Dougie's smug smile.

"That was me, man. I couldn't let him get the BigBoy contract. Went back after everyone left, knocked him off his fucking float, ripped the light off the wall, and threw it in the pool. Took two seconds. Even had enough time to come back to camp to seduce you."

Annie gasps as he winks at me, and I feel a wave of nausea hit, my face burning.

"OHMYGODWHAT?" Annie shouts.

I lower my head in shame. "Scott broke up with me. I was sad, and he comforted me." I feel deeply ashamed as I tell Annie. "Nothing happened."

"No, because you were being too much of a loser all 'oh, I miss my boyfriend!'" Dougie puts on a high-pitched voice like he's pretending to be me. "News flash! Your boyfriend didn't even break up with you! That was me!"

I narrow my eyes at him. "You what?" I swallow.

"I took your laptop. I had to see what you were writing in your little blog once Annie had blabbed about it. I'm so smart that I actually broke into your laptop and hacked your phone from it. I blocked your boyfriend's number and replaced it with one that belongs to me, then set up the profile to look like his. LOL. I did it all while you were out playing nuns with Annie." Dougie crosses his arms in front of his chest and gloats. "Since then, every time you've been texting him, you've actually been texting me."

Guilt washes over me for half a second before a realization hits me, and I cringe with shame, because this must mean that Dougie's received all the texts I wrote to Scott. All. Of. Them.

"So you received *all* the texts I sent to Scott today?" I feel like I might actually die. They won't need to kill me after all. I'll just combust.

"I did, your ladyship." Dougie smirks at me, and I resist the urge to scream, cry, and throw up.

I put my hands over my face. I'd actually like to have an out-of-body experience. I can feel the heat coming off my cheeks and ears. I must be scarlet by now.

"You dark horse," Annie whispers.

"I don't want to talk about it," I whisper through gritted teeth.

Celeste gives me a sympathetic look. I bet she's seen many a person fall swooning at Dougie's feet before.

If Dougie was texting me, though, that means Scott didn't break up with me, right? I feel a glimmer of hope, if I can get out of here, maybe things with Scott could be okay, too? I just have to focus on the small matter of escaping alive first.

"Wait, so you didn't kiss him?" Celeste checks.

"No," I mumble.

"Well, that must be a first!" Celeste says. "Dougie's literally never been rejected before!"

I look up and glance at her and Annie, both of them are smiling at me as my shame turns to pride.

"That must have stung. Seducing's always been your best skill." She looks up at Dougie, challenging. Their friendship shattered now anyway; she clearly wants to get him where it hurts.

"Shut up!" Dougie snaps, and I fear she's gone too far. "I'm sick of people thinking I'm just this dumb guy who screws around and looks pretty, and that's it!"

"I never thought you were stupid," Celeste says to him sensitively. "I loved you. You were family to me."

"You were the only person who never underestimated me," Dougie says wistfully. "Timmy was always doing it. Mystic Millie always did it. Ethan was always *such* a smug prick. All of them getting BigBoy before me. What the fuck man."

"BigBoy condoms could have had me as their feminist ambassador," Winona butts in. "They could have made history, but instead they picked the most ridiculous and unsuitable people.

I don't mind Dougie having it; he's earned it. But honestly, the moment Dougie told me BigBoy wanted Ethan as their next ambassador BECAUSE of the DM scandal, he had to go."

"Now the contract's got to be mine," Dougie beams. "I'm not letting you guys stop me. Especially not Kerry, not now that I know how frigid she is anyway."

"DOUGIE!" Winona shouts. "What did we say? That's not feminism!"

"Sorry." Dougie hangs his head in shame.

Next to me Celeste grabs my hand and gives me a squeeze. I squeeze back, we look at each other, Annie's eyes sparkling, and I know they've got a plan.

"I just feel like you don't necessarily have the feminist moral high ground when you've done murders?" I suggest, feeling emboldened.

Annie and Celeste nod in agreement.

"Also are you really about to kill your *best* friend? Over condoms?" Annie adds, tilting her head.

"She's not my *best* friend," Dougie says. "That's just the stuff our parents put out there when we were growing up. I can't stand her."

"You're such a shallow dick! What the fuck?!" Celeste says.

"SHUT UP!" Dougie shouts, pulling an unsheathed BigBoy condom out of his pocket and flexing it.

Celeste and Annie cuddle closer as he comes toward us, the condom stretched around his knuckles. I want to duck and hide from him or run away, but Winona's still got her crystal dildo weapon and she's eyeing us all, ready for any movement. Celeste squeezes my hand and I realize my whole body has started shaking.

"We thought it would be pretty neat if you all died in the same way Timmy did. Like Celeste coming full circle with her serial killing," Winona says, behind Dougie.

"Which one first, Winnie?" Dougie asks, stretching the condom as he paces in front of us.

"God, Dougie, I don't care. Can we just hurry up? I'm supposed to be on the eleven o'clock news talking about 'the tragedy.' If we can get these guys done by then I'll have even more to talk about."

"What if they offer Winona the BigBoy contract?" Celeste asks, her voice shaking. "She's got way more followers than you now and a feminist angle would be novelty."

"Even if they did, she'd just pass it over to me. Wouldn't you, Winnie?" Dougie says.

"I mean if they ask . . . I don't know." Winona makes a vague hand gesture.

"I thought you said you wanted *me* to be the ambassador?" Dougie walks away from us, approaching Winona. "That's why we were doing this."

"Don't be stupid, Dougie, why would I go to all this trouble just for you?" Winona says.

"What?" Dougie's face falls, his shoulders sag and he looks broken.

When he turns back around to us, Annie sees her chance. In a flash she's up, spraying something in his face, and he's choking while Celeste darts across the room, also spraying something, but at Winona. I hear the tinkle of her crystal dildo falling to the floor as she coughs and splutters.

"GRAB THE KEYS, KERRY!" Annie shouts at me, and without thinking I delve into Dougie's pocket. It's a place millions of thirsty folk would be besides themselves to dig into, but I can honestly say I'm not that fazed.

My fingers close around the metal of the keys as Annie and Celeste continue to spray, a terrible cloying smell filling the room. It's like a mixture of pee and manure. I look over at Winona clutching her eyes while Dougie falls to the floor, clawing at his face, trying to get whatever it is out of his sinuses.

I race over to the door, my fingers fumbling around the key while I try and get it in the lock. Finally the key slides in and I turn it, flinging the door open wide and racing outside. Annie and Celeste are next to me in a second.

"RUN!" Annie shouts.

I pick up my pace, determined to keep up with them, my adrenaline off the charts as I look behind me to check Dougie and Winona aren't close.

"AFTER THEM, YOU FOOL!" I hear Winona shouting to Dougie as he coughs and splutters behind us, stumbling around, still trying to recover his vision from whatever was sprayed in his face.

"What was that you sprayed at them?" I ask.

"Bitches Get Riches body spray," Celeste replies breathlessly as we race through the disco set. "There was a mistake in production. I got sent the bottles of it when we were here and they must have used the wrong ingredients because it's so gross. I'd left some cans in the green room."

"It's foul," Annie concurs.

"Agreed," I say, glancing back and seeing Dougie and Winona, racing toward us. "Shit! They're coming!"

"Did anyone get their phone?" Annie asks.

"Nope," Celeste shouts.

"No," I admit.

"Into the farm set," Annie points. "Maybe we can lose them in there."

The three of us run onto the set and duck behind some hay bales, Celeste in between me and Annie. We link hands, holding tight in a line. My knuckles turn white as I grip Celeste's hand tighter and the sound of footsteps gets closer.

"Celeste?" Dougie whispers. "Hey, Celeste, look I don't want to do this. She made me. We can escape. We just have to be smart. Trust me."

Celeste looks from Annie to me, her face hopeful, but Annie and I shake our heads, and she knows we're right. I can hear him prowling around, but I can also hear the second set of footsteps and I know Winona's with him, even if she's saying nothing. I'm panting so hard from all the running that I'm sure the sound of my breathing's going to give us away.

The footsteps get louder and then stop. The three of us look at each other, I'm sure we're about to be found. It's Annie who moves first, gesturing toward the hay bales. She counts to three with her fingers, and as she puts the final finger down we jump up, launching the hay bales at Dougie and Winona with a strength I didn't know I possessed. Winona gets knocked over by one of the bales while Dougie manages to stay upright, fighting through the hay with his hands. We're at least stopping him coming closer though.

I feel something hitting the back of my head and turn to see that Jessica, Mini-Heather Three, has thrown an inflatable alpaca at me.

"Jessica?! What?" I blink at her, startled.

"STOP THROWING HAY AT MY BOYFRIEND!" Jessica screams back at me.

"What?" I ask again as Annie and I scrunch our faces up, as we keep throwing hay forward.

We need to get as much between us and them as possible. Winona's becoming buried while Dougie still fights it off though.

"Jessica was my helper on the inside. Weren't you, babe?" Dougie says smugly, before spitting out a fistful of hay I manage to aim into his smug mouth as he speaks.

I lob another bale of hay at him in an attempt to knock him back down.

Under her arm, Jessica has the smoke machine that she used to make Mystic Millie look more mystical onstage. We're trapped between her and Dougie. In response, she starts blowing smoke at us, but a gust of wind takes it back in her direction and she's left coughing and sputtering.

"Dougie, rescue me!" she gasps.

"Sorry, baby, it was just a festival romance," he says callously, trying to fend off our rapidly diminishing stock of hay "It was never a long-term thing."

"WHAT?!" Jessica advances toward us with rage.

I'm not sure if her aim is us or Dougie to be honest, but Annie tuts and grabs a boot, throwing it at Jessica's head. She falls over, dropping the smoke machine. Inspired, Celeste grabs the other boot and chucks it at Dougie. It wallops him on the head, and he finally falls.

"Poor Jessica," I say.

"Think we were just saved from hearing the world's worst

breakup speech, though," Celeste says, as Annie and her high-five.

As the smoke begins to clear, I spot Winona's arm starting to emerge from the hay that knocked her down ahead. She's stumbling, her feet tangled in the mess, but she's moving.

"Shit," I mumble.

"I'll take Winona," Celeste says, grabbing a ring light with one hand and clutching the body spray sticking out of her pocket with the other. "You two take Dougie."

"I'll help." Jessica surprises us all by emerging from the floor behind us. "Fuck Dougie."

Celeste goes over to Winona, body spray poised.

"No! No! Please I can't smell that stuff again! It's so bad! My eyes are still stinging! PLEASE!" Winona begs, and slinks away, looking small and sheepish on the floor.

She tries to get up, but she must have hurt her ankle because she limps and trips back over. Using the body spray as a threat, Celeste ties Winona's ankles together with the cord from the ring light. Jessica hands her another that she uses to tie Winona's hands together.

"Women are so powerful when they work together. Don't you think, Winnie?" Celeste smiles at her.

Annie and I approach Dougie as he stirs from his boot to the brain.

"QUICK!" Annie says, jumping on the tiny red pedal tractor.

I hop into the trailer and grab one of the large plastic chicken models. It clucks in my hand as I brandish it, ready to use it to fend off anyone that comes near me.

We race toward Dougie, Annie pedaling as fast as she possibly can. Finished with Winona, Jessica starts lobbing inflatable farm animals at him, disorientating him. An alpaca bounces off his head as Annie rams into the backs of his knees on the tractor and he falls forward, landing heavily on his arm. I hear a snap.

"MY ARM!" he wails. "I think it's broken! How am I supposed to lift now?"

He struggles to stand, but Annie rams into him again with the tractor, and he's back on the ground in seconds. In the distance, I hear the sound of sirens and look up to see the flash of blue lights. Relief washes over me.

"That's it!" Annie says decisively, getting off the tractor and jumping on Dougie while he's down. "Everyone, just sit on him until the police get here."

Celeste, Annie, Jessica, and I all do as we're told, and despite his strength he's unable to get up. He struggles and strains for a few minutes but eventually just lies back on the floor with a grunt.

Within seconds the festival site is swamped with police cars and DI Wallace strides across the empty field with the kind of pompous air of someone coming to save the day that we've already saved.

"Winona Philips and Dougie Trainor, we're arresting you on suspicion of murder," he begins.

Annie, Celeste, and I climb off Dougie, letting the police officers take charge. It's an arrest that DC Short seems to be showing a very personal and intense interest in.

Within seconds, Heather appears on her small Festival of Fame golf buggy, red-faced and sweaty. Then again, she's never actually one to get her hands dirty clearly.

"What's going on?!" she demands.

"We received a tip-off that led us to believe that Winona Philips was hiding out here and was the perpetrator of several crimes along with her co-conspirator, Dougie Trainor, pertaining to the death of multiple people," DI Wallace reels off arrogantly.

"What was the tip-off?" Annie asks.

"I don't need to tell you that," DI Wallace says, a pettiness overtaking his previous authority.

"Was it my livestream video, though?" I ask as Annie and Celeste turn to me.

"It was!" DC Short exclaims, excited. "Your stream was screen recorded by people who followed you and then after it finished it was shared over social media with pleas from people to get you guys help and get Dougie and Winona arrested. It's been shared one hundred thousand times so far! The internet was frantic!"

"Are we trending?" Winona shouts.

"You used ReelLife?!" Annie gasps, eyes sparkling. "I'm so proud of you!"

"Don't get used to it," I say, petrified to look at my account now.

"So, the tip-off and the reason why you showed up here was because we'd figured out that Winona was doing it and we caught her confession on livestream?" Annie double-checks.

"Yep," DC Short says because DI Wallace is never going to admit to it. "The power of social media, really is impressive, huh?"

"What the hell took you so long?" Annie glares at him.

DI Wallace's face grows steadily redder as Annie gloats.

* * *

330

I'm sitting in the back of an ambulance, huddled in a foil blanket, but honestly I think I'm fine aside from a sore hay-throwing arm and shock. I can hear Annie and Celeste in the ambulance next door giggling away, reliving their various heroics.

DI Wallace has taken Dougie and Winona back to the station so now it's just us, the paramedics, and what feels like millions of police and forensic officers. I know I've got some admin to do. I go to WhatsApp and block and delete the number that's been on there masquerading as Scott—Dougie's number—and go to my privacy settings, unblocking the number that I know really belongs to him. I open a new message chain to him, but I don't know where to start.

What would I say to him if he was here? What would he say? He would probably say—

"KERRY!" I do a double take hearing his voice outside and jump up straightaway, shrugging off the foil blanket and racing out of the ambulance.

I see him immediately, searching the Instagram sets and shouting my name.

"SCOTT!" I shout running toward him.

I didn't know I had more running in me, but it turns out that for Scott I do. He sees me and starts running, too, pushing through police officers and forensics to get to me. We reach each other both too slowly and too quickly, and I find myself stumbling into him, crumpling into his shoulder as he kisses my head and squeezes me tight.

"I've been so worried! I was trying to message you all day but nothing was going through. It kept saying my messages weren't delivering and all the calls were going to voicemail and then I heard about the video and you going viral. I was so confused!" he says in one breathless burst.

"I thought you'd broken up with me!" I blurt out, trying to explain as quickly as I can.

I run through everything I know that Dougie did, hacking my phone and pretending to be Scott.

"Why do that, though?" Scott looks so confused.

"He knew I was jealous because of all the videos of you and Jen and he wanted me to think it was over because . . . well . . . I think he was kind of into me? He kind of tried it on . . . but I think it was probably just as a distraction so he could get away with murder. . ." I feel my jaw clench and my face fix into a grimace. "Nothing happened! I promise!"

"Of course it didn't," Scott says, hugging me close to him and stroking my hair. "Nothing happened with Jen, either. I was so worried when I saw what people were saying on Reel-Life. I needed to talk to you and explain. None of it is what's actually happening in real life!"

"I know," I say, because deep down I do know. "But it didn't stop me getting jealous. Is that bad?"

Scott pulls away and looks at me, brushing hair off my face. "No," he says, stroking my cheek. "I can't lie, I'm feeling a bit jealous of Dougie right now myself."

"As murderers go, he *is* hot." Annie nods.

I hadn't even realized she was there.

"Not helpful," I say.

"Shhhhh." Celeste giggles, kissing Annie's cheek from behind and wrapping her arms around her waist. "Let's leave them to it."

"Maybe sometimes jealousy just happens. I thought *I* was a bad person for feeling it but maybe it's just natural. And feeling bad about it probably just makes it even worse," Scott says. "At least that's what I'm telling myself."

"God, you're so wise," I say. "What do we do about it, though? I'd never want you to stop hanging out with Jen. She's in the band."

"Just have to trust each other," Scott says with a shrug. "Maybe you should stop hanging out with Dougie, though. Not because he made a pass at you, just because he's a murderer and stuff?"

"Agreed," I say, giggling with relief.

"I love you, and you love me, and there's going to be hot people in our lives but you're who I want to tell everything to, who I want to watch shit films with and laugh with and sit in silence with." He smiles, his dimples popping, as I nod. "You're my person."

"And you're my person." I smile.

He leans in, his hand still on my cheek, and our lips meet.

Epilogue

"I can't believe this time last week we were solving a high-profile murder investigation and now we have to go back to school," Annie whines, rolling the *Paw Patrol* bike next to her as she talks.

"*We?*" I ask Annie. "I seem to remember very clearly spending a lot of time *alone* solving the murders while you hung out with your new girlfriend."

"I can't believe I have such bad taste in men," Heather says, raising her head high with great effort as she stalks in through the main entrance wearing a pair of wedges combined with wide-legged jeans and a T-shirt that reads, *Over the Influence(rs)*.

As is customary on the first day of term, the whole school turns to watch, bowing down to her fashion choices. It's comforting to see her back at the top of the school hierarchy where she belongs.

"I can't believe you were literally throwing yourself at a serial killer!" Audrey shrieks.

"Like you wouldn't have done the same for the Adorable Adonis? You were hooked on *Romantic Rambles* so hard that you watched each episode three times!" Colin mocks, falling into step next to her. "*I'm* just livid we missed all the excitement. I've always wanted to go to a séance."

"It really wasn't that big of a deal," Annie says casually. Her phone beeps in her hand, and she smiles at it, mooning over whatever Celeste has sent her. I know I wasn't sure about Celeste at first (and then I thought she was a killer), but I like her now. She's badass, and she and Annie make a really good team.

"Is that your girlfriend *again*?" Colin asks. "That's like the third time this morning!"

"She's trying to pick an outfit for the first day of her apprenticeship," Annie says.

"Oh my god, I'm so jealous. She's hanging out on sets with models doing makeup while we're . . ." Heather looks up the school steps to the main door.

"It's good Joanna saw sense and let her out of her contract," I say.

"Joanna's already moved on. She shut the agency and started a successful dog-grooming business," Annie points out. "She said she'd wanted to do it for a while. We're probably not going to be taking Herbie there any time soon, though."

Heather stops in front of the school steps to pose for pictures as the younger kids pap her like she's a celebrity.

"Annie, put me on your socials so more people can see!" Heather says between poses.

"Sure," Annie says, scowling. "But this isn't exactly the hard-hitting content I was going for."

After reaching a million followers and discovering that her feminist hero was actually a fake, Annie's decided to try to become the new feminist hero we all need. It's a steep learning curve with people correcting her and calling her out when she gets stuff wrong. She's never been great with criticism.

"You know Kerry's actually got more followers than Annie now," Colin says, showing Heather my follower count.

"It climbed by, like, thousands yesterday when she posted her blog article on there," Audrey confirms.

The blog post was obviously boosted by all the followers I got from the video, and I was really nervous about posting something I'd written to that many people, but it turned out the internet loved it. From the messages I've received it's not even the bit about the murders people enjoy the most. Most people are identifying with my observations about how being yourself can become harder and harder when all you're seeing all day is curated snippets of everyone else's lives.

As we reach the top of the steps, I spot Scott and the band, and give them a wave. He walks over to give me a kiss and rests his arm around my shoulder. Jen follows him over a few minutes later, and I feel a nervous gurgle in my stomach. The two of us haven't spoken since everything that happened on ReelLife. I take a deep breath as she opens her mouth.

"I'm so sorry," Jen says. "I didn't realize what people were saying online. I feel terrible."

"It's fine, honestly. I know." I hold my hand out to her. "There's nothing to worry about."

"You're like, really cool," Jen says, giving me a hug before going off with the rest of the band.

"Like, too cool," Annie mutters, giving Scott the evil eye. She's still not entirely forgiven him, but she's not sure what for.

It's not as if she was aware of what was going on at the time, either.

"You *are* pretty cool," Scott says, giving me a kiss.

Heather, having finished holding up traffic at the main door, leads us into the corridor as a group. The smell of dirty sneakers and sweat hits our noses again, like it never went away. After last week I'm finding it kind of comforting, though, I can't lie. Besides, nothing's worse than Bitches Get Riches body spray.

"I can't believe that was the last time we're going to be walking into school on the first day of a new school year," Colin says emotionally.

"Wow that's . . . a lot . . ." Scott says, and Colin nods mournfully, but I don't think they're quite on the same page with this.

"Oh no!" Annie cries. "We're going to have to do it again. I wanted to get a ReelLife of us all going in together, looking fierce. PLLEAASSEEEE?"

We all stare at her in disbelief and carry on walking.

"Or for the gram? We could do it for the gram? 'Come with me on my last first day of a new school year'????" Annie's shouting, but everyone carries on. Ignoring her.

I feel a bit sorry for her as she stares at me with pleading puppy eyes that could rival Herbie.

"Oh god, FINE," I say. "Come on, then."

The two of us walk back outside and pose on the steps while Annie makes a boomerang of the two of us. She posts it to ReelLife with the caption "The Tampon Two Forever ♥."

Acknowledgments

I'm extremely lucky to be surrounded by a team of people who love Annie and Kerry as much as I do and support me even when life feels frankly impossible.

First, thank you, Chloe Seager, my number one champion, friend, therapist, hero, and agent. I'm so grateful I get to work with you, and making you laugh is still one of my favorite bits of the job. Thanks to all at Madeleine Milburn, a most exceptional and talented team.

Massive thank-you to Sara Schonfeld for embracing the wonderful weirdness of Annie and Kerry and being so supportive of me and them. Thank you for always being so hilarious to work and brainstorm with. And thank you to all at Harper who have worked so hard on bringing my two favorite detectives to US readers!

Thank you to Eleanor Laleu for the incredible cover art and for bringing Annie and Kerry (and little Herbie) to life so well.

Thank you to my husband, Nick, and Angus the cat—the little family that I write for and who support me. I'm so glad you're my family and I promise the next book won't be so hard. (I'll keep saying it till it's true.) Thank you for making everything in life more fun.

And finally, the most important thank-you. Thank you to everyone who read *Murder on a School Night* and loved Annie and Kerry as much as I do. It means so much to see people enjoying their adventures. It is such a privilege to write books, and to have them reaching such fantastic readers. I'll never stop pinching myself.